Racing to the Dawn

Jack Lyons

ISBN: 979-8-9859457-0-6

This book is dedicated to my friends and family who have always loved and supported me

Cover design and illustration by Ivan Semonchuk - Getcovers

Edited by Sara Jane Herbener – Savvy Communication

ISBN 979-8-9859457-0-6 (paperback)

ISBN 979-8-9859457-1-3 (e-book)

Printed in the United States of America For sales, distribution, and more information about the book, visit

www.JackLyonsAuthor.com

Chapter 1

*T*he Harrier fighter jet shook violently, smoke filling the cockpit as Jim frantically maneuvered the aircraft to attack the enemy troops below. He was desperate to defend the pinned-down Marine squad below, who were in danger of being overrun and wiped out. No one else could help them. The jet was barely responding to the controls, smoke was filling the cockpit, and warning lights and alarms were blaring from the dying aircraft. Tears of anger and frustration ran down Jim's face as he slowly turned the jet to engage the enemy again.

Jim Stabbert, call sign Reverend, awoke on his gray metal bunk on board the amphibious aircraft carrier USS *Boxer*. The hum of the ship was gone, no air movement or noise of machinery, only a small illumination from the emergency lights.

"The ship is experiencing a power failure," the wall-mounted speaker blared. "All hands to their emergency stations."

"Hrnn . . . ?" His bunkmate, Captain Stacy Krug, shifted in the rack above him.

"Yeah, again. Get up," Jim said, sliding his feet out of the rack and onto the deck. While it was a tight fit, he had a room, even if he had to share it with another junior officer pilot. The enlisted personnel had to live in a berthing space and listen to up to seventy-five people snoring and farting all night.

He grabbed coveralls off the hook on the bulkhead and slipped them on, snagging his boots to put on in the passageway. Two grown men just could not get dressed in the small stateroom at the same time.

Six months into the deployment, Jim's dreams were a nightly occurrence. Fears and anxiety, suppressed during the day, came out to play while he slept. It was a burden he kept to himself.

"Trice up and push out, swab," Jim growled on his way out.

"Fucking lifer," came a muffled mutter from the upper bunk.

Jim knew Krug was a consummate professional, despite his bitching behind a closed door. He would be dressed and out of the space in moments. He would probably beat Jim to the muster station, although Jim still hadn't figured out how he accomplished that.

Jim slipped on his boots and tied them quickly, then headed down the passageway leading aft. This was officers' country; very few enlisted members would be around. That was preferable, as most of the men and women stumbling out of their racks at three thirty in the morning looked more like hammered dogshit than like officers should. In various stages of uniform dress, they were rubbing their eyes and shaking their heads, pulling themselves together enough to at least look like leaders, even foggy-headed as they were.

Along the passageway, Jim encountered the Marine air wing commander, Lieutenant Colonel Steven Wayne, call sign Duke after the cowboy actor. Wayne gave him a brusque nod. Both were headed for their assigned emergency muster stations. Pilots without airplanes were fairly useless on board a ship; their place was up in the air. Still, they needed to be accounted for in an emergency.

The pace was not as hurried as if this were an actual emergency like a fire or collision. Something had gone wrong in the engine room again, that much was obvious. Probably a mechanical failure of some sort, or a sleepy sailor on the midwatch had thrown the wrong switch—or the right switch at the wrong time. The deep, dark engine room was all a mystery to Jim, but thankfully it wasn't his problem.

Traveling through a couple of watertight doors and then up and down a few ladderways, Jim made his way toward the ready room, the designated muster spot for pilots. The combat ship design was segregated and sectioned off for survivability in the event of damage. It was definitely not for the ease of its occupants.

Arriving at the last stairway, hearing the distinctive whistle of hands sliding down steel rails, Jim stood to the side. An enlisted sailor wearing wrinkled, greasy blue coveralls came hurtling out of the darkness with a fluid motion, then moved down the passageway at a good clip, an engine room snipe on the way somewhere in a hurry.

Jim glanced up the ladder to see if anyone else was coming. Noting the way was clear, he headed up and through the hatch to the pilots' ready room. Entering the small space with chairs in six rows, five across, he saw Krug and slipped in beside him. Krug—whose call sign was Judge because he had a law degree from Northwestern—had his head down and eyes closed. He cocked his head when Jim sat down.

"How'd you get here before me?" Jim asked.

"Secret passages."

"You'll have to show me," Jim said.

"Wouldn't be secret, then, would they?"

Lieutenant Colonel Wayne stepped up to the podium in the front of the room, saying, "Thank you all for joining us."

"Report all pilots accounted for," he added to the blue-uniformed seaman in the corner, who was wearing sound-powered headphones. As the sailor spoke into the rubber mouthpiece, Duke turned to face the groggy pilots. "Even if their speed is that of geriatrics."

Duke glowered at the men and women under his command, then growled, "Let's step it up, Marines; we are not home yet. As we have this time, and since we only lost two hours of sleep, we can go over assignments. Reverend and Judge, you will be providing air support to the Marines patrolling Nasiriya. Fish, Ratchet, you will be . . ."

The commander's voice went down the rolls, reading out each assignment in turn. Jim knew that close air support was one of the most dangerous assignments. It was critical for the forces on the ground to know they could call in air cover when needed. Without that support, they might face being wiped out by superior forces.

Jim had flown more than fifty missions, providing ground support, since the *Boxer* had arrived on station. The pace was grueling, with little to no downtime, and never being able to relax had started to take its toll. Jim was always on the razor's edge of alertness, being wrung out day to day by boredom punctuated by moments of terror.

Jim had graduated near the top of his class from the US Naval Academy at Annapolis, then followed with a commission and flight training with the Marine Corps. At twenty-four, he was one of the best the country could produce: a patriot, educated in the ways of warfare and leadership, believing in the Corps and his country. Strict parents had raised him by the values of hard work, responsibility, and duty. Adapting to the demands of the Marine Corps had not been difficult. Jim believed wholeheartedly in the Corps' guiding values.

Jim had always thought that the highest calling was to serve his fellow man and country. The Marine Corps motto, "Semper Fidelis"—Latin for "Always Faithful"—had spoken to him deeply when he was growing up. So when the time came to choose Navy or Marines at Annapolis, it was a no-brainer. He had loved and excelled at the infantry training, leading men in difficult and arduous tasks. But the call of aviation was where he had found his true purpose.

Jim had wanted to be a brother among brothers and a leader amongst men. In school, the duty part was more theory than reality. But pride filling your chest, songs in your head, and inspiring speeches can't convey the grinding, relentless marathon that is a combat deployment. As a pilot, Jim was blessed to at least be sleeping on a ship indoors. The grunts in the field, he knew, were baking and freezing by turns, day and night.

The lights suddenly came back on, making everyone blink, and the air, which had become stifling inside the metal ship, started to move again. It would be some hours, though, before the ship fully cooled down again.

"Head out, and good luck, people," Duke said.

Jim and Krug headed back to officers' country along with the other pilots.

"Cuppa joe?" Krug asked.

"Yeah, that sounds good," Jim replied.

In their room, Krug had a small coffeepot with the remains of what had been a considerable stash of specialty beans from Seattle. The floor-sweepings coffee served in the mess hall couldn't even come close. Such small things, pleasures that reminded one of home, made the day a little easier.

Feeling better once he was properly caffeinated and had taken a cold-water shower, Jim headed to the working deck and geared up. He would be flying the Harrier jet classified AV1, with Judge in AV2. Walking around the aircraft, he turned his attention to the young woman observing him.

"Peters," Jim said to a young woman in a blue jumpsuit, "we good to go today?"

"Yes sir, all checked out and ready for arming." The stocky, blonde young woman, at only twenty-five, was the chief of the plane, in charge of all aircraft maintenance.

Soon they had completed the arming of the missiles and bombs.

"Good to go," Jim said.

"Bring her back in one piece, sir."

"Roger that."

Jim left and headed to the flight deck to wait for the plane to be lifted by the huge elevators from the working deck into position. He found Krug already there.

"Ready to go?" Jim asked.

"All good," Krug replied, staring out at the passing ocean.

The heat was rising, the sea was still and flat, the sun barely an inch above the horizon. No breeze, and already ninety degrees in the shade.

"Think anything will come up today?" Krug asked.

Jim thought about it. "The grunts are pretty good at their jobs. You never know, though, what might pop off around the oil fields. We'll see when we get up there."

The taciturn Krug only nodded in reply.

The USS *Boxer* was classified as an amphibious carrier because the fighter assets were mainly US Marines instead of US Navy pilots. While the conventional aircraft carriers had the faster F-16 and F-18 jets, the Harrier fighters did not need to use the deck catapults to launch that the others required. Harriers could lift off vertically from the smaller decks of amphibious carriers.

Both pilots headed to the Harriers waiting on the flight line. Jim's was in front, pointed toward the bow of the ship. Jim saluted the crew chief, clambered into the seat, hooked in the hoses of his pressure suit, and started his preflight inspection: fuel level, oxygen, control responses, radio check with the tower. All was in order. He stowed the checklist placard and closed the hatch. He couldn't wait to get off the deck and into the cooler air above the sea. He did one last visual check with the crew chief and got the okay from the tower. He glanced at the photo of Maggie, the beautiful schoolteacher he had met when training in Pensacola, and gave her a wink.

Throttles up and brakes set.

"AV-1, Reverend ready," Jim said into the microphone inside his oxygen mask.

"Roger, AV-1, stand by," tower control replied, adding a moment later, "Ship at speed, five knots wind on the bow, no crosswind. On your mark."

"AV-1 departing."

Jim made the necessary adjustments to position the aircraft's nozzles down. Then he pushed the throttles to full power, feeling the vibration of the plane increasing as it slowly lifted off from the flight deck. The rush filled him, as it did at every launch.

A versatile fighter, the Harrier was a British design that had been around for more than forty years. While not as fast as other assets in the arsenal, its VTOL—vertical takeoff and landing—capabilities made it unique. The plane could land and be supported from practically anywhere, which meant it could be hidden in the countryside or placed close to enemy lines and didn't have to be exposed to the vulnerability of an open airfield. The fighter's uniqueness was its greatest strength.

Jim felt the push of the g-forces on his body from moving the throttles to flight mode, and the Harrier leapt forward, the downward thrust of air jets through adjustable nozzles creating the lift. Jim pulled back on the control stick and adjusted the nozzle lever to forward flight. It was here that the hovering jet's flight became more streamlined and smooth.

After adjusting the airspeed and heading for the rendezvous point, Jim listened more closely to the radio chatter from the tower and from AV-2, Krug's aircraft. Jim banked north toward the mainland Iraq coastline twenty miles away; at quarter speed, Krug would have no problem catching up. At six thousand feet of elevation, he could see Krug pull up on his port side.

"AV-1, five by five," Jim said. "Accelerate to .7 Mach."

"AV-2, five by five, roger."

The responses were quick and precise. Excessive

chatter was discouraged. The jets formed up and headed inland.

"Spear command, *Boxer* AV-1 Harrier patrol in the country," Jim said, checking in with the ground force control. The port city of Basra had come and gone in minutes as they sped over the brown landscape.

"Understood, AV-1. Proceed to Nasiriya best speed. A Marine patrol is taking fire. Requesting air support."

"Roger, command. Three minutes out," Jim said. "Judge, accelerate to .8 Mach and let's head in."

"Roger. Accelerate to .8."

The two planes banked and accelerated in tandem. Jim felt the rush of adrenaline, his senses sharpening. If Marines were in trouble below, he and Krug would do their best to add critical weight to the Marines' firepower. Drowsiness or thoughts of home were banished, all intent focusing on the task at hand. They were the devil dogs of war, slipped loose from their chains.

The time to station seemed to last forever but in truth was only a few minutes. Jim began scanning the hills and plains below, the aircraft dropping from the skies at one thousand feet per second.

"AV-1, ground control." The sound was louder in his helmet with his heightened senses. It was the voice of a forward air combat controller on the ground, who would now be directing the assault.

"Go, ground control."

"We are engaging enemy forces estimated more than one hundred. They have our patrol pinned down in some ruins four klicks north of Nasiriya, assisted by heavy weapons and accurate mortar fire. Mortars are believed to be west of the position. Blue smoke is marking friendlies. Anything outside that is to be engaged as hostile. Weapons free."

"Roger, command," Jim said, then looked out the windshield, scanning the ground.

"Blue smoke, two o'clock." Krug's voice jerked Jim's head around to note the location.

"Roger that. Judge, fall back. I'll do the first run. If you see any tracers or rockets, engage the target."

"Roger that. Falling back."

Jim could sense the disturbance in the air as Krug moved his aircraft back to a tail guard position.

"Half-track, twelve o'clock," Krug said.

Jim checked that the Intrepid Tiger II electronic jammer was working, helping discourage any guided rockets targeting the fighter, and began his run. From there on, instinct and muscle memory did the work, developed from countless hours of training and flying. Jim noted trucks and three tanks. He selected the CRV-7 rockets and loosed them in bursts, hitting one tank and one truck.

Secondary explosions could be felt as he blasted over the target area.

"Tank down. Where was that hiding?" Krug asked.

It was a good question that Jim didn't have time to think about. All of the Iraqi armor was supposed to have been eliminated months before.

"Doesn't matter where it was, only that it's here," Jim said. On his bank to the right, he could see Krug firing on a position, the rockets streaming out of the pods mounted underneath the wings.

"AV-1, AV-1, ground. Be advised friendly Apaches inbound from the south," came the voice of ground control.

"Roger, ground. Have engaged two tanks and one weaponed half-track. Beginning the second run. Break . . . Judge, condition," Jim said.

"Rev, this is Judge. All good. Got the third tank. No following tracers. More targets spotted. Advise western run this time."

"Form on me two klicks to west, same drill."

"Roger, Rev," Krug said.

Jim lined up in preparation for the run.

"AV1, this is Scorcher-45 Apache," a new voice came in over the radio. "Good hit on armor. We have located mortars one klick west of ruins and engaging, using Willy Pete follow-up if possible."

"Roger that, Scorcher. Will be on the lookout," Jim said. "Willy Pete" was white phosphorus. These specialized shells had been in use for decades and were a dreadfully effective tool of war. They would explode and distribute white-hot fragments on the target area, destroying personnel and machinery.

Soon Jim saw the cloudy plumes of the white phosphorus rockets impacting the ground. Vaguely he could see the outline of one Apache and then red tracer fire from the south toward the helicopter.

"We're taking fire. Scorcher-46 hit." The pilot's voice was calm, his training kicking in even while under enemy attack.

Jim's eyes tracked the line of tracers back to its source. It appeared to be a mobile antiaircraft vehicle of some sort. An old adage of combat is that tracers work both ways.

"Scorcher, break right. Judge, two degrees west, engage the ground target."

"Roger, Rev."

As Jim banked his plane to line up on the mobile mounted heavy machine gun, he could see one of the Apaches spinning and losing altitude.

"Ground control, Apache is hit and going down. Selecting napalm."

Jim selected two of the four napalm canisters under his wings by toggling a small switch on the jet's console and then engaged the targeting computer. Screaming in at very low altitude, Jim waited, then triggered the release of the containers of the highly flammable mixture.

"Release," Jim said, taking evasive maneuvers after nailing the target.

The tracked vehicle, though hidden between two sand dunes, never had a chance once it revealed itself by firing on the Apache. Wide, rolling flame engulfed the sandy hills and the machine between. What had been safety now became an oven, roasting the machine and its crew.

"Rev, more antiaircraft, nine o'clock," Krug said.

Red tracers sped by Jim's plane, filling the air like fireflies. He knew that the tracers were spaced with up to twenty non-illuminated rounds between them, throwing up a wall of lead.

"Break left!" Jim ordered sharply.

"I'm hit! I'm hit!" Krug shouted.

"Climb! Climb evasive," Jim said, hoping they could outrun the range of the tracer rounds. The sheer volume of rounds was incredible. How many guns were down there? They had flown into a veritable hornet's nest.

Jim could feel impacts to the aircraft. Warning

buzzers were going off. Leveling the fighter, Jim looked around quickly to the wing. He could see some damage, but he still had control. The single fuselage-mounted engine wasn't happy, but he knew he could keep the aircraft up even with the new holes in it. The primary damage seemed to be in the left wing and rudder, the back end of the plane jiggling around, feeling sluggish.

Jim scanned his altimeter. He thought he was finally out of range of the enemy fire. Now he could set his mind to analyzing the current combat problem. The SPAAs, tracked antiaircraft guns, and MANPADS— shoulder-fired antiaircraft rockets—had been thick and fast. This seemed to be a trap, executed with the looted armaments from Saddam's bunkers that had disappeared all over Iraq. The enemy had used the Marine patrol for bait, pinning them down until the air support came in, where it could be knocked down in overwhelming firepower. At least that seemed to have been the plan.

"Judge, report." Jim snapped the command to his wingman.

There was no response.

Jim scanned around him to spot Krug's aircraft. Still there was no response on the radio. Then, banking despite the protests of the damaged jet, he spotted a plume of smoke from the ground.

"AV-1, AV-1, Scorcher-2."

"Go for AV-1," Jim responded.

"AV-1, I believe AV-2 was hit. Punched out . . . looked like a missile from the ground . . . there were two or three of them coming up. I spotted the antiaircraft and put all my rockets into those. Smoke trail north of you."

"Roger that, Scorcher-2," Jim said. "Ground

14

control, AV-1. AV-2 down. I repeat, AV-2 Captain Krug down. Report of seeing him punch out, but no chute confirm."

"Roger, AV-1. SAR inbound. See if you can make it a little less hot down there."

Jim knew the search and rescue team, SAR, would risk a lot for downed pilots, but they probably wouldn't undertake a guaranteed suicide mission.

"Will lay down suppressive fire around the crash site," Jim said.

"Roger, AV-1," the Apache pilot said, adding, "You're pouring smoke out of your right wing."

Jim could feel a general shaking that turned into a shudder when exceeding a certain point in the turn.

"I'm still flying but severely restricted," he said.

"Head back, AV-1. We will locate AV-2," the pilot of the SAR aircraft replied.

"AV-1, that ain't no magic plane," ground control said. "Don't know if we can get to you before the bogeys if you go down."

Jim ignored the advice and continued banking, easing off the controls only when the plane started to shudder. His eyes found the fuel gauge. The readout was steady. The fuel tanks didn't seem to be hit. He adjusted the throttles; increasing his speed seemed to make maneuvering easier. He smelled smoke in the cockpit.

As he completed his turn, the battlefield below was active, chaos in motion. An Apache swooped down on positions in the sand, tracers from its gun filing like ants into the hills. A small secondary explosion came from the ground at the impact point. Again tracers came from the ground, fewer than before but enough to be trouble, from two positions trying to get at the nimble Apache.

Lining up where the fire originated, Jim slipped to starboard and soon had the enemy like ducks in a row. Selecting the remaining rockets, aiming carefully, he released them at the position. Even as they were in the air, he switched to the napalm canisters, holding back on them as he followed the rockets in. Protecting the other air combat assets was crucial. The Apaches and Cobras, both attack helicopters, could keep closer and protect Krug better than he. Jim could move faster and higher, providing protection for them and the Marines on the ground.

Explosions on the antiaircraft SPAA were bright flashes. Moments after he saw them, Jim released the napalm canisters, sensing they were on target. Almost immediately, the plane began to shudder and pitch violently, much worse than before. Something was wrong—very wrong.

Jim struggled to control the aircraft, pulling up to gain altitude, the nose barely responding. All of the lights on the console were flashing. Then they all went out at once.

"Eject! Eject!" a recorded voice blared in his helmet headset.

Flying so low to the ground, Jim didn't wait. He reached up and pulled the eject lever. The result was immediate. The plane was violently shaking, its tail dropping away, creating a negative g-force of weightlessness. The canopy blew away as Jim jammed his head back as hard as possible. Rockets under the seat blasted it out of the plane. As the blood ran down from his brain, Jim willed himself not to pass out.

It didn't help.

Jim couldn't see. His face was to the ground, with a mouth full of sand. Everything was painful, from the bottom of his feet to the top of his head. Hearing was sporadic, choppy. Slowly flexing his fingers, he knew he was hurt but was not sure how badly.

He could remember ejecting out of the airplane, but not much after that. Unsure of speed or orientation when he ejected, he might easily have been dead if the cockpit had been pointed at the earth. Just a sticky crater.

Dead probably didn't hurt this much.

Finding his limbs still working, Jim tried to sit up. Pain radiated a quick flame up the sides of his chest and through his right groin muscle. Jim lay back again, breathing shallowly. He had a perverse understanding of how a dog must feel the first time an electric collar zaps it. He made a promise to the pain: *I won't do anything quickly if you don't do that to me again.* After a few minutes of feeling the edges and limits of his injuries, he was able to gently slip off the helmet and slowly push to a sitting position.

Looking around at his surroundings, he saw the edge of a small sandy hill. His parachute was draped behind him, tangled in some rocks and shrubs. The sharp stones nearby had scuff marks on them, showing the impact point of his descent from the air.

Undoing the parachute harness, he scanned the landscape, trying to figure out where here was. He could hear machine gun fire pretty far to the west. Jim knew he should find some cover before some unhappy enemy infantry types showed up and wanted to chitchat.

He could tell he was out of the central zone of fighting, and now he was free of his harness. Jim slowly dragged himself along the ground to the crest of the hill.

The journey took time, as aching ribs and the groin injury occasionally made themselves known, stopping him, if only not to wet himself from the pain. He was respecting the damage to his body now.

Struggling to the top of the loose, sandy hill, Jim slid his head up behind a small bush, not wanting to present a target if a sniper happened to be monitoring his landing site. Smoke was rising from multiple spots out in the distance. A number of Apaches and Cobras were working over the area. There was not much heavy ground fire, but there was still some small-arms resistance.

An Osprey in the distance was coming in fast and low, losing speed when it moved to hover mode. He watched as the fixed-wing aircraft became more helicopter than plane, its twin wing-mounted propellers rotating ninety degrees. It had to be landing for another pilot.

"That's my ride home," Jim muttered.

Reaching into his flight suit pocket, he pulled out his emergency search and rescue radio and turned it on.

"Pilots, report. This is SAR-2."

Jim keyed the mike. "SAR-2, this is AV-1. Over."

"Go, AV-1."

"I have eyes on you. I am about three klicks south of you. Over."

"Roger, AV-1. What is your condition?"

"SAR-2, I am injured but conscious," Jim said, then thought, *Obviously.*

"Roger, AV-1. We will complete the pickup and proceed to your location. Conceal yourself as best you can and monitor this channel. Prepare a smoke marker but do not deploy."

"Roger, SAR-2."

Jim slumped to the ground, the message given. He then slid back down the hill toward some brush that might offer cover. The twenty feet seemed a mile, but in a relatively short time he was able to get there, finding a small alcove of rock.

Jim wedged himself into the small divot. He noticed a strange smell, which he would always think of as "snakey" from growing up in the country. Pulling a plastic bag out of a pocket of his flight suit, Jim ripped it open, spilling a flare and smoke canister onto the ground.

"AV-1, SAR-2 en route to your position. We have your signal. Deploy smoke."

"Roger, SAR-2. Deploying."

Jim pulled the smoke grenade from the bag, pulled the pin, and tossed the grenade about six feet from the bushes. The canister flared and began emitting orange smoke in a steady, billowing stream. The whump of the Osprey's rotors echoed, and he started to crawl out of the hole. Instinct made him look to the right. A fat brown snake was curled up and tensely observing him, curled in a striking pose, right in his only path to the Osprey.

"Ah, man," Jim muttered, staring at the new problem.

"AV-1, SAR-2. Do you copy? We see your orange smoke. We are landing fifty yards from you. Can you meet us?"

Jim lay there, not daring to move yet. The snake, in its menacing presence of coiled speed and death, was motionless except to taste the air with its forked tongue. Its viper's eyes coolly regarded him. The noise from the Osprey was louder as it set down just over the hill.

"Fuck it," Jim said, reaching out quickly, holding the radio toward the snake. Jim felt the impact in his hand as the snake struck the radio. Before it could retract to strike again, Jim pushed down hard with the radio and pinned its head to the ground.

"Captain Stabbert, where are you?" The voice of the pararescue jumper could be heard over the hill, along with heavy footsteps.

"Over here," Jim shouted, bearing down as much as he could on the snake's head. The rest of the body was writhing as the snake struggled to pull itself out.

The PJ came over to Jim's position. "Let's go, sir."

"Got a problem. Snake," Jim replied, struggling to keep weight on the thrashing serpent.

The PJ looked down at what Jim was doing.

"Holy shit, that's a cobra."

"Great," Jim said sarcastically. "Wanna take a picture?"

The PJ pulled a Kabar knife from his combat vest and smoothly sliced off the head of the snake where it met the body under the radio. The headless body continued to writhe and twist on the ground.

"I'd rather get the hell out of here, if it's all the same to you, sir."

Jim dropped the radio and held up his hand. The PJ released his grip on his M4 carbine and let it hang from the sling around his neck. He pulled Jim out from under the bushes and to his feet.

"Can you walk, sir?"

Jim thought about it. He should have been in screaming pain, but with all the adrenaline in his system, he couldn't feel much. A little dazed, he pondered this. The PJ, likely tired of waiting, scooped him up in a fireman's carry and started off around the hill.

"Keep your eyes closed, sir."

Jim obeyed. He was aware of sand whipping around them and of being carried up the ramp and deposited onto a stretcher inside the Osprey.

"Good to go," the PJ said after strapping him in.

Jim opened his eyes, then quickly closed them again. His mouth felt dry and gritty. Numbness began coming over his body. He tried not to think about the silent, blood-soaked figure of his friend Krug across from him.

Blank eyes stared into his soul.

Jack Lyons

Chapter 2

Jim stood in the lobby of the San Diego airport, his uniform perfectly pressed, a bouquet of roses in his right hand. The balmy sun was warming his back. A fresh haircut and straight razor shave he had gotten that morning at his favorite barbershop in Coronado made him feel complete. A trim but muscular man topping out at just under six feet tall, with bright green eyes and dark skin, Jim cut a dashing figure of a young military officer, a flesh-and-blood recruiting poster for the Marines. He was aware of the looks from people passing by.

After two months of healing both overseas and in San Diego, he was finally fit for duty. Phone calls and emails had brought him to this point, waiting on a beautiful girl not seen in person for months. Their correspondence had started innocently while he healed, and with letters and phone calls, it had fully bloomed. Without seeing or touching each other, the two had become very close.

He spotted her gait before seeing her face: five feet two of fantastic in a yellow sundress. Quick bustling movements set her apart from the crowd, his firecracker Maggie Whimple.

"Jim!" Maggie squealed when she spotted him. She rushed toward him, all tapping heels, swirling skirt, and bouncing brunette curls, then leaped into his arms from almost five feet away.

"Mags."

Maggie was peppering his face with kisses and his ears with exclamations.

"Oh, you look so good" . . . *kiss, kiss* . . . "You feel good too" . . . *kiss, kiss* . . . "Have you lost weight?" . . . *kiss, kiss* . . . "You hungry? I'm hungry" . . . *kiss, kiss* . . .

Maggie felt light in his arms, soft and strong at the same time, smelling of sunshine and jasmine. She found his mouth and pulled his lips to hers in a deep, soft, warm, wet, sweet kiss. People passing stared and smiled, and Jim didn't care. He felt as if he could hold her there forever.

"You smell good, jarhead." Her southern drawl hit hard on the *jar* before the *head*.

"You smell better," Jim said.

"All right, put me down. People are staring!"

Her eyes were level with his. He could see his own reflection in her blue-rimmed irises with a twinkle of mischief within.

"Let 'em," Jim said, but he put her down all the same.

She kissed him again, and he gave her a squeeze.

"Ow, you're sticking me," she said.

"It happens."

Maggie blushed. "No, your pin or something."

Jim looked down and saw that the front of her sundress had caught on his gold flight wings.

"Hmmm." The sound vibrated in his chest.

"Watch it, mister. Everyone else is watching too. So help me."

Jim stooped and deftly unhooked the ruffle of her dress from the wings. In doing so, he accidentally brushed the back of his hand across Maggie's nipples through the thin material.

"Hmmm, now," she whispered. "'Take me to bed or lose me forever.'"

"*Top Gun* was a Navy movie."

"Shut up!" Maggie laughed, then teased, "Maybe I should find a sailor, then?"

Jim scooped her up in his arms again, picked up her suitcase, and swept out the door, Maggie laughing. Soon he was placing her in the topless Jeep Wrangler. Maggie had talked a blue streak on the short walk from the airport.

"Daddy and Momma say hello. They're fine. School is good. Glad it's winding up. The kids are sweet, but wiping noses and—and all that is—"

He kissed her again, saying fondly, "There's my Magpie."

She smiled coquettishly.

Jim jumped into the driver's seat and fired up, pulling out of the parking lot. The sunlight gleamed, and the breeze caressed them on the drive. Maggie laughed as her curls flew up around her face in the swirling air.

"Where we going, handsome?"

"Coronado," Jim replied. "I got us a room on the base. Not too far."

"Good," Maggie replied.

He reached for her hand and held it as they drove. The absence of the doors and top let them feel a part of the glorious morning. The tires hummed, the engine purred. All was right in the world.

The next few days flew by, with sex, napping, sex, dinner, sex, and beach time. Jim loved showing off the town he had made his home. From dinner in the Gaslamp Quarter to lunches in little Mexican shops all over the city, he showed her what the beautiful town had to offer. Jim was stationed here with the USS *Boxer*, and now he was to be assigned to teach new pilots in San Diego and at the Harrier base in Yuma, Arizona. So he would at least be in one place for a while.

"So this is what real Mexican food tastes like," Maggie exclaimed after her first bite of a carne asada quesadilla.

"Yeah, the Taco Tico has nothing on this."

Jim always liked to see Maggie eat. Her enjoyment of the food was visceral.

"Make sure you leave all your fingers," he joked.

"*Mmmm*, it's so good," Maggie said, rolling her eyes, guacamole on her chin.

It was the same for the spectacular fish tacos at his favorite bar in Ocean Beach, the Tilted Stick. Pushing back her plate and washing down the last bite with her cold Corona, Maggie sighed with contentment.

"Much more of this, and I'll have to go shopping for new clothes."

"I think we've worked off the calories as much as we can."

Maggie smirked at him.

The constant beach sun had turned her skin to a deeper brown. Her blue eyes, lit by the setting sun, looked at him across the table. Jim gazed into their depths constantly. She was the most beautiful woman in the world. Jim was happier, he thought, than he had any right to be.

Later, in bed, with the ocean waves murmuring through the open window, Jim lay beside Maggie, slowly stroking her back, the soft skin still warm from the sun. Gently, he traced her spine and shoulders, then caressed her round, tight bottom.

"You're putting me to sleep," she said.

"Good," Jim said, smiling. "It'll give you time to heal."

Maggie laughed. "It's a sweet hurt, though."

In truth, both of their sexes were raw from their constant lovemaking. But each time they touched or kissed, that meant less than nothing.

"I want to stay here forever. Like this, with you," Jim said.

Maggie looked up at him from just under his chin, her brown curls framing thoughtful eyes. Turning over delicate fingers, she began touching his face with her fingertips, tracing the jawline. Minutes passed and neither said anything more as they gazed into each other's eyes.

"Why don't we make it so?" Jim asked at last. "I sleep better with you beside me."

This was true. With Maggie beside him, Jim had slept soundly for the first time since the crash, untroubled by the nightly flashback dreams.

"I have to leave tomorrow," Maggie said.

"Who says?"

"I have a life back there. Friends, family."

"I love you, Mags."

"I love you, Jim."

"I want to marry you. I want to be with you until the day I die." As he said it, Jim felt his heart tighten at this sincere confession of feelings laid bare.

Maggie was silent, an amused expression on her face.

Jim continued. "Before you came into my life, I was completely focused on my work. I lived for it. But this last time, when I was away, over there, I only thought of you. It was my escape, my oasis. I thought of being here with you, touching you, being around you. The smell of your hair, the feel of your skin, the sound of your laughter, your happy chattering talk about everything."

Jim sat up and slipped his hands to the sides of Maggie's face. "When Stacy died—Maggie, that could have been me. They gave me a medal and said I was brave, but I wasn't. After we flew into that ambush, I was scared. I did it anyway. I went back into the fight. But all I could think was how, if I died that day, I would miss the life I wanted to have with you. I don't want to continue to live for duty. I want to live for love, for being with you."

Jim looked into Maggie's face, seeing tears sliding from those blue eyes. He slipped a hand around her waist and onto her hip, pulling her closer to him.

"I look into your eyes and see my future," he said. "A future I want to have. I'm a good man, Maggie, and I'll be a good husband and father. I love you."

Inches from her face, he looked deeply into her eyes.

"I love you, Maggie Whimple, and I know you love me. Marry me."

Maggie sat up, pushing him back.

"Damn, Jim, you've gone and made me cry," she said as she fumbled for the tissues on the nightstand. She blew her nose and dabbed at her eyes, then looked up at him.

"You're supposed to get down on one knee, asshole," she said. "And not be bare-assed."

Jim grinned, sliding off the bed until both his knees were on the floor. He reached for her ankles and pulled her to him.

"Maggie Whimple, will you marry me?"

"Yes, stupid. But when we tell this story, we were by the ocean."

Jim kissed her long and deep, and then they were one again.

The following days were a whirlwind. First they looked for a place to live near the base and were lucky to find one in Jim's price range, a pretty little cottage set about with eucalyptus trees and green grass. It was part of a property that included a larger house where the owners, a retired Navy captain named Paul Sotta and his wife Jenny, lived. The Sottas showed them around.

"My wife and I started in a place like this. You been married long?"

"The ink is still wet on the license," Jim replied. "We'll have a bigger ceremony later."

Maggie fluttered around the rooms with Jenny. The house was a well-made little Craftsman with one bedroom and wooden floors. It had a cozy kitchen and a private view of a pool set back from the main house.

"You a pilot?" Paul asked.

"That a question?"

"Nope, not really." Paul smiled at Jim. "I flew in Korea and Vietnam. Three tours each and back home."

Paul looked at Maggie chattering with his wife.

"Looks like her mind is made up."

"Looks like," Jim agreed.

"Why don't we go have a beer and some man talk?"

The rent worked out better than Jim had hoped. Paul, who was pleased that they would be in the area for at least a couple of years, gave a discount to the new couple. Jim explained he would be a liaison trainer of sorts, stationed in San Diego and flying the short hop to the training base in Yuma, Arizona, a couple of times a week. There were benefits to being thought of as a war hero, even though he certainly didn't feel like one.

Maggie and Jenny walked up, chattering. Jenny, a pretty blonde woman with a ready smile, was arm in arm with Maggie.

"Is it done?" Jenny asked.

"Well, I don't want to jump into anything too quickly," Paul said, winking at Jim. "Maybe we need to do a background check. Call Steve over at the office."

"Steve Hertzig is a close friend. I grew up with him in San Diego." Jenny lowered her voice and said in a mock whisper, "Former CIA."

"Former, my ass," Paul said, reaching for his beer.

"Well, I love the house," Maggie said.

"It's done, then. Will you stay for dinner?" Jenny asked. Then, not waiting for an answer, she continued, "Fine. Maggie and I will get to know each other, and you fellas can do the same."

Jenny took Maggie by the hand and went into the main house. Jim watched them go. Paul smiled at him.

"Did you have other plans?"

"Guess not," Jim said, turning back to Paul.

"Jenny pretty much gets an idea in her head and doesn't let go. So I call her my terrier," Paul said.

"Sometimes I call Maggie my 'Magpie,'" Jim said. "Chatters a lot and likes shiny things."

They both sat in the fresh evening air and listened to pots and pans rattling in the kitchen.

"I like it when she chatters her happy talk," Jim said after a moment.

"I know what you mean. Here's to new couples and new friends."

Paul tipped his bottle, and Jim tapped it with his own. Life was better than he deserved.

Jack Lyons

.

Chapter 3

The days fell into a nice routine, with Jim reporting most days for work at the Naval Air Station North Island on Coronado. The year that passed all too quickly was the happiest Jim had ever known. Work was going well; Jim had found that not only was he an effective teacher, he enjoyed it.

A couple of times a week, he jumped into a jet and headed off to lecture in Yuma, where there was a new crop of pilots every eight weeks. There he would evaluate training and bombing qualifications. On those days, he was sometimes home a little later than he preferred, but at least he slept in his own bed with Maggie.

One Friday he had to run over to the "Big Navy" base, 32nd Street Naval Station, for a meeting, and then the rest of the day was free. He called Maggie to see what she wanted to do for dinner.

He and Maggie had gotten into the habit of having dinner with the Sottas on Fridays to celebrate the end of the week. The two couples had become quite close. Maggie and Jenny were two peas in a pod. He and Paul could speak and understand each other. In a world often unfamiliar with combat and the men it made, he felt lucky to have found someone he could share a beer with—or a silence as it came.

"Hello?" Maggie's voice came from the phone.

"Hello, beautiful."

"*Baby!*" she squealed.

He loved that she always answered his calls as if she couldn't believe he would take the time to call her.

"Hi, sugar," he said. "I'm headed home and wanted to know if you needed anything for dinner."

"Well, let's see. I stopped by the farmers' market on the way home from school and bought the best-looking zucchini I ever saw from the nice man there, Paulo. You met Paulo once when we were there together. So anyways, I thought we would have that, with pasta and some wine. Still, I forgot to get the wine and couldn't remember what type we had that I liked, the white I think, for zucchini and pasta. And Steve is coming with his new lady friend . . ."

Jim listened and smiled. This may have sounded like chatter to someone else, but he knew it was happy talk. His wife was delighted and wanted to talk and tell him all about her day.

". . . so I need some wine and a little bread, maybe a loaf from that bakery by the house. Jim? Jim?"

"I'm here," Jim replied, jostling the phone a bit as he paid the toll at the base of the bridge. A lot of the conversation had been lost in the wind riding over the bridge, but at least he had gotten the important bits: wine and bread. "I'll pick them up and be home soon."

Half an hour later, Jim pulled into the driveway, parked, and headed around back. Paul was already relaxing at the patio table by the pool. Light jazz was playing through hidden speakers around the man-made grotto.

"Beer?" Paul asked Jim as he walked by the table.

"Thought you'd never ask," Jim said, scooping one

from the small cooler one-handed, popping the tab, and taking a deep drink. "Ah," he sighed, enjoying the cold beverage. "Let me drop these off and join you."

"Take your time."

Jim walked into his cottage, spotted Maggie and Jenny working at the kitchen counter, facing away from him. Soft-footed, he sneaked up behind them, then reached out and goosed Maggie.

"*Gaak!*" Maggie exclaimed with a jump, then twirled to face him. She pulled him close for a deep kiss, Jim lifting her with one arm.

"Mmmmwah," Jim vocalized, setting her down.

"Get a room," Jenny said wryly, smiling at the couple.

"Baby, did you get the wine? How was the drive? Was it nice for the Jeep today? Are you thirsty?"

Jim set down the bags and kissed her again, only partially stifling the stream of questions.

"Mshs," Maggie said through the kiss, "bread and we have olives and fresh cucumbers. Go outside and sit with Paul, and we will be out in a moment."

Jim went back to the bedroom, took a quick shower, then changed into shorts and a favorite worn T-shirt. Passing by the kitchen, he grabbed his beer and the plate of crackers and cheese Jenny handed him without breaking her conversation with Maggie.

Heading to the table, Jim set down the platter, took a seat, and sipped on his beer. He and Paul chatted for a moment, enjoying the little sunshine left and listening to the soft music. The breeze softly rustled the leaves around them and made a perfect end to a San Diego day.

"Busy at work?" Paul asked.

"Steady," Jim replied. "A meet and greet today for

the new pilots coming in. Logistics with the ordnance department and the commander of training."

"Seems a pretty good gig, being able to be here and jump a jet to Yuma."

"There are some perks, to be sure."

"Noticed that ribbon on your fruit salad when you came in, blue stripes on white. A Silver Star, if I'm not mistaken. I hadn't seen it before. Usually you're in your flight suit."

"Yeah," Jim said. "It's from the last deployment, when I got hurt."

"They don't just hand those out. I won't push you, but if you'd like to talk, I'd like to hear the story sometime."

"Sometime, then," Jim agreed. The memories were still a little too raw, even over a year later.

"Sometime is good enough."

"Hello, all." A voice came from the corner of the house, followed by a tall, heavyset man in tan slacks and a blue button-down shirt.

"Steve, hello," Paul said, rising with an extended hand. Jim also came to his feet as greetings were exchanged.

"This is our friend Jim Stabbert," Paul told Steve. "His wife Maggie is in the cottage with Jenny, preparing supper."

"Beer, Steve?" Jim asked.

"Got any bottled water?" Steve asked.

"Sure," Jim said, grabbing a bottle from the ice and handing it to Steve as they all sat.

"So, Jim, how are you finding San Diego?" Steve asked, taking a sip of water.

"Well, I've been here off and on for four years. It's

pretty much as it was, perfect except for the traffic. Paul tells me you've been gone for a while."

"Wrapping up a two-year consulting assignment," Steve replied, sitting down at the table. "I grew up here. It wasn't much more than a lot of little towns then. Jenny and I used to practically live at the beach. Our parents were friends, and we grew up almost as brother and sister. There were a whole mess of us running around together: Italians, Portuguese, Mexicans. Jenny was one of the only blonde white girls, *guera*, in the bunch. It was a great place to grow up."

"You've traveled since then?" Jim asked.

"Yeah. I've ranged pretty far on business for the government, all over the world. San Diego always drew me back. Big as it has become, it's always been my home."

"I can see why."

"Paul tells me you're newly married."

Jim grinned. He couldn't help it when his marriage came up. "Maggie and I have been married for about eleven months now. After I got back from deployment, a lot of things got clear in my head. She was who I wanted to be with."

"How did you meet?" Steve asked.

"I was doing pilot training after the academy and met her in Pensacola. She was down for spring break with some girlfriends, and it just went from there."

"To true love," Steve said, raising his bottle.

"I'll drink to that," Paul said.

"Are you boys talking about football yet?" Maggie asked, coming to the table with a bowl of salad.

"Just bragging on your cooking," Jim said.

"I know that's a lie. Hi, I'm Maggie," Maggie said,

extending her hand to Steve, who rose to take it.

"Steve Hertzig," he said. "Your young man here, he said you're the best cook in three counties."

"Two liars in as many minutes, but thanks."

Jenny followed with plates and food, and everyone found their places. Jim stood up, opened the chilled chardonnay, and began filling glasses.

"None for me," Steve said.

Jim moved on to Maggie's glass.

"Me either," Maggie said.

Jim gave her a quizzical look but put the wine back in the cooler, then put his napkin in his lap and looked around. Maggie was looking down but almost vibrating.

"What's the matter, honey?" Jim asked, concerned.

"I'm pregnant!" Maggie exploded, giggling and covering her mouth.

Everyone started talking at once. Jim sat stunned.

"Well, say something, Jim," Jenny said.

"Guhhh," Jim said.

"Jim?" Maggie said hesitantly, observing him intently.

Jim was aware that everyone was looking at him. He knew he would have to do something or hurt Maggie's feelings. Jim stood up, leaned down, and gave his wife a big kiss on the lips. The others applauded. Jim sat back down, relieved that he had gotten through that hurdle.

"Well, that was nice," Steve said. "Cheers."

They tapped glasses and began to eat. As Jim ate, he kept gazing at Maggie. Manners dictated that he should engage in the conversation with the others, but he couldn't take his eyes off her. Maggie gave him a little kick under the table and smiled at him. He matched her smile, and Maggie reached out and held his hand under the table.

As the night went on, Jim engaged more in the conversation, though his thoughts and eyes never went far from Maggie. He was ecstatic at the idea of fatherhood, that he and Maggie had made a child that would be a part of each of them. The dinner was eaten, goodbyes were said, and Jim and Maggie headed home, Maggie leading him by the hand to the cottage and then the bedroom.

"You were rude tonight," Maggie said teasingly.

"I know. Think they'll forgive me?"

"Probably. Take me to bed or lose me forever," Maggie said, smiling as he lifted her sundress up and off. They kissed as his own clothes found their way to the floor. He joined with her, gazing into her eyes.

"I love you, Maggie."

"I love you more," Maggie said.

Chapter 4

Jim pulled the control stick and slid his Harrier jet in line with the North Island airfield lights. His day had gone late in Yuma, but there was still some light left from the beautiful sunset over the Pacific. He made the necessary adjustments and guided the jet to touch down, then taxied from the runway to the hangar.

Shutting down the engines, he lifted a picture from the console. It had replaced the one he had lost in Iraq. This one showed Maggie smiling and wearing the same bikini as before, only this time she cradled the pronounced bulge of her stomach, with his baby growing inside.

He loved that picture of Maggie smiling and glowing.

Jim climbed deftly from the cockpit and returned the ground chief's salute. Slipping out of his flight suit in the hangar's change room, he turned on his cell phone. A message from Maggie showed on the voice mail. He tapped it and listened.

"Hi, honey, I'm over at the doctor's. Call me when you get in. I had the best day today," Maggie said. "Jenny and I went for lunch after school let out and then to the doctor's. I saw a dress in a shop window on the way over here, and I liked it—it would go with the hat from home. I got it, but I can't wear it until after the baby comes. Still, it is so tight and—and I know you'll love it and then—"

Jim smiled and hit the button to call her back as he got into his Jeep.

"Hello," a voice said. Not Maggie's voice, a man's voice.

"Hello, did I get the wrong number? I'm sorry." Jim pulled the phone back and looked at the screen. It was Maggie's number.

"Wait," the man said. "Jim, this is Paul."

"Oh, hi, Paul," Jim said as he pulled onto the road leading out of the base. "Could you put Maggie on? I just landed, and I'm headed home. I want to know if we need anything for dinner."

Jim waited for an answer as he steered through the traffic. There was none.

"Hello, Paul, are you there?"

"Are you near the base hospital, Jim?" Paul said at last.

"Yeah, I'm driving right by it now."

"I wonder if you could stop by and give me a lift home."

"Sure, Paul. I'll be right there."

Jim pulled into the hospital parking lot and parked the Jeep in an empty spot. Walking up the steps to the main entrance, he spotted Paul sitting on a ledge, eyes serious. The expression on Paul's face caused Jim to stop walking and just stand there.

He was talking to me on Maggie's phone! Jim thought, alarmed.

Jim ran up the remaining steps to Paul in a flash.

"Paul, where's Maggie?" Jim asked, breathing heavily, his senses immediately on edge.

The older man's face was grim and set.

"Jim, I need you to listen as we walk," he said, standing up.

"*Where's Maggie?*" Jim shouted.

"In there, in surgery," Paul replied, pointing down the hall.

Jim was moving faster now, into the hospital, scanning the scene. Paul caught his arm firmly, pulling Jim around with his own momentum. Jim tried to shake him off, but Paul held fast.

"Jim, listen to me!" Paul said forcefully. "She's in surgery, and you can't get to her. Come with me. Now."

The pain in Paul's eyes cut through the questions in Jim's head. He straightened up and followed Paul down the hall. They came to a waiting room. Steve was sitting there, staring at the floor, tears in his eyes.

Through clenched teeth, Jim asked, "Will someone please tell me what's going on? What's happened to Maggie?"

Steve and Paul exchanged looks. Finally Steve nodded, rose and turned to Jim.

"Jim, there's been an accident. Jenny and Maggie were hurt."

Jim felt his legs wobble and his chest constrict. Steve got hold of his arm and guided him to a chair. Jim looked up at Paul, who was leaning against the wall, his left hand over his eyes. His shoulders were shaking, but no sound came from him. Steve had a hand on Jim's shoulder and looked down into his eyes.

"Jenny's gone, Jim," he said.

Jim felt cold and numb, staring at the pale tiled floor.

"What happened?" he asked Steve.

"A truck, out of control," Steve said. "They were

crossing the street. Jenny apparently pulled Maggie out of the way, so she . . . got the worst of it."

Jim sat back, not quite in control of himself. After a moment, though, he took a deep breath and his long military training kicked in. He would no longer let his panic guide him. He would identify the problem and overcome it. He walked over to Paul, put his arms around him, and squeezed him tight.

"I got this," Jim said, to himself as much as to the man in his arms.

Paul shook for a moment in Jim's arms, then returned his hug, saying nothing. Tears came to Jim's eyes.

"Are you Jim Stabbert?"

Jim looked to his right and saw a man in hospital scrubs.

"Yes," Jim said, pulling away from Paul.

"Your wife is out of surgery."

Jim took a closer look at the man. He was about forty-five years old, with a crew cut and a lean runner's body. He looked at Jim through brown eyes, calm and steady.

"Major Stabbert, I am Captain Grace. I'm the head of surgery for this hospital. I operated on Maggie."

"How is she? Can I see her?"

"She is stable for now, she is in recovery, and you will be able to see her soon."

Jim let out a long sigh.

"Major Stabbert, I'm afraid we were unable to save your child. The trauma was too much. We performed an emergency C-section, but she just wasn't able to make it."

Jim felt a burning in his chest. *Push it down, push*

it down.

"She?" Jim asked, looking into the doctor's eyes.

"She. I'm sorry, Major. Would you like to come with me?" The doctor took him by the arm and started to lead him down the hall.

Jim looked back at Paul, who was now embracing Steve. Paul looked up at him.

"It's going to be okay, Jim," Paul said, his tears telling a different story.

Jim turned back down the hall and followed the doctor to a doorway.

"She's in here, Major Stabbert. You can go in. She's going to be groggy. We haven't told her about the baby yet. I'll go with you and . . ."

"I'll tell her," Jim said, quietly but firmly.

The doctor hesitated a moment, then said, "I'll be right down the hall if you need anything."

Jim nodded, and the doctor walked away a few steps. Jim put his hand on the door, steeling himself. He walked in.

Maggie was in a bed, hooked to tubes and monitors. Her eyes were closed, and bandages were on her head and up her left arm. Jim felt a lump in his throat. It was hard to breathe. He walked to her bedside and gently took her right hand, careful to avoid the device clipped to her finger and the IV in her arm. Jim looked up at the heart monitor and the others—not knowing what some of them measured—then back at her.

"Maggie," he said softly. "Maggie."

Maggie stirred under the sheet.

"Jim," she said. "Jim, where am I?"

Jim stifled a sob as he looked at the bruises and cuts on Maggie's face.

"You're in the hospital, baby. You were in an accident." His voice felt thick and rough.

"Hospital, oh . . ." Maggie pulled her hand from his and felt her stomach, her shoulders rising up in pain. Her eyes sought his, wide and questioning. "The baby . . ."

Jim gritted his teeth and said, "Don't worry about that now. Just rest."

Maggie relaxed. "All right, Jim."

She took his hand again. Looking into her eyes, Jim had never felt so scared and useless in his entire life.

"Jenny?" Maggie asked.

"Just rest, Maggie." Jim lifted his head up, his mouth gaping, trying to draw air.

Maggie squeezed his hand.

They stayed that way for a moment, Jim feeling the tears roll down his face. He kneeled beside the bed, kissing her hand.

Maggie stroked his face and said, "Shhh, baby. It's gonna be okay."

He couldn't hold it back anymore. Jim's sobs racked his body, wrenching, anguished cries. He pressed Maggie's hand against his face. He was supposed to be comforting her, and he couldn't even control himself.

"Shhh, baby. It'll be all right," Maggie said in her soft drawl. Then, after a moment: "They're both dead, aren't they? Jenny? The baby?"

Jim couldn't answer her, his throat producing only sobs and gasps for air. He nodded his head.

How can she be so calm? How can she be so strong? he thought.

He stayed that way for a while. How long, he couldn't say. Eventually, the room stopped spinning, and the shadows began to lengthen. Jim struggled to his feet and leaned over Maggie. He could see his tears on her face. Somehow, she smiled.

"Kiss me," she said.

He did, as gently as possible.

"I love you, Maggie," he said.

"I love you more," she replied.

Jim watched as the light went out of the light of his life's eyes.

Jack Lyons

Chapter 5

Driving to the funeral service, Jim observed the traffic. Regular people going about their ordinary lives. How could they be so unaware that a light had just gone out of the world? Maggie was gone, and they just went to work, got lunch, and chatted on their cell phones as if nothing had changed.

Jim had told his and Maggie's families the news and then made all the arrangements. After his breakdown beside Maggie's bed, no more tears had he shed, feeling only emptiness. He'd put the pain in a box and tucked it away.

The man who had killed Jenny, Maggie, and their child—their killer—was a foreign national from Mexico, illegally in the country. Pablo Champos, a middle-aged rich man driving an expensive truck in a country he shouldn't have been in, had caused the carnage. Witnesses said he had appeared high or drunk and in the middle of a rant of some sort, yelling into his phone, at the time of the killing.

The funeral home was filled with family and well-wishers, including people from the grade school where Maggie had worked in San Diego. He greeted them all and thanked them for coming. A lot of them had tears in their eyes, but inside, Jim had turned to stone. He put on the necessary face for the world, but it was only a mask, hiding his anguish and the nothingness inside.

After the service, burial, and reception, he returned home. Walking by the pool, he found Paul sitting at the table where they had shared many dinners and drinks. Paul seemed to have aged ten years in the past couple of days. Jenny's service had been the day before, an overwhelming show of support for a hometown girl who had touched many people's lives. Paul hadn't been up to a second funeral in as many days. Jim didn't blame him a bit.

"Hey, Paul," Jim said, walking over to the table.

"Hey, Jim." Paul's eyes moved up to Jim's face.

"Is it helping?" Jim asked, gesturing to the table, which was littered with beer cans and tequila bottles.

"Little bit, a little bit," Paul said, then sighed. "Not really, though."

"Mind if I join you?"

Paul looked at him through bleary eyes.

"Yeah, go ahead."

Jim picked a beer bottle out of the cooler and sat down, draining it quickly and picking up another. He finished half of that one, then took a huge swig from the bottle of tequila on the table.

"You in a hurry?"

"Hurry to catch up, maybe," Jim said.

"Hmmph."

Jim looked over at the newspaper lying on the table. The handle of a pistol was sticking out from underneath it.

"What's with the pistol?"

"Trying to decide whether to blow my brains out or go kill that son of a bitch, *then* blow my brains out," Paul replied.

Jim finished his beer and grabbed another.

50

"You gonna try and talk me out of it?" Paul asked Jim, his eyes red-rimmed and belligerent.

"I was thinking about whether I would join you," Jim said.

"Naw, the paper would say we were fags."

Both men cracked up, laughing at the crass absurdity. The unbelievable tension and grief inside them was desperate for a way out.

Footsteps on the gravel next to the house made them look up. Steve appeared with brown bags and a large bag of ice.

"I thought I'd find you here," Steve said.

"This is a drinking party, Steve. I don't know that you'll like it," Paul growled.

Steve pulled two cases of beer out of one bag and two handles of whiskey out of the other. He dumped the beer into the large cooler and covered it with half the ice. Pulling one, he opened the can and raised it to the two men.

"I haven't had a drink in thirty-five years, my promise to Jenny after I wrapped my car around a telephone pole," he explained to Jim. "My word is complete to her now, and I don't want to go to some bar and drink with assholes who didn't know her."

"Well, there are two assholes here who did," Jim said. "Have a seat."

"To Jenny and Maggie," Steve said. "We will never know their like again."

"And to Dawn, my daughter, who never got to see one," Jim added.

The men clinked bottles and began to drink in earnest.

"He's gonna get away with it," Steve said, staring

at the pool.

Both Jim and Paul looked at him in disbelief.

"Fuck you mean, 'gonna get away with it'?" Paul demanded as he struggled to his feet, slurring his words.

Steve finished his bottle of beer and reached for another one.

"I said, the fuck you mean by that?" Paul demanded, slamming his palm on the table, unsteady on his feet.

Steve opened the beer and sighed.

"He's an asset," Steve said. "No one told me so, but I've been doing this a long time. He wasn't here by accident. Someone's running him for intelligence, for his connections and knowledge. I made some inquiries. It's what wasn't said."

"You don't know that," Jim said as he rose, taking Paul's shoulder and guiding the older man down.

"Yes, I do," Steve said.

The men sat in silence, sipping from their drinks.

The night went on, the men beginning to swap stories about the ones they had loved, the ones they had lost, trading lies and truths about war and fights and childhoods. Steve and Paul were switching from reminiscing about Jenny to arguing over her favorite song.

The beer flowed and the whiskey poured. Paul and Steve were both trying and failing to sing a coherent verse. This led to an argument, the two men trading some pushes and punches until Jim shoved them both into the pool. They came up spluttering, and Steve pulled Paul to the shallow end, where they moved into the maudlin portion of the evening. Crying and embracing, they swore they would be brothers united in their love of Jenny. Jim got into the pool and helped the older men out as best he could in his own drunken condition. The three men lay beside the pool, trying to catch their breath.

"I want to go to the desert," Jim said suddenly. "I fly over it enough. I want to go there."

"Now?" Steve asked, wringing out his socks.

"Now," Jim said.

They looked at each other for a minute, then grabbed the cooler and what was left of the beer and loaded into Jim's Jeep, with Jim at the wheel, more clear-headed now than he had any right to be.

They drove east on I-8, seeing almost no other cars in the predawn hours. The smell of chaparral and eucalyptus washed over them. The miles flew by, the Jeep powering up the mountains and gliding along their tops. Jim sat with grim determination, Steve stone-faced beside him. Paul spent much of the trip being noisily sick, hanging over the back of the spare tire, painting the road behind them.

Soon Jim could see the first lightening of the sky descending from the mountains. Taking the exit off the highway at Ocotillo way too fast, he hung a left and continued to accelerate. Neither of the passengers said a word despite the high speed. Jim sped through the small town and out into the Anza–Borrego Badlands highway. The powerful engine was pulling them along the two-lane road, the headlights illuminating the bushes and sand around them. Redness in the sky behind the rocky, sandy mountains gave notice of the world's turning.

Jim slowed the Jeep and continued at a more manageable speed as he saw a dirt turnoff ahead and took it. He eased through the scrub, rocks, and cacti lining the dirt track, weaving through rocks and boulders and canyons, the Jeep's engine the only sound. Effortlessly, he navigated around and over obstacles in the dusty trail at the bottom of the canyon. The sky was becoming lighter, the headlights not really necessary. Jim drove along the rutted road winding out of the canyon onto a dusty plain.

Jim shut off the Jeep and stepped out into the bleak landscape: a wide-open plain covered in dirt, sand, and scrub. Austere, lonely, quiet; the motor, ticking as it cooled, was the only sound. This place was big enough to swallow a man and everything in him . . . even his grief. He walked up the slight slope to the base of a cliff and began to climb, scrabbling up to a small ledge thirty feet above the ground.

Jim looked to the east as the first rays streamed over the horizon, and he smiled.

In accomplishing nothing, he had accomplished everything. He could still smile.

It was so clear to him.

He was still alive. He could be alive, he could remember Maggie.

Now he thought about the criminal who had killed his wife and daughter, the man wrapped up by some US intelligence agency, protected from the consequences of his actions, from justice.

Jim closed his eyes and felt the sun bathing his face like a blessing.

He was alive, and Maggie wasn't.

With the sun peeking over the skyline, his confusion was gone. He was filled now in this empty wilderness. The feeling had started in his stomach and risen to his chest, then his whole body. He knew he had to live and survive, to taste what Maggie couldn't. To feel what Maggie would never feel again.

And, if what Steve said was true, to bring justice to her killer.

Chapter 6

"He's being held in a safe house in Arizona," Steve said, looking across the kitchen table at Jim. "But he might be moved at any time."

"So it's real, then. Champos won't see the inside of a courtroom here?" Jim asked.

There had been no mention of Champos from any news source in the weeks since Jenny, Maggie, and Dawn had been killed, and no word from the authorities. Steve had reached through his contacts in the intelligence community to find out what was happening, what was being done—or not being done—to the man who had killed Jenny, Maggie, and Dawn.

"No. He gives up what he knows about trafficking and corruption, and then it's done."

"They're letting him go? Scot-free?" Paul asked.

Steve turned to Paul.

"He will be turned over to the Mexican government, possibly, if we need a trump card in a deal or treaty. Champos knows a lot about corruption in the political system in Mexico: who gets paid, who does the paying."

Jim looked out the window to the soft sunlight.

"It smells to me that he was being kept here, probably by one of the alphabet soup agencies," Steve said. "Got him a new identity and covered him."

"Until he messed up," Paul said bitterly.

"The US government covers murderers now?" Jim asked Steve, leaning forward.

Steve looked at him flatly.

"Okay, stupid question," Jim said.

"There it is, gentlemen, all of what I know. Except that this man is absolutely a murderer, and not just of Jenny, Maggie, and the baby. He has been debriefed at length: women, children, and men, you name it, he's killed it. He has been involved in brutal torture and rape. He is a sociopath, only interested in himself and nothing—no one—else."

A long moment passed as Jim considered his words. Finally he spoke.

"I only have one question, Steve."

"Yes?"

"How do I get to him?"

"You don't."

"Not good enough," Jim said.

"You being in prison for the rest of your life isn't an option," Steve said. "Maggie wouldn't want that."

"Maggie wouldn't want to be dead either, but she is," Jim said, his jaw tightening. "This sit right with you, Steve? Him getting away with killing our people? Your Jenny, my Maggie and our daughter?"

Steve slumped in his seat, then leaned forward. "Fuck you, Jim."

"Fuck you back, Steve."

"Fuck you both," Paul said, his eyes clear and angry. "Jim and Steve, I don't care what you do. I'm gonna kill that son of a bitch if it is the last thing I do on earth, even if it costs me everything, including my life."

Paul stared hard into the two men's eyes. "Choose if you're in or out, but one way or another, that piece of shit is gonna die."

Two weeks later, Steve walked into Paul's house, his
arms full of boxes and papers. In the past two days, the
home in the quiet, wealthy neighborhood had been
transformed into a planning area. Whiteboards listing
scenarios that were eventually discarded adorned the
living room walls. Steve plopped the box down and
unrolled a map on the dining room table. Jim and Paul
gathered around him.

"The house where he's being kept is a safe house
on an abandoned military installation . . . here," Steve
said, pointing to the brown speck on the map.

Jim leaned forward and took in the terrain and
location, brown surrounded by blue.

"Isla Guadalupe?"

"Owned by Mexican military intelligence," Steve
said.

"He is in Mexico, then?"

"Yes, transferred yesterday. Agents are holding
him there while he is jointly debriefed."

"Is it a big island? Busy?" Jim asked.

"It's very small, less than a hundred square miles,
and has only a scattering of permanent residents. The
island hosts a few environmental scientists some of the
year. They have been gone for a couple of months. Their
arrival back will be delayed due to some made-up
concern. Expedition yachts and dive boats are not being
given permits either."

Steve moved the map and placed a more detailed
cross-section photo down on the table.

"Two small Mexican naval patrol boats are

moving all marine traffic away, so no vessels can approach without authorization. The island has a small airfield and radio installation. In fact, it is used to detect missile launches and monitor chatter from the Pacific and Asia. The NSA and the Mexican intelligence service have a cooperative post there on the other side of the island."

Jim looked at the layout.

"It looks sleepy, not much going on."

"A lot is unseen. There are listening arrays in the ocean surrounding the island. Monitoring for submarines, mostly." Steve scanned the map, then pointed. "Here, on the east side of the island, is where the target is. A couple of cottages with this big one near the ocean."

Jim looked at the photo, the cluster of houses. He then looked at the commercial satellite map. There were no houses.

"Commercial map shows nothing," Jim said.

"If you had a top secret, joint cooperation to find submarines and missiles, would you allow it to be photographed?" Steve asked. "I heard that the NSA hacked the satellites that go over it so that the image you see without any marks is the one shown to everyone. The installation is the reason for the pier and airstrip."

"Every satellite?"

"The only ones that could get an actual image, not digital, are the high-resolution photograph satellites that drop actual film. We haven't used them since the seventies, and when another country sends one up, we send armed squads to take them out."

"What do you mean, armed squads? To a satellite? Why?"

"Space commandos. To fight the other soldiers

near the satellites if necessary."

Jim stared at Steve. "We have commandos in space to protect photographic satellites?"

"No, of course not. Mostly they are there to protect the satellites which are actually missile silos, pointed at rival countries, able to launch in under nine seconds."

"Tell me you're joking."

Steve returned Jim's stare but said nothing.

"Getting back to the map, here's the information," Steve went on after a moment. "Champos is being held in this larger house near the cliffs. The only way out of this compound is through the other houses. They lock him in at night, there's nowhere to go on the island anyway, and there is a mating ground of great white sharks in the water. No swimming away, even if it was close enough to do so. So, got any ideas?"

"You know I do," Jim replied. "It's custom-made for a fighter pilot."

Jim sat back in the kitchen chair. He thought long and hard about what he was getting into.

"Can you trust your contacts that much? You tried to talk me out of it. Are you in this till the end?" he asked at last.

"I'm dying, Jim," Steve said. "Cancer. A gift of operating in dangerous areas around dangerous things. Another year, maybe, is all I have left, and then all my knowledge and experience will be gone from this world. Jenny was everything to me, like Maggie was to you. I was busy roaming the earth, protecting my country, or maybe we would have had what you had.

"I was gone, and she met Paul, who made her happier than I ever could have. But I never stopped loving her and wanting what was best for her. I've seen these deals a hundred times: the compromises, the exchanges. This guy killed the one person I loved most. When I finally close my eyes at the last, I want to know this piece of shit is dead."

Jim nodded; he understood the pain he was seeing.

"What about you, Paul?" Jim asked.

"Whatever it takes," Paul said emotionlessly, without hesitation.

"For you to have a glimmer of surviving the rest of your life outside of a prison, you need an option of escape," Steve said. "I can arrange a ship to pick you up a hundred miles off the coast of the island. They won't ask any questions and are reliable. But here's the tricky part. You'll have to ditch the plane in the ocean at the right time in the right spot to get picked up."

Jim looked at the map and calculated the distances in his head, reviewing travel time and possible problems. Any number of things could go wrong: not getting in the air at all, being intercepted by the Mexican air force, being engaged by the US Navy or Air Force.

"How would you do it?" Steve's voice snapped Jim out of his own head.

"What?"

"You're the pilot. How would you do it?"

"It's definitely different from anything else I've done. Not only the target, but dealing with pursuit from my own country."

"Assume taking off from Coronado. How do you do it so that they don't know you're doing it?"

"The range is well within that of the aircraft. What if I can disable the tracking device on the plane itself and then figure a way to keep pursuit off of me? Maybe fake a crash via radio, which will initiate search and rescue, causing confusion? If the weather cooperates, I could fly low or into a rain squall, somehow evade detection. It's all about buying time. I won't engage with other pilots. That's not part of the deal. There is the locator beacon on the aircraft. If I eject, that's one issue to solve. Disable it somehow?"

"Your IFF transmitter could be cloned, maybe," Steve said. "That could buy you some time."

"Cloned?"

"Yes, maybe even multiple transmissions. That would cause some hesitation, if your plane were seen to be in numerous places. We could put them on a couple of civilian planes. You turn yours off, and they turn on. You'd have the signal jumping all over the place."

"You know how to do that?"

"I know a guy. Or two," Steve said.

"What's the timeline? Till they move him?" Jim asked.

"A week, a month, a year, who knows? How long to empty out his head, is what it depends on. As far as I know, they'll keep him there until he's wrung dry. And there will be multiple verification checks for the information he provides. They might have him evaluate occurrences in the country. At a certain point, though, the information is out of date. Champos's usefulness will degrade over time, and then what they'll do with him is unknown."

Jim reviewed the information in his head, looking for pitfalls and problems.

"In five days are the night bombing qualifications for pilots," Jim said. "They'll be hitting San Clemente Island, leaving out of Coronado."

"You know you're not coming back, right?" Paul

said, sitting down across from him. "It would be naive to think you won't get caught. The best we can hope for is that you are thought of as dead."

Jim looked at Paul over the table. Yes, it was true. He would be throwing away all that he had worked for. He nodded slowly as he accepted the obvious.

"Yes, but where will I go?"

"You'll be dead, as far as anyone in the US is concerned," Steve said. "I can provide transport and a new identity, a start, somewhere. But to not end your life in prison, you'll have to fake your death, and you'll have to stay dead."

"Where can I go? Where will no one ever look for me?"

"It's best you don't know for now. You can't take anything but what you normally would take for a flight. No extra money, diplomas, family photos, letters, nothing. It has to look as if you planned a normal day at the office."

Chapter 7

Jim awoke early; he had gotten a fitful sleep, turning in at four in the afternoon to rest for the night training operations. Waking in the darkness, he pulled on his uniform. His flight suit was in his helmet bag by the door. Wallet, watch, and keys went to their respective places as the coffee brewed in the kitchen.

Nothing was out of place. A typical day—but the day that would change everything.

Jim withdrew the picture of Maggie from his pocket and slipped it out of its protective plastic sleeve. He stood there looking at it in the kitchen of the house they had shared, where the new life they were beginning had shined so brightly.

"You mattered," Jim said to Maggie, who wasn't there. "*We* mattered."

Slipping the picture back into its sleeve, he placed it into the breast pocket of the uniform that had once meant so much to him. He filled a travel mug with coffee and walked out of the life that used to be his.

The hangar housing the Harriers was nearly empty of personnel in the dead of morning. Jim waved at the crew chief and his men, leaving for the mess hall before flight operations. The student pilots' airplanes were going to come in from Yuma after a refueling stop in Coronado. They would be getting up for their flight prep soon, scheduled to rendezvous over the ocean with Jim and his wingman for firepower demonstration runs on the gunnery range.

Jim walked around his aircraft, his eyes taking in the lines of the deadly, predatory plane. The weapons attached under the wings were two AGM-84 Harpoon air-to-surface missiles and two LAU-5003 rocket pods with nineteen CRV-7 rockets each. Jim ran his hands over the two Mark 77 napalm canisters, the lethal complement rounded out by the 25mm Gatling gun with 300 rounds of ammunition. The demonstration of the warfighting capabilities of the jet for the student pilots was intended to be thorough.

Jim nimbly climbed up the removable ladder and reached into the cockpit. Locating the IFF transceiver cord, he attached it to the black box Steve had given him, fitting it between the connections. This would supposedly allow him to switch off the electronics that enabled others to track his plane.

Walking over to the second aircraft, Jim undid the maintenance hatch covering the access to the engine controls. A few moments of fiddling with connections ensured that the vibration of the engine starting would work loose at least one of the cables controlling the fuel mixture. He had seen this fault in an aircraft before, and it had given the sailors fits to troubleshoot. So this would hopefully ground the other plane and ensure he would be alone in his mission.

Jim said a little prayer that this would work. Would the very competent ground crew be able to identify and repair the problem in time for the other jet to take off with him for this mission? He hoped not. He also sincerely hoped that the unusual fault would not result in disciplinary action for the technicians.

Soon the rest of the flight personnel were coming in, headed to the conference room for preflight.

"Colonel," Jim said as he nodded at a trim man in a flight suit. "Going up today?"

"No, Major. Pulled a muscle in my back," the colonel said, looking over Jim's shoulder. "Lieutenant Little will be your wingman. Iris, come here, will you?"

Jim turned to see an intelligent-looking young woman with a tanned face. "Iris? That's an unusual name."

"Hello, Major," Lieutenant Little said, extending her hand. "It's an acronym, actually: IRIS. Stands for 'I Require Intense Supervision.' I used to drink a bit and get into mischief."

"You've just returned from deployment, is that right?" Jim asked.

"Came back from leave last week," the young woman replied. "I've completed the initial instructor training, so I'm ready to go."

After the briefing, the pilots suited up and climbed into their planes. Jim tried to relax as the two aircraft were towed out of the hangar. He scanned his controls almost unconsciously. He kept wondering when IRIS's plane would start its trouble.

"Cleared for takeoff, IV-1, IV-2. Proceed to the main runway." The flight controller's voice from the airfield tower in his helmet's earphones brought Jim back to attention.

He increased the power on the engine and could sense, rather than feel, IRIS doing the same. Their planes started to move.

"Shit," IRIS's voice said over the radio.

Jim felt himself relax. "Report."

"Plane's acting wonky. All kinds of alarms," IRIS said. "Wait—okay, settled out. Let's move again."

Jim powered up his plane and moved forward. He willed the alarms in the other plane to start again.

"Dammit! It's on power-up; it looks like the same issue the fleet memorandum went out on," IRIS said. "Didn't you have to write that one up, Major?"

"You're scrubbed, IRIS," Jim said. "Tower, IV-2 is no-go. Mechanical issues. IV-1 will proceed."

"Roger, IV-1," the colonel's voice said from the radio. "Students are in the air already approaching rendezvous. Proceed as planned, less IV-2."

"That sucks. I guess the noobs won't get to see wingman tactics," IRIS said regretfully.

"Another time, Lieutenant," Jim said, grateful that this part of the plan had worked. "See you when I get back."

Jim powered up further and began his run to take off. He rose into the air, banking over the San Diego Bay and into the airspace above the Pacific on a northerly course. The dark early morning skyline of San Diego was beatific, its citizens sleeping. He would miss this feeling of being a protector of his countrymen.

Within minutes he had overtaken a private jet on his starboard wing at a predetermined point. He knew Paul was the one flying it. The jet waggled its wings, and Jim hit the switch on the IFF transceiver box he had wired in according to Steve's instructions.

"Command IV-1, having some alarms and trouble with—" Jim said into the radio, as planned. He shut down his active systems in the aircraft—no radar or radio transmissions—and then the running lights. He reduced altitude, going lower than he had ever dared before in the

States, flying just over the Pacific, hoping to stay under Navy and civilian radar monitoring. The private jet was now transmitting his Identification Friend or Foe code, and anyone tracking it would be drawn away to the east.

Jim could hear the Navy flight controlling station calling but didn't respond. He knew the Gulfstream jet was going at top speed inland now, away from the ocean, toward the desert. A new voice on the radio came through, terse, demanding that he respond.

"Unidentified aircraft, this is the USS *Kauffman* you are approaching, on bearing 248 degrees. Respond and state your intentions."

Oh shit! Jim thought. A Navy frigate was wondering why something was moving at them fast over the ocean. He thought quickly. If he allowed his identity to be confirmed, he would have the whole air detachment after him. Jim thought hard. What did he know about the *Kauffman?*

That's a frigate on TAR duty. Reservists, out for training.

"Aircraft, you are approaching a warship of the United States Navy. State your intention or you will force us to engage." The voice was calm, yet demanding.

Jim heard the voice continue with background noise. Then he realized the person speaking to him hadn't released the transmit button on the radio handset. Jim listened to the exchange while scanning the skies for an option.

"What do you think, chief?" the voice on the radio said.

"Light 'em up," another voice said. "Probably a drug mule."

They'll track me with fire-control radar and try to

destroy me, Jim thought grimly. To port, the sparse moonlight illuminated a line of rain clouds. The clouds could hide his aircraft from air control radar, but he knew the more powerful fire control radar would be able to punch through the cover easily.

Jim pushed the jet close to its top speed, flashing through the clouds at almost six hundred miles per hour, tensing, waiting to hear the alarms on his aircraft alerting him to being tracked by offensive weapons. But the radio was silent. The frigate had apparently decided not to engage.

Pointing south, he lined up on the coordinates of the target, Isla Guadalupe. With 180 miles to go, he would be there in less than thirty minutes. Cutting it close, but he expected to be on target by four o'clock . . . and gone before anyone could figure out what had happened.

Chapter 8

The ocean was dark as Jim flew straight toward the coordinates. Nothing moved in the sky in the dark morning hours except him, a predator streaking to its prey.

Pursuit had been expected, possible outrage, screams and orders on the radio, but all was silent. He thought about all that it had taken him to get to the position he held. Years of training and sacrifice, earning the trust of his country. All to be tossed behind and swirl away in the darkness left by Maggie's murder.

And it was murder, the callous ending of his wife and child's lives. The future that could have been, stolen from all of them, a murder of indifference. Plans made a shambles by one man, protected now by the country Jim had dedicated his life to. Someone had done the math, with whatever complicated equation, that this man who had taken everything from Jim—and from Paul and Steve—was not going to face justice.

Supposing there had been a trial, a punishment, the machinery of civilization to deal with this killer. In that case, Jim could have accepted the workings of the society he lived in. Civilization operated on the concepts of crime and punishment. That machine had been subverted; governmental justice didn't and wouldn't happen in this case. All that had been left to Jim was the reckoning.

There was no question of the guilt. Now came the

punishment. An eye for an eye, a tooth for a tooth. That was another code he'd learned and understood from his father's knee. A death for a death, the ancient code imprinted on a warrior's DNA.

Jim saw the dark bulk of the island before him. He slipped the jet to port as he aligned with the target somewhere in the gloom. He turned the AGM Harpoon missiles to active. While either would be more than enough to obliterate the structure, Jim intended to use both. He would make sure that the job was done.

The targeting computer assessed the coordinates in a moment, using algorithms written by engineers and transferred to a computer, then refined to be part of a lethal system to calculate the fire controls. Jim stared at the information for what felt like a long time.

The slightest twitch of his finger, a synapse of his brain controlling it. The last second before the last choice, one that could not be undone. Taking a human life. This act, if undertaken, would be a complete abandonment of country, of duty, of a sacred oath. Jim took a breath, full and deep. He could still call this off.

He stopped, switching the missiles off. Banking away still more than a mile from the target, Jim took a second to consider what he was doing. Heading south, he throttled back, then banked the aircraft in a slow turn to line up on the island and the cluster of buildings that held the murderer.

Moving in low, Jim could see the structures on their cliff, a few lights illuminating them. Approaching the island, Jim dragged the small black lever to his left. This control directed the nozzles downward, allowing the Harrier to do what no other jet could do: stop midflight to hover.

Jim could see the cliff, a sheer drop below the compound, waves crashing three hundred feet below. He guided the jet closer, under the ridge, the change in wind buffeting the aircraft a little but nothing he couldn't compensate for.

Slowly rising, Jim watched as the rocky cliff scrolled by until it gave way to the stone house. Jim could see into a dimly lit living room through glass double doors. The jet continued rising. A bedroom went by, then the railing of a balcony on top of the building.

And then the figure of a man.

Jim stopped breathing. There, through the windshield, he could see a man with a lighter held to his face, staring in disbelief at the hovering jet. Jim had seen that face, memorized it, and obsessed over it.

Champos.

Jet fighters never see their adversaries, not like this, face to face. It was surreal, looking into the eyes of a small, unassuming man smoking a cigarette in the middle of the night.

Jim almost unconsciously switched the fire control to the GAU-12 25mm five-barrel rotary gun mounted under the plane's belly, the cannon located almost under his left foot. He felt a slight vibration, different from the rest of the aircraft noises, that let him know the barrels were spinning, awaiting his decision. Time slowed.

As Jim looked at the man frozen in front of him, he doubted himself, his motivation, even his very sanity . . . until Champos snapped out of his shock and turned. That act of fleeing, from danger, from accountability, triggered a predatory instinct in Jim. Blinding rage, boiling up from a hidden place inside him, replaced doubt.

He made a choice, directed his will. His brain fired the synapse and twitched the finger. The machine gun roared as the jet pivoted to starboard, the heavy 25mm machine gun bullets fired out at 3,600 rounds per minute. The tracers illuminated the night, showing the destruction of Champos and of the top of the building behind him, hot metal streaking into the darkness to deliver the final verdict of a just cause to an evil man.

Jim held the fire button down, steering the aircraft instinctively, suddenly realizing he was screaming as he fired. He guided the bullets until the firing suddenly stopped; exhausting the three hundred rounds in the ammunition pod only took seconds. At that moment, his screams stopped and he began to sob. He hadn't cried since Maggie had died in her hospital bed. The tears now flowed freely, tears of rage and anger, tears of sorrow, tears of happiness and regret.

The time was four thirty in the morning. The quiet slumber of the island had been shattered. For an instant, Jim could see the building where Champos had stood, now lit up by flames. He was grinning despite the tears, knowing he had reached out to someone "untouchable" and delivered vengeance.

The tears stopped and dried as he turned from the scene of destruction, switching to flight mode and accelerating to maximum speed. In a moment, he had aligned to a new bearing back over the Pacific Ocean, heading to whatever future lay in the dark void before him.

Time vanished for a while as the release of so much raw emotion resulted in a physical shudder in his body, feelings of shame and revulsion creeping through him. Shame at betraying his country and oath. Revulsion at ending a life, even the life of the man who had killed his wife and daughter. Buffeted by emotions, Jim flew numb and operated on training.

Finding the needle in a haystack that was a ship at sea was going to be challenging, but it was his only hope of survival in the emptiness of the sea. He turned his attention to the task. He had GPS coordinates to aim for, in the hope that an incredibly complicated series of events had occurred to bring the ship to where he needed it to be. He checked his fuel gauge: it was down to half capacity. The flight range of twelve hundred nautical miles was theoretical and dependent on operational conditions. He planned on a maximum of one thousand.

Jim felt tension in his stomach, the body's reaction to a mind being aware of the physical trials to come. Even assuming the ship was where it was supposed to be, that it had not been delayed by a variety of factors from mechanical breakdowns to lousy navigation, and even assuming he could find it, which was dicey at best, he would have to eject from his jet, land in the cold, dark water, not break his neck or drown or die of shock or get eaten by something with fins and teeth, then have the ship find him in the vastness of the dark water. From training and time at sea, Jim knew that trying to spot a man in the water was a complicated task, especially at night.

Jim focused his mind on what he could control: getting to the rendezvous point. At six hundred miles off the coast of Mexico, it was three hundred miles past international boundaries. He had about five minutes to arrive on site. Jim turned his radio to the commercial UHF frequency given to him by Steve days before. Unfortunately, the ship could only transmit on this particular frequency to a limited range. Still, he was getting close, thank God.

Jim scanned the sea around him, looking for any sign that there was activity in this area of the ocean. He had overflown a surprising number of fishing vessels and other ships going about their business. He'd seen passing oil tankers transferring crude oil between them, their powerful floodlights marking them out like a disco party at sea. Other ships could be seen by the red and green lights of their bridge wings and bow lights. Jim knew that each different configuration of lights indicated the size and direction of the vessel.

The ocean around him was dark and empty. Jim considered turning on the radar, but the risk of the energy transmission being seen by ground monitoring stations was one he did not want to take unless it was absolutely necessary. There was no way of knowing for sure what vessels were in the area. Possibly being seen by a warship was too big a risk.

Jim looked at his GPS coordinates. Nearly there. He banked the jet into a slow turn, scanning the darkness for any sight of the ship he was supposed to meet. Suddenly, right below him, the bright lights of a fishing trawler came on, blinked three times, then stayed steady.

Jim released the breath he hadn't even realized he'd been holding and realigned the heading, switching to hover mode about a hundred yards from the ship.

The aircraft shuddered as the nozzles pointed at the water, pushing it aloft upon the air pressure provided by the powerful engines. Jim pointed the nose of the jet away from the ship, since he knew the ejection would launch him forward. He could see the crew climbing into the small, fast rescue craft on the side railing of the vessel, ready to pick him up.

Jim waited until the small craft was in the water, then positioned his hands over the main systems control switch and the ejection control handle. Then, after taking a couple of deep breaths, he hit the main control switch, shutting down the aircraft, and simultaneously pulled the ejection handle.

The canopy blew off with a loud noise, and then Jim felt the pressure of the rocket-powered seat flying up and out of the aircraft, followed by weightlessness and falling. The sharp jerk of the parachute opening made him glance down at the plane settling into the water below him.

The ride down to the water was over in an instant. The cold sea soaked him as his training took over. Jim released himself from the parachute restraints and inflated his life vest. Slipping through the water, he pulled himself to the search and rescue transceiver on the raft and disabled it. He then slashed the raft with a knife, sending it to the bottom with the plane.

Strong hands pulled him into the rescue boat, dumping him into the bottom like a landed fish. Jim lay there, gasping, panting, and shuddering at the cold and the adrenaline dump, as the boat raced back to the ship, where it was recovered quickly and secured in its cradle.

"Well, you don't see that every day," a familiar voice said.

Jim looked up to see Steve standing on the deck of the ship, smiling at him. Jim smiled back and slipped off his flight helmet, tossing it over the side.

"No, I guess you don't," he said.

"Let's get you below and out of that flight suit, Jim," Steve said, reaching to help him.

Jack Lyons

Chapter 9

The transit by ocean was a slow and languorous ride into the future. Jim had abandoned both his uniform and his military grooming. The last part of his old life slipped away with them.

As the vessel slowly made its way across the Pacific, it stopped to fish when the tuna were found. The crew was made up of mostly male members and assorted clansmen of Malaysian and Chinese descent. Jim came to understand that Steve had been instrumental in smuggling them out of China and resettling them in Malaysia. Steve's loyalty to them, at significant personal risk to himself, would give them a chance to live and prosper. They gave that loyalty back now, transporting Jim and Steve across the ocean.

Jim helped on deck, pouring himself into physical labor each day, barely stopping for meals, until he dropped exhausted, most of the time sleeping on the deck in the tropical weather. Days turned into weeks. His body grew leaner and browner, and his hair and beard grew longer than they had been for years.

"A place to put your sorrows and worries," Steve said one day as they both leaned against the handrail, looking out on the sunset over the smooth water. The dark bulk of an island miles away before them, the sun sinking behind it, made a scene out of a Tahitian poem.

Jim nodded, then pointed to the island. "Are we

pulling in here?"

Steve regarded the island. Jim, looking over at him, noted that the sunshine and enforced removal from the stresses of modern life had been gradually browning and relaxing him.

"That's Hiva Oa, of the Marquesas Islands. It's where Gauguin died, you know."

"Who?"

"Paul Gauguin, a French impressionist painter from the late nineteenth century. He painted a lot of pictures in what was then French Polynesia. He died in Atuona, the main town on the island, and is buried there."

"Afraid my art history is a little sparse," Jim said.

"Gauguin was a bit of an asshole," Steve admitted, leaning against the rail. "But it's a beautiful place. I intend to die here too."

"You're getting off here?" Jim asked, concerned. He hadn't realized he'd be losing this man, whom he had come to know and respect, so soon. It would be the loss of one more tie to his old life. Perhaps the last.

"It's time I accomplished the last of my obligations," Steve said. "I set up an identity that will take me through what life I have left. A businessman from Canada, in retirement, walking in beauty and kindness."

Jim felt oddly numb, the scene before him of an idyllic island in the middle of the Pacific a counterpoint to him finally facing what his own future would hold.

"You could stay here if you wanted," Steve said after a moment. "This island is far enough away from anything that it is doubtful you would be found—if, in fact, anyone looked for you at all. The documents you have are perfect. I built both our new identities to withstand all but the best scrutiny."

"What are my options? We haven't fully discussed them."

"Well, you shouldn't really go back to the settled world. You would probably be fine, but who knows? I have cut ties with almost all my information sources. As far as most people are concerned, my car plunged off of the Torrey Pines cliffs and no body was recovered."

"Sounds dramatic."

"A body washing away in the ocean, never to be found, is the perfect cover. It saves trouble. No dental records or DNA."

"Will anyone buy that?"

"Will anyone care?" Steve replied, leaning against a handrail.

"Maybe somebody worried about a fighter jet gone missing and a dead intelligence agent."

"If they wanted to find me, they'd probably have to look for years, and I'll be gone by then. Some could probably do it, but I doubt anyone will be too concerned. Champos alive was an asset; dead, he's just another asshole. So, how about it, Jim? You want to stay here or go somewhere else?"

Jim considered the life of an island resident. Maybe if he were another man, one who didn't love adventure and the challenges it brought.

"I don't think I could see myself spending the next forty years on a small island, even one as beautiful as this. I'm not ready to go gentle into that good night."

"You would rage against the dying of the light some more? I wonder if that makes me the wise man," Steve said, smiling.

"You know Dylan Thomas?"

"I know a poem I liked when I read it," Steve said. "I can offer you another option, a place where many people disappear. You could use your skills and still feel what you long for in regards to living. But wherever you go, you need to get used to your new name. You have to understand that Jim is gone. To start a new life, you have to get rid of your old one. Your name and history are in the papers I have given you. David Somers. That's what you'll take with you."

"To where?"

"Africa. Specifically, the Congo. I have contacts there who can always use a man with skills. It means going into a place of war and chaos, but then, that's always a good place to hide: war and chaos."

Jim looked out over the water. The peaceful scene did not relax him. The emptiness inside him had changed. He'd thought he had been ready to die, to give up, lie down. But as he looked into his heart, his life hung on an instant.

"Africa," Jim said finally, turning to the man beside him. "I will remember what you did for me, Steve—for Maggie."

"Good luck, Jim," Steve replied. "I hope you find what you are looking for."

The ship ride to the African continent took another month, stopping along the way to fish, fuel, and resupply. The crew kept their distance, and Jim didn't mind. They were used to not asking questions, and Jim was getting used to not talking.

In Tanzania, the port city of Dar es Salaam was a foreign and overwhelming experience after the long months at sea. The port and customs officials looked at Jim's papers for an extended time. Finally, the captain laid down a nondescript envelope filled with cash alongside the ship's documents and casually turned around so that the officials could collect their bribe in peace.

Jim said brief goodbyes and walked down the gangway into the bustling mass of humanity. Dirt streets and buildings of cinder block covered with sheets of tin stretched away as far as the eye could see as he walked to the taxi stand.

"Imperial Hotel," Jim said to the driver of the ratty taxicab through the window.

"Yes, boss, no problem," the ancient, emaciated driver replied.

"You take euro?" Jim asked. Euros were the only cash he had.

"Yes, boss, no problem. No problem."

Jim got in the back of the taxi. The interior was clean, with cool AC drying the sweat on his back. The radio was playing some sort of African pop station. He watched as the taxi wove its way through the streets, a riot of colors and people going about their daily lives. A streaming jumble of people walking, talking, selling all manner of things in the street, the scene was teeming with life. He had lost himself in observing the tableau when the taxi pulled up to an old colonial-looking building.

"Imperial Hotel, boss."

Jim paid the fare and stepped out onto the street. In crisp, pressed short sleeves, the doorman nodded and smiled at him as he walked into a lobby out of an old movie. The high ceilings had ancient fans, and dusty pictures hung on the walls. Looking around, he saw an attractive desk clerk behind a huge, polished wood counter.

"Checking in, sir?"

"Yes, I believe there is a reservation. David Somers."

"Excellent, sir. Passport?"

Jim handed over the paperwork. The clerk took it, then turned to the massive wall of cubbyholes behind the desk. She selected an envelope, turned, and handed it to Jim.

"Mr. Somers, this was left for you, to be delivered upon your arrival. The room will be 120,000 shillings."

Jim balked at this immense-sounding sum of money. "What is that in euros?"

The clerk smiled at his disbelief.

"Approximately fifty euros," she said. "Will you just be staying the night, or would you like a longer stay?"

Jim smiled back, breathing a sigh of relief.

"One night for now. I may need to extend. Is cash acceptable?"

"Yes, sir, but we will require an additional 120,000 shillings as a deposit."

Jim handed over the required money.

"Very well, sir. Enjoy your stay," the clerk said as she handed him the key and envelope.

Jim took the offered items and went through the lobby to the stairs. He went up to the second floor and found his room. Unlike those in more modern hotels, the door had a key lock. Once in the room, he set down his small bag, sat on the bed, and opened the envelope.

Mr. Somers,

Please call the number below upon your arrival. I would be most pleased to make your acquaintance. You have been highly recommended by our mutual friend.

—J

Jim picked up the room phone and tried to dial the complex series of numbers but could not seem to make the phone work. He went down to the lobby and asked the clerk for assistance. She seemed to have no issue dialing the numbers and handed him the desk phone with a smile. Jim nodded his thanks.

"Hello?" The voice on the phone was a man's, refined, with an English lilt.

Jim realized he only knew a letter, not a name. "Is J there?"

"This is J. To whom am I speaking?"

"David. David Somers," Jim replied, the name strange in his mouth.

"Ah, from Canada. Are you settled in the hotel?"

"I've checked in, yes."

"Very good. Well, relax a bit, and I will meet you there in the bar. Say, six this evening?"

Jim scanned the lobby and saw a door marked "Bar."

"That should work for me," he said. "See you then."

"Righto, ta," the voice said, followed by a dial tone.

Jim handed the phone back to the clerk, who accepted it with a smile. With five hours to kill, he went to his room to shower and take a nap.

That evening, the bar was empty of customers, but it was full of history. A genteel shabbiness was reflected in the rich woodwork and worn carpet. Oil paintings on the wall depicted manly triumph and nature rendered as something to be conquered, then admired.

Jim ordered a beer at the bar and sat down at a booth to enjoy it. Sharply at six, a well-dressed older man walked into the room. His eyes quickly located Jim, and he nodded. He waved to the bartender, then walked up to Jim, hand extended.

"David Somers? I am Jacques Franklin." His bright, intelligent, grey-green eyes searched Jim's face, and he seemed to like what he saw. Releasing Jim's hand, he sat across from him. A moment later, the white-shirted bartender approached and set a cocktail on the table.

"Thank you, Nigel," Jacques said.

The bartender gave a dignified nod and retreated to his domain of dark wood.

"So, Jacques . . ." Jim began uncertainly.

"Yes, you have found the Jacques," the man began, then paused to take a sip of his cocktail. "My, that's lovely. So here you are. Our friend informed me that you would be interested in a position. There just so happens to be one available. Your skills include piloting, I understand?"

This stream of speech was rapid-fire and to the point.

"Yes, I am—was a pilot."

"Once was, then will always be. Though not once saved, always saved, possibly. Do you still know how to fly planes, then? What types?"

Jim regarded the man before him. He realized he

didn't have a lot of choices here.

"I can," he said. "Fixed-wing and jet. I was trained—"

"Oh, no, I do not need to have a résumé, nor do I really want to know too much backstory. It can muddy the waters, you know." Jacques leaned forward in his chair. "I just need a pilot who can navigate and put a plane full of cargo where I need it to go."

"What kind of cargo?"

"Does it really matter? I could pretend that it will all be sparkling clean and aboveboard, but the lines over here tend to get blurred sometimes."

"You own a transport company?"

"I own a company that needs to transport things. A slight difference."

"What sort of aircraft are you using?"

"Usually a Cessna 208B Cargomaster, for now," Jacques said. "Sometimes, with a larger cargo, an Antonov An-12 is used. Do you think you could fly those?"

"I'm familiar with the Cessna line, and at the end of the day, a plane is a plane."

"Confidence with no basis in fact. Excellent," Jacques said, raising his glass. "I have a flight in need of a pilot tomorrow morning. Be ready for your driver at four o'clock tomorrow morning. He will pick you up in the lobby."

With this pronouncement, Jacques downed his drink, stood up, and made his way out of the bar. Jim watched him go, wondering at the speed at which life had just changed.

Jim awoke at three o'clock. His dreams had been intense again. All across the ocean, he had sweated and clawed through them. Sometimes he dreamed of combat or some other sort of fighting. Sometimes he dreamed of Maggie screaming for him or Maggie dying alone. Sometimes Krug was speaking to him from his gurney aboard the helicopter, his eyes staring accusingly from his blood-soaked face. "Where were you?" Maggie or Krug would ask in these dreams, over and over. "Where *were* you?"

Jim showered, dressed, and packed up his meager possessions. Making his way to the lobby, he turned over his room key to a sleepy clerk. Then he helped himself to a cup of hot tea and sat in a chair to wait for his driver.

"Mr. David?" A slim man approached him.

"Yes."

"With me, please, sir." The slim man picked up Jim's bag and walked out of the hotel.

Jim followed, gulping down his tea and placing the cup on the table by the door. The 4x4 pickup at the curb was already running. Jim got in, and they were off into the quiet African night.

"Mr. Jacques asked me to give these to you," the driver said, handing him a box.

"What are they?"

"Malarone. Anti-malaria pills. Take one a day."

"What's your name?"

"Haki," the man said. "Please take a pill now. Here is water. The malaria is very dangerous."

Haki handed Jim a bottle of water with condensation beading on the sides. Jim took it, popped a pill out of the blister pack, and swallowed it down.

"You may have nightmares, but better than sleeping forever," Haki said, steering through the dark streets of the city.

Jim leaned back in his seat. He knew about nightmares and what came after. Almost every night, he woke from one, reached for Maggie, and felt only empty sheets. He doubted that a pill could hurt more than that.

Jim had tried to keep track of where they were going but had given up. The roads they drove on were completely empty. The only lights were from the truck itself and some stores along the way. He could feel, rather than see, when they finally left the city, the heat becoming less and the smell becoming that of open spaces.

Jim was dozing when he felt the truck come to a stop and heard the engine turn off. He looked up to see a single light above the door of an old metal Quonset hangar. They were in some sort of scrubland, the sounds of birds beginning in the trees and bushes around them.

"In there, Mr. David," Haki said, pointing to the hangar.

Jim got out of the truck and grabbed his bag out of the bed. Haki pulled away slowly, leaving him. The sight of the truck disappearing into the darkness of the African night caused a feeling of isolation and aloneness to grip Jim. The foreign sounds moving in the dark compelled him to move to the door of the hangar. He tried the handle and, finding it unlocked, went inside.

"Hello?" Jim said to the gloom.

As he moved farther into the building, a few lights illuminated the hangar space. Jim could now see the Cessna 208B, being loaded by three African men. They turned and stared at him with unfriendly eyes. Jim could feel the tension in the room and started to consider his options.

"Wewe ni nani?" the man closest to him demanded in a brusque tone.

Jim put down his bag and walked into the light so the men could see him.

"I'm sorry, I don't speak Swahili," Jim said. "Is Jacques here?"

"Kwenda kupata bosi," one of the other men told the one who had spoken. He went to the back of the hangar.

"David!" Jacques's voice carried through the tension, causing everyone to visibly relax. He turned to the men. "Waungwana hii ni David atakuwa kufanya kazi na sisi kama majaribio."

They came forward to shake Jim's hand. All were lean but muscular men, all with smiles now. They introduced themselves.

"Haji."

"Erevu."

"Babu."

Jim shook their hands in turn, and they returned to their loading.

"There, we are all friends now. Come to the office and we will talk about the flight," Jacques said.

Jim followed him through a door to a sparse office. There were maps on the wall, a desk, and a table with chairs, one of which held a husky, grey-bearded white man sleeping under a hat, with his feet on the table. Jacques filled a cup of tea for Jim, handed it to him, then walked over to whisper into the husky man's ear.

"Mimi nina kwenda kula wewe."

The man instantly sat bolt upright as Jacques stepped back, laughing. He looked around the room wildly, settling his gaze on Jacques.

"Mchekeshaji ni uwezekano wa kuwa moja ya mwisho akicheka," he growled.

"Your Swahili is awful, Christopher," Jacques said. "David, this is Christopher Richardson. Christopher, this is David Somers, your copilot for the day. You need to familiarize him with the Cessna."

"What did you say to him?" Jim asked Jacques.

"He said he was going to eat me," Christopher said, walking over to shake Jim's hand. "Jacques here is only a generation removed from cannibalism."

"Only the white meat is good enough for me," Jacques said, crossing to the map on the wall. "Now, down to business. Here we are in Kibaha on the eastern side of Tanzania."

Jacques indicated a point on the map, then slid it west to a spot deep in the green of the Congo.

"You will be flying first to Mpanda for fueling, which is here," Jacques stated, indicating a spot on the map closer to the Congo border. "You will be there around eleven or noon, depending on conditions. At that time, after refueling, you will depart for Pweto to drop off a legitimate cargo of mail and medicine. But along the way, you will stop here, near the village of Toya, land on the road, leave the cargo, and take off again."

"Are we meeting anyone?" Christopher asked.

"Maybe," Jacques said. "There will be a white post with red and black stripes by the road. Push out the cargo there and continue on. The recipient is responsible for picking up their goods, so it doesn't matter who is there or if no one is there."

Jim began studying the map.

"I guess there are no official government airports for contingencies?" Jim asked.

Jacques and Christopher looked at each other and began laughing.

"I knew I was going to like you," Christopher said, wiping his eyes.

Chapter 10

The preflight check of the plane was quick but thorough. Christopher walked Jim through the controls and starting sequence, nodding satisfied when Jim showed he could pick up the layout quickly. They got the plane started and were in the air as the morning changed from darkness to gray.

"So, I probably shouldn't ask what we're transporting, right?" Jim asked.

"Doesn't matter. If you're hanged, innocent or guilty, you're still hanged. Probably some guns, some other stuff. The Congo's a shitstorm right now, everybody fighting everybody. You got rebel groups all over the place. We sell them what they need."

"No restrictions?"

"Of course. They have to have money and be vouched for. The country doesn't really have any way to enforce the skies right now."

"Ever run into problems?"

"Crashed a couple of times," Christopher replied. "Had to hike out once when we got some shitty fuel and lost both engines. That was pretty hairy."

"How long?"

"Two nights, three days. Had already made the drop-off, so we didn't lose anything but the plane. Recovered it later. Look down there."

Jim leaned forward and looked at the empty

landscape.

"What that is, is a whole lot of nothing. Some villages up in the hills here and there. But there are still large predators out there. Crouching up a tree while listening to big things roaring and barking all night tends to disrupt the sleep," Christopher said.

The beige and brown landscape was rapidly turning green and brown. Jim took over control of the aircraft as Christopher stretched and undid his seat belt.

"You good for the coordinates?" Christopher asked.

"Yes, I've got it."

"You'll be seeing Lake Tanganyika in a few minutes, can't miss it. You'll see it long before you get to it; it's huge. Start the course correction then, with the lake on your starboard side all the way into Mpanda airport. I'm going to lie down for a nap. Wake me when we get to the lake. Should be there in about an hour."

"Got it," Jim said.

He kept his eyes on the landscape below him and peripherally on the controls and indicators. From experience, he continually scanned the horizon for other aircraft and the ground for places to set down if necessary. Some dusty roads in the hilly terrain would do.

The vast lake came into view on the horizon. After about forty-five minutes of flying parallel to the blue water, Jim saw some type of settlement below. He was consulting the map when Christopher edged back into the pilot seat beside him. After putting on the headphones, Jim asked him about the settlement and why it wasn't on the map.

"It's not a town. It's a refugee center. Nyarugusu

camp. All the people fleeing from Burundi and the Congo."

"It's huge," Jim said.

"Well over one hundred thousand people, the last I heard. There are a few of those camps. When the big boys fight, the little people get squished. Fight, die, or run. Those are the options over here."

"What about us? Which side are we helping?" Jim asked.

"We aren't helping. We're supplying. And whoever can pay."

Jim pondered the camp in the distance as Christopher took back the controls of the aircraft. Another thirty minutes had them lined up and descending into Mpanda airport. The smooth landing and transition to the staging point were uneventful. As the plane was fueled, Jim took the opportunity to eat and relieve himself. Before long, they were up in the air with Jim at the controls.

"We fly over the lake, then a seemingly straight course to the Pweto. Only the slight side trip, and that should be quick, twenty minutes down, tops."

"Roger that," Jim replied.

Christopher cocked his head and looked at Jim. Jim became aware he was being observed.

"What?"

"'Roger,'" Christopher said. "That's a US military term. Not Canadian."

Jim looked back at Christopher.

"I . . ." Jim stammered.

Christopher held up his hand.

"Don't know, don't care, and don't want to know. Minding my own business is what has gotten me through over here. Just be aware that people listen in this business we are in."

Jim nodded and went back to consulting his map.

"Looks like the road is coming up in about five miles, right over that ridge there," Jim said, pointing.

Christopher made a slight adjustment to the controls. Reaching up, he reduced the throttle.

"We'll be coming in fairly low," he said. "I've landed here before, and it's relatively smooth. So I'll do a flyover and make sure nothing is in the way to make us crash."

"Like cars?"

"Like buffalo, giraffes, elephants, things like that."

Jim looked out the windshield, the road visible now, a brown smear across the grassland, hemmed in by tall, thin trees. Christopher guided the plane about a hundred feet above the road, scattering a small herd of animals as they glided over.

"Those looked like hogs," Jim said.

"Red river hogs, native to the jungles," Christopher said. "They'll get out of the way. Giraffes and buffalo can be stubborn. The hogs are smart. They run. I've had times when I had to fly by shooting a pistol out the window at fifty feet to scare giraffes."

"Hit any?"

"Naw. If by any chance I killed one, I'd screw up my landing strip with the carcass."

Christopher banked the plane, making a neat loop, and lined back up on the road. Nothing was visible now on the brown strip.

"Think you can take us in? I want to offload, and if we do meet anyone, I'll be able to communicate quicker than you."

"My aircraft," Jim said, taking the controls.

The plane came in smoothly, Jim guiding with one hand on the yoke and one on the throttle, reducing the power to the engine and bleeding off speed by raising the nose of the plane. The Cessna settled smoothly on the roadway.

"Good. Now head for that open area and swing us around. Point us back down the way we came and be ready to take off in an instant if I tell you," Christopher said, pointing up the road.

Jim guided the plane to the spot indicated and turned it around.

"Shut her down but stay in the seat."

Jim nodded and shut down the engines.

Christopher got up from his seat and went back to the cargo area. Jim looked around and could see nothing but forest and scrub plants surrounding them. Christopher opened the doors and got out. Jim immediately started sweating as humid air and a musky scent of vegetation filled the plane's interior. Christopher quickly walked around, checking for damage and scouting the area.

"This is it, no one about. I'll offload. You stay put."

"Are you sure?" Jim asked. "It's a lot to unload alone."

"I'm sure," Christopher said. "I feel better knowing we can get out of here quick if needed. Every second may count."

Christopher started unlatching cargo and carrying it off the plane and into the high grass. Bundles and bags went quickly, Jim watching the man work as the sweat soaked his shirt. Many younger men could not have matched the pace. Jim scanned the area. Soon his attention was drawn to slight movement in the high grass to his left.

"Chris," Jim said as the man came back to the plane.

"Yes?"

"Something in the grass, port side."

Christopher looked out the side window.

"Probably our contact, maybe an animal," Christopher said, staring into the quiet landscape. Minutes went by as the men strained to see or hear anything in the quiet clearing. Only the hum of insects and the wind whispered to them.

Finally, Christopher reached into a metal storage box and removed a large black military rifle, a FN FAL. Christopher checked the rifle's chamber and headed out the back of the plane.

"Habari, habari," Christopher called out toward the scrub.

The silence from the scene around them seemed oppressive. The absence of animal noises was forcing Jim to strain his ears. He could see that Christopher's body language seemed tight, that something was wrong.

"Habiri, ambaye ni hapa!" Christopher said as he moved his rifle into a ready position.

The first shots were close but wild; Christopher dropped to one knee and fired indiscriminately into the high grass, emptying the rifle's magazine in bursts.

"Start it up!" Christopher screamed as he scrabbled backward toward the plane, reloading.

Jim was already hitting the button to start the engines. They roared to life. The propeller began to spin, the process seeming to last forever. Jim could hear Christopher firing behind him, the concussion from the rifle shaking Jim's nerves. Pinging sounds from bullets penetrating the thin skin of the aircraft hastened Jim's movements; he pushed the throttles to maximum while trying not to cringe too much in the seat. He felt very vulnerable as the rounds kept hitting the side of the plane behind him and passing through.

The plane jumped as it started to roll. Jim looked back to the cargo area just in time to see Christopher get the doors shut and then lie down on the deck as the plane gathered speed while still absorbing bullets.

As soon as they reached the minimum speed for liftoff, Jim pulled back on the yoke, causing the plane to rise from the ground. Firing still came from the ground but was fading. Breathing deeply, Jim willed himself to slow his heart and manage the adrenaline pumping through his body. At one thousand feet, he leveled off and looked back to check on Christopher.

"Chris! Chris!" Jim yelled. His voice was lost in the noise of the aircraft.

Christopher was curled into a ball against the side of the plane. He wasn't moving. Jim jerked the yoke to the side, causing the plane to rock. Christopher raised his head and begin to pat his body. He looked at Jim and smiled, then lay back for a moment on the deck, panting for air.

Jim turned his attention to the controls, consulting his kneeboard for the coordinates to their next stop, Pweto. His eyes scanned his controls and indicators, searching for any signs of damage or trouble with the aircraft. Besides a slightly higher level of breeze in the cabin, he could find no evidence of damage. Jim turned to see Christopher holding out a can of soda. He took it. Christopher put on the headset and slid into the seat beside him.

"The sugar will help when the adrenaline wears off, so you don't get the shakes," he said.

Jim watched as Christopher drained his own soda in one long draught and tossed the empty can behind him.

"My aircraft," Christopher said, taking the controls.

Jim nodded, releasing the yoke. His hands were starting to shake. He opened the can of soda and savored the cold sweetness as it rushed down his throat.

Christopher flew for a while, both men mentally adjusting to what had just happened and the realization that they had made it out alive and unharmed. Christopher glanced over, and Jim returned his look. Both men began laughing uncontrollably.

"You did good," Christopher said finally, wiping his eyes.

"Too scared not to. Did you see anything?"

"Just some muzzle flashes from way too close."

"Does this sort of thing happen a lot?"

"No, usually it's pretty quiet. Just a transaction. Maybe a little tension, but that was pretty unusual."

Jim checked his kneeboard and consulted the map.

"So, any cargo left? The holes in the plane are going to be hard to miss."

"Couple of crates of ammunition. I was waiting to see how the aircraft did before figuring out the next move. Pweto is close enough, but considering that the fuselage damage will attract attention, we should probably go to Tanzania."

Christopher studied his own map and pointed with his thumb, showing Jim the dot.

"Sumbawanga is probably our best bet. Decent

airport, easily bribed officials. We'll go back over Lake Tanganyika, kick the cargo out while we're over it, and figure out a story to tell the airport inspectors."

"Gonna take a while to get used to these names," Jim said while adjusting the controls for the new heading.

The plan went well, other than a door sticking while they were over the huge freshwater lake. Jim was able to pry out a bullet that had become lodged in the door mechanism. He waited until they slowed and were not over any fishermen. The last thing he wanted to do was crush a small boat with a crate of bullets. Jim slid the remaining cargo to the sliding door and kicked the boxes out into the deep blue water below.

The trip only took about an hour to complete. Landing in the small dusty Sumbawanga airport close to dusk, Christopher guided the plane to the parking area and went to deal with the bored officials. The explanation involved a great deal of shouting and arm-waving.

The story they had worked out between them was that during a trip to Pweto, they had experienced engine trouble and had to land on a dirt road in the Congo backcountry. While making a slight adjustment on the engine, they'd been attacked by rebels and had to shoot their way out. The official seemed to accept the story after his "fee" was paid.

"What do we do now?" Jim asked Christopher as they returned to home base.

"Now we head to a hotel and get drunk."

Jack Lyons

Chapter 11

"Y ata, which is here," Jacques said as he pointed to the map.

"It's not marked."

"Barely worth the ink, but worth the trip. There is a small clearing that should be sufficient to land the Cessna."

"Should be?" Jim said.

Jacques shrugged.

"Erevu is from there," Jacques said, tilting his head at the happy-faced man next to them. "He is going home and is hitching a ride with you."

Jim nodded at Erevu. The two of them had become somewhat conversant in a French/English/Swahili patois over the several months that Jim had been flying for Jacques. Erevu was smart and friendly, an instinctive and skilled mechanic on the planes. Jim had found him eager to learn and had enjoyed expanding his own knowledge while teaching.

"Sisi kwenda kwa nyumba yako, Erevu?" Jim asked. "We go to your house?"

"Me home, David."

"To see your many wives?"

"Yes, boss." Erevu smiled, nodding. "Take many rifles to fight the Mai-Mai."

"Mai-Mai?"

"Mai-Mai, kutomba yake." Erevu said and spit on

the floor.

"Yes, yes. Fuck them. Now clean up that nasty spot," Jacques said, pointing at the spittle.

As Erevu stooped to clean the floor, Jacques walked with Jim to the plane, watching as the last crates were loaded.

"Mostly just rifles and bullets," Jacques said. "Some small luxury goods and medicine. The profit is not much, but we will be buying some goodwill. A good thing to have, goodwill. You feeling up to this?"

Jim was surprised, though he shouldn't have been. It was an honest question. He had changed since coming to Africa. He'd been letting himself go, drinking heavily with Christopher or alone, putting on twenty pounds of fat from booze and overeating. And a late night with Christopher in a bar had introduced him to something that would actually take the dreams away: heroin. The first rush was a miracle. He felt better than he could remember. At first he'd only snorted a little, but it had become his evening and morning routine as the drug dug its claws in. Jim knew what was happening but had somehow convinced himself, at the same time, that it was under control. Christopher had told him that he had been using it for years, just to get by.

Besides the added weight, Jim had changed physically in other ways. He was not really on top of his hygiene. Bushy hair and a scraggly beard had replaced his clean-cut military look. He looked like a wild man, and when drunk he acted like one, doing stupid things like fighting. If his strict, wholesome parents could see him, they wouldn't recognize the jaded physical and moral wreck their son had become.

He could never have imagined becoming who he

was now, just another lost man on the Dark Continent.

"I'm fine," Jim said, his words going against the booze sweat he was off-gassing and the sunglasses worn to hide his bloodshot eyes.

Jacques coolly regarded him for a long while.

"So, Yata is pretty deep in the jungle?" Jim asked, changing the subject.

"Deep, dark jungle, the kind that can swallow you up if you're not careful," Jacques said, still looking at Jim.

"What do you mean?"

Jacques held his gaze for a moment and then spoke. "You've done well here, David. It's rare to find competent men of talent anywhere, but here in this place, in this business, it is exceedingly so."

Jim nodded. He knew that he did the work well, and he was satisfied that he had found a place for now. He tried not to think about his old life. But after each day of flying, drinking, and drugging, he returned to the hotel and spent time staring at his picture of Maggie. That picture was the one tie to his old life that he could not give up. And each morning he looked in the mirror at the long-haired, bearded face of a stranger.

"Your health appears to be suffering, though. Are you still taking your malaria medication?"

"Yes."

"It will take some time for you to build up to the environment. Malaria here can put anyone down, especially where you are going now. The river in that part of the jungle breeds mosquitos the size of buzzards."

"Must be the heat. Takes some adjusting to it," Jim said absently. He was looking over at the plane on the runway, mentally running through a checklist to ensure that it and he were ready.

Jacques regarded him for another moment and then shrugged.

"Well, maybe a break when you come back. Zanzibar is not far, and it is much more civilized than this backwater."

Jim turned and walked to the plane. He didn't want to discuss his health, mental or physical. The nightmares were vivid and unrelenting, the heroin providing only momentary relief. And now the dreams of Maggie and Krug screaming, dying, begging for his help, had been joined by a dream that she was safely asleep in his arms. In this dream he could feel her warmth, smell her hair. Then he woke to cold reality.

Those dreams were almost harder than the nightmares.

In a strange way, though, they helped him adjust to his new life. Remembering Maggie, dreaming of her softness and warmth, gazing at her picture, reminded Jim of why he'd chosen this path. Jim didn't regret the act of revenge. In fact, he felt he could not have lived with himself if he hadn't gone through with it. Now this was his life, to live as best he could—and as overwhelming as the environment of Africa was, with new sights, sounds, and smells at every turn, Jim was getting used to it. You could get used to anything, he supposed, though the heat was a killer and not helped by his alcohol and drug habits.

Jim got on the plane and nodded to Erevu in the seat beside him. Erevu gave a smile and a thumbs-up. Jim went through the checklist, fired up the plane, taxied to the runway, and lifted off into the African morning. In the hours of the flight, over the great lake and then the jungles, Erevu kept pointing excitedly. He had worked on many planes, but he'd never been up in one before. Jim found himself amused and smiling at the man's enthusiasm, and he could feel a bit of the excitement for something he had long taken for granted.

The land turned to deep jungle and hills beneath them. Most of the flights before had been to the south of the great rain forests of the Congo. Rivers, small and large, occasionally cut through the massive expanse of green. Small patches of brown dirt were few and far between and made a stark contrast to the dense canopy.

"We're almost at the coordinates," Jim said after hours in the air.

Erevu jumped in his seat and put his hands to the headset over his ears.

"Home? Nyumbani?" Jim asked.

Erevu nodded and began chattering in Swahili, pointing toward the ground, speaking too quickly for Jim to understand. Jim angled the plane to make out a clearing below, not far from a narrow strip of river and some small structures. Jim flew over the village and eyed the clearing; it was small but doable for landing.

Jim turned and lined up, coming in for a relatively smooth landing, considering that the runway was a dirt-and-rock road. He angled the plane around to point in the direction from which he would take off. Erevu was looking out the plane window, his initial excitement turning to a look of concern, his body tense.

"Problem?" Jim asked as he shut down the plane.

"No, people," Erevu said tensely, still looking out the window.

The men sat in the plane as the engine shut off. All was quiet except for insect noises. Getting out of the plane, Jim and Erevu looked around. The heat was stifling. Jim could feel the sweat on his back soaking his shirt.

"Njoo nje!" Erevu shouted.

Jim watched as the man began to move toward the village of large huts evenly spaced in the clearing from the jungle, calling in Swahili for people to come out. The village seemed deserted. Jim was getting an uncomfortable feeling.

He walked back to the plane and opened the cargo door. Reaching into the plane's interior, he removed the FN FAL rifle and a bag full of magazines, which he slipped over his shoulder. He reached for the canteen inside the plane and had just raised it to drink when he heard Erevu scream from within the village.

Jim dropped the canteen and rushed from the plane toward the sound, his rifle held low and ready. Using the closest hut for cover, he peered around the corner.

The village was a dusty cluster of grass-topped huts surrounded by jungle, edged on one side by the small river. Large trees were scattered at the village's edges, with a few also at its center.

Seeing no movement, Jim continued around the corner and deeper into the village. No people or animals were evident in the twenty or so huts arranged around a larger central building. Jim could not see Erevu anywhere. The smell of old woodsmoke from cooking fires outside of the houses became stronger. The village did not feel dangerous, but it did not feel like a place where people lived either. Just empty.

And then the smell hit Jim like a punch, making going forward a daunting prospect. It was the scent he had come to associate with the worst of Africa: the smell of death.

Walking up to the open door of the central building, Jim saw Erevu inside in the middle of a scene of horror. Bodies of people covered the floor in disarray as men, women, and children lay in death in the center of their village. Erevu was kneeling, holding the body of a woman in his arms. Tears were streaming down his face, and as Jim watched, he began to keen. The woman's once pretty face was marred by death. Her body was missing both arms above the elbow, the ragged flesh oddly pinkish against her dark skin.

The sight of those ragged stumps made Jim realize something he'd overlooked at first: many of these bodies were missing their arms. Slowly he looked up: what he had taken in the half-dark of the hut's interior to be branches or vines hanging from the ceiling and walls were human arms.

Flies swarmed everywhere in the hut, buzzing and alighting from the bodies. A cloying miasma of blood, shit, and rot was thick in the air.

Jim staggered back from the scene, away from this place of suffering and the end of suffering. He walked to the hut farthest from the center and sat with his back against an exterior wall. Setting down the rifle, he breathed deeply. The lush, earthy smell of the jungle filled his nose, but still he could smell the death. The smell was like a physical thing trying to sear its way into his brain.

Jim had known things like this were occurring in the area, had heard of it. This was the reason the guns were coming here. For people to try to protect themselves from whomever had done this.

He didn't know how long he sat there, only that

the shadows had moved.

"Will help bury?"

Jim opened his eyes to see Erevu standing with a pick and shovel in his hands, their points resting against the ground. Erevu's manner was calm, his brown eyes looking levelly into Jim's.

Jim got up without a word and reached for the pick. He followed Erevu to a place near the edge of the village. The men began to dig graves. They found some food and water to sustain them, along with a lantern so that they could continue when darkness fell. Jim lost track of the bug bites that pierced his skin. Some DEET spray from the plane helped, but still he was assailed by the onslaught of flies and mosquitos. When the holes were dug, he and Erevu began picking up and moving bodies and pieces of bodies from the building to the graves.

Pick broke earth, shovel turned earth, hands picked up bodies and placed them into the hole, earth then covered the vessels of flesh that once were people. People who laughed and cried and lived and died.

They dug many graves that long, hot night. Mothers and daughters, fathers and sons lay together in the ground. Jim couldn't be sure how many they moved, how many they put in the same hole. He just followed Erevu's lead and worked until the last body was in the ground.

As the darkness began to fade with the dawn's light, Jim could feel his body reaching the end of its endurance. The men had not spoken throughout the ordeal. Both had put away their emotions to accomplish the grim task.

When the work was completed, Erevu led Jim

down to the river, to a wooden platform on the water's edge, which held a small table and a basin. It was full morning now, and birds flew about the small brown river. Jim went forward to dive in, but Erevu put a hand on his chest.

"No," Erevu said, pointing. "Crocodile."

Jim followed Erevu's extended finger to see a long brown shape across the water. He shook his head in disbelief at the strangeness of this dangerous place where people lived their lives.

Erevu took a bucket from the dock and dipped it into the water. He poured the river water into the basin, then repeated the action until the basin was full. He handed Jim a sliver of soap and a small rag and waited as Jim stripped and cleaned himself as best as possible, then dunked his clothing in the water, wringing out the dirt and other stains that he didn't want to think about. With no other option, when done Jim put the clothes back on, the cool dampness feeling welcome after the long night.

"You go," Erevu said.

Jim looked at him, trying to make sense of the words through the fog of exhaustion.

"We go," Jim said.

Erevu walked to the plane, and Jim followed. Erevu opened the cargo door and began pulling out crates and placing them on the ground. Despite his exhaustion, Jim began to help. When the boxes of rifles and ammunition were unloaded, Erevu turned to Jim.

"You go," he repeated.

Jim knew that the cargo had already been paid for. There was really no reason to stay.

"We go," Jim said again.

Erevu shook his head. "I no go. You go, or you

die. My home . . . my country. Mai-Mai will be back. I fight."

Jim could see that he wouldn't be able to convince Erevu to leave. He was too weary to make sense of an argument. Everything that the man had worked for and loved was gone. Jim nodded, shook Erevu's hand, and closed up the plane. As he turned, Erevu spoke again.

"Be careful of Jacques, David. He is for himself first and last. My thanks to you."

Not knowing what else to do or say, Jim took a last look at the village and the brown mounds of the graves he had helped dig.

If Jacques was disappointed to see Erevu go, he didn't let it keep him down for long. The other men, Haji and Babu, heard the news, nodded, and wandered out of the building to take care of the plane.

"Are they from the same village? I didn't ask," Jim said.

"No, but they might as well be," Jacques said. "Babu grew up in a village that was annihilated like that one, but he escaped. At five years old, he walked alone from the jungle to Kinshasa. He was lucky; an orphanage there was able to take him in."

"Haji?"

"Same basic tribe as Erevu, but a different part of the country. They are all Bantu peoples, specifically Luba or Baluba, which includes about thirteen million people in the Congo and spans three hundred to six hundred different ethnic groups. Nobody really knows for sure. The one thing they all share is a common history of violence. Africa is, was, and shall be violent, which is why we are in business."

Jim blinked, looking out over the airfield. He swayed a bit, unsteady from the events in the jungle.

"Go get cleaned up and lie down, David. Get some rest," Jacques said. Jim looked back at him.

"It is Africa, David," Jacques said, his eyes momentarily sad. "It is just Africa."

Jack Lyons

Chapter 12

J im and Christopher were looking over the map, where a large swatch of green deep into Congo was circled in grease pencil.

The cargo was different this time.

"Who the hell can afford a *tank*?" Jim muttered, shaking his head.

Christopher looked at him with a raised eyebrow. Jim shrugged at the glance; neither of them was very interested in that answer.

"So, low altitude drop with no landing?" Jim asked.

"Yeah," Christopher replied, staring at the map.

"A prop plane?"

"No, Jacques is lining up an Antonov-124 out of Nigeria," Christopher replied.

Jim looked at Christopher with interest.

"Buying one?"

"Let's say renting. A couple of Nigerian pilots are borrowing the plane from their government for a day or so. Jacques will coordinate landing it here and loading the extras for the tanks."

"What kind of tanks?"

"Scorpions. Two of them. Coming in from Egypt or somewhere, through Nigeria."

"American?"

"British," Christopher replied. "Light tanks."

"And what extras?"

"The ones in the crates outside." Jacques's voice behind them caused them to turn around.

The men walked to the mouth of the hangar and looked at the truck pulling up. Two large wooden crates were visible in the back.

Christopher looked over the bed of the truck. "Flotation screens?"

"The tanks can move through water as amphibious vehicles. Very useful for operations around the lake," Jacques explained to Jim. "A navy and a ground force."

"So why not just drive them there?" Jim asked.

"Why ask why?" Jacques replied, grinning as he adjusted his pressed suit. "People tend to notice tanks driving through their villages."

Jim considered the response and decided he had been nosy enough for now. The early morning bump of heroin, with the addition of some amphetamines, was keeping him level.

"So, to do the drop, we'll need a loadmaster in addition to pilots," Jim said. "Are the Nigerians going with us?"

"Unfortunately, no," Jacques said. "They will be bringing a loadmaster to assist in securing the vehicles, but having them involved beyond that will not be possible. They're being paid a small fortune just to get the plane here. Or, rather, to Dar es Salaam."

"Quite a lot of eyes at that airport," Jim muttered.

"The load-out and refuel will be done inside a hangar. The only ones who will see the plane will be paid not to see."

"These going to the government militia?" Jim asked. He regretted saying it as soon as it came out of his mouth.

Jacques looked at him with a steady gaze. After a lengthy silence, he asked, "Does it matter?"

Jim remained silent. The memory of Erevu's slaughtered village was still fresh. He knew he shouldn't be asking these questions. Asking questions—other than "Will I get killed?" and "When am I getting paid?"—was stupid in this line of work. Anything else came up against good business and continued breathing.

"No, these are going to an individual concerned with the security of holdings in the area," Jacques explained finally.

The answer was a little too convenient, but it was the one Jim needed to hear. He regretted shooting his mouth off. Jacques walked back to the office, leaving the two men alone.

"You catch crazy somewhere?" Christopher asked.

Jim shook his head. "Sorry, must be the heat."

"Must be. Let's hope there's no more of that heat. This is not a place to start growing a conscience. You got any doubts in your head, you let them pass or keep them to yourself. Understand?"

The air was cooler in the midnight hour as Jim took the controls and eased the plane onto the runway at Dar es Salaam, then up into the air. While he had not flown this type of plane before, his new profession demanded adaptability. After a brief instructional session with the Nigerian pilots, complete with some sticky notes translating the Russian controls, Jim had figured out enough to fly the aircraft.

The two squat tanks in the back had been quickly loaded on their pallets, along with an additional pallet of ammunition and spare parts. The Russian jet handled the weight well and flew surprisingly gracefully. Of course, he wouldn't put it up against a fighter for acrobatics, but it was docile once on course.

Christopher came into the cockpit and sat in the copilot chair. The earlier tension had gradually faded as both men attended to their tasks. Christopher shuffled through the folder of documents in his lap and held up a photo.

"This is the approach here, as we discussed," he said, pointing to the picture of a valley nestled between two unremarkable hills next to Lake Tanganyika. Jim checked his instruments and then looked at the picture. He had gone over the plans with Christopher before departure.

"I got it," Jim said, returning his attention to flying the plane.

An hour later, they readied and prepped for the drop. The early-morning daylight revealed the rolling hills of the northern Congo plains stretching out and up from the deep African lake. Jim aligned the big plane to the required coordinates and began his run five miles to the south, as discussed with Christopher.

"Dialed in for approach," he said. "Chris, radio check."

"Five by five, Jim," said Chris's voice in the radio headset. "Initiating door opening."

"Understood," Jim replied. He was getting better at repressing the instinct to say "Roger that."

Jim felt his nerves tighten and his attention focus more sharply as the console light went on to let him know the large rear door was opening. He controlled his breathing to calm himself, the stress of a dangerous and challenging task sharpening his senses, making him feel alive up here in the air.

A flicker appeared in the sky, instantly drawing his attention. A flash of something, then nothing. He returned his gaze to the instruments.

"Slowing aircraft to drop speed," he said into the radio.

"Righto."

Jim eased the throttles back, bringing the jet closer to the edge of where it would be unflyable. Jim was aware, as all pilots were, that no plane was magic. When the speed of the air flowing over the wings dropped too low, physics would take over, and the plane would simply fall out of the sky.

"Target speed," Jim said.

Over his headset Jim heard Christopher's response: two clicks of the mic button, signaling he understood. Jim moved the yoke forward to bring the plane closer to the earth, watching the altimeter marked высотомер.

Thank God the numbers don't need translating, Jim thought as he leveled off the plane.

"Target altitude," Jim said into the radio and was rewarded with two more clicks.

A roar across the windshield shocked him, a terrible sound of fury, and something blotted out the light. Jim would have jumped out of the seat if he hadn't been buckled in. Only by his training was he able to keep his body calm enough to maintain the aircraft.

"What the hell was *that?*" Christopher's voice yelled on the radio.

Jim didn't reply. His eyes were frantically scanning the sky. He knew they had just been buzzed by a fighter aircraft.

"A fucking MiG!" Christopher screamed.

Jim took a moment to process this as he eyed the landscape below.

"What's he doing?" Jim asked.

"What?"

"Is he lining up on us or not?" Jim asked, processing options in his head as the hills he was looking for came into view. His body tensed, sweat pouring. He would have given a few years of his life for a bump of the white powder. Blood was roaring in his ears.

"No, not lining up," Christopher said.

"Proceeding with drop."

"*What?*" Christopher yelled, incredulous.

"Two minutes to target."

"Get the fuck out of here!"

"Anywhere you want to go and explain the tanks in the back if we get forced down?" Jim yelled back. "Or would you rather explain to Jacques how we lost them?"

There was silence on the radio as Christopher considered this.

"One minute to drop," Jim said, not waiting for a reply, guiding the aircraft steadily. He could see the site now, a flat spot between the hills.

"Ready for the drop," Christopher replied, his voice tense.

Jim gauged the drop site, keeping his wings level and an eye on his altitude and speed. The unknown intentions of the MiG fighter were making concentration on the task at hand almost impossible. They were only a few hundred feet off the earth. Any miscalculation or error at this point could make them crash. He angled the nose slightly up to bring the plane's rear down while feathering the throttle to keep the speed up and prevent a stall. The engines sounded as if they were protesting the dangerous maneuver.

"Drop," Christopher said.

"Drop away."

Jim felt the plane leap with the weight release of the tanks and their parachutes. Then the three heavy pallets loaded with ammunition and equipment slid out to float toward the earth as well.

"Away now, David," Christopher said. *"Now!"*

Jim quickly pushed the throttles up, applying power to pull out of the low-altitude trajectory. The big plane responded quickly.

"Hang on," Jim responded, watching the light on the console that signaled the closing of the cargo door turn from red to green. He banked the plane east, back toward the lake and the border.

"Beautifully done, sir. A nicer drop I have never seen."

The voice on the radio was polished, refined, with an accent Jim did not recognize despite its British inflection. Jim concentrated on flying. Every sense was heightened, sharpened by the danger and adrenaline.

"Aircraft, you are in the airspace of the Democratic Republic of the Congo. Identify yourself," the voice said in Jim's headset. Jim thought he could almost hear the voice smile.

Christopher clambered into the copilot's chair and hurriedly buckled in after slamming the headset onto his head.

"Aircraft, I see you are flagged for Nigeria. Are you lost?"

As Jim watched, the MiG fighter came from behind them and slid into view on the port side. Jim could see the pilot looking at him through the windshield.

"One of you looks a bit pale for Nigeria," the voice said. "I trust you understand that you will not be welcome if you return?"

Jim knew they were close to the boundary of Tanzania, as they had been over the lake for a few minutes. The MiG dropped away; Jim could not track where.

"Three minutes to the border," Christopher said. "Climb, and then we can dive if necessary. I think he's just screwing with us."

"Who the hell is he? Didn't realize Congo had an air force."

"A mercenary. Congo hires them for good money to be their pilots, fly their jets."

"Aircraft, you are close to the border," the voice said. "Guess you don't want to play. Take my regards to Mr. Jacques."

Jim felt and heard the impact of rounds piercing the rear fuselage of the plane body behind them. He immediately angled the plane down and to the left to evade the attack.

"Farewell, then," the voice on the radio said. The MiG waggled its wings, then did a barrel roll and disappeared.

"We're over the border. Thank God," Christopher said, leaning back into his seat.

No alarms were sounding, and the plane felt steady. Christopher went back to check the damage.

"Four holes on each side," he called out. "We should be fine."

"We should be down in another hour," Jim said. "But do you think Dar es Salaam will be safe?"

"No way," Christopher said. "Head to the alternate

site. I'll call Jacques and let him know."

The rest of the flight was uneventful. Landing at the remote alternate airstrip, they were met by Jacques and the Nigerians. The Nigerians immediately began to shout about the damage to their plane.

Jim just walked away and sat in the SUV, watching the scene through the windshield, physically spent. Jim watched as Jacques talked to the men, obviously trying to placate them. The shouting grew until Jacques pulled out a pistol and fired it into the ground at the men's feet. A brief exchange ensued, money changed hands, and the men boarded the plane.

Jacques and Christopher joined Jim in the vehicle. Immediately Jacques began questioning Jim and Christopher about the MiG, asking the same questions again and again. Finally they arrived at the hotel, where Jim was dropped off and headed directly to the bar to drink himself nearly blind, enough so that for the first time he used a needle in the arm instead of snorting. Booze and drugs were probably the only two things letting him cope. He thought he might be losing his mind.

More than a month went by with Jacques gone, resolving the issues with the Nigerians while trying to find out more about their own problems. How had they been intercepted, and would it be a problem going forward?

Finally Jim was called from his hotel—and his bender—to meet Jacques and Christopher at the hangar.

"How did the MiG pilot know your name?" Jim blurted. The thought had nagged since the last time they had talked.

Jacques looked at him over the office desk for a moment, then shrugged. "How does anyone know anything? He asked someone, and someone told. Maybe he looked and he saw."

"Kinda vague."

"Vague is good in this business, you know that."

"Did the shipment get picked up?" Jim asked, rubbing his face. He felt exhausted all the time now.

"Yes, the client was very pleased. Thankfully it was remote enough that no other forces could get there first. There has been a request for something new, though: many weapons and ammunition for a rebel/freedom fighter offensive. It will take all of our inventory and then some to fill it. In actuality, it's government-backed."

"Which government?" Jim asked.

"Good question, but not germane at the moment," Jacques said breezily, ignoring Jim's curiosity. "We will make this delivery and then take some time off to see where things settle."

"What's the plan?" Jim asked, his brain foggy. He rubbed his arms, which were covered in long sleeves to hide the track marks.

"I have located an older but serviceable C-130 Hercules aircraft. I am in negotiations at the moment, but they should be concluded soon. You and Christopher should be able to fly the entire package over the border, drop it off, and return. At that point, we will close up shop and briefly retire. If you do not want to do that, I have contacts that can keep you in your profession in other parts of the country or the world."

Jim considered this information for a moment.

"What about the MiG pilot?"

"He is a South African based out of French Algiers, a mercenary pilot in the employ of the

Congolese government. Jean Grance Transell is his name."

"Thought the accent was odd. Would have figured that Russian-trained pilots were easier and cheaper," Christopher said.

"Russians don't generally speak Swahili and French."

"Will we be dropping again or landing?" Christopher asked.

"Landing at night. Some of the things you're transporting are too delicate and precious to drop, though we will rig the pallets with parachutes in case a jettison is absolutely necessary. We would lose a lot of money if anything were broken, however. A *lot* of money."

Jim raised his eyes. "Landing at an airport?"

"On a road. You will be in communication with the ground team, and they will light up the target with flares. The ground team is trained and experienced in this sort of thing."

"So, government troops?"

"Trained personnel, not civilian fighters. We'll leave it at that."

"I get at night because of the MiG, by why landing? What's so delicate?"

"It's not only delicate. The delivery must be confirmed to the right person. Without that confirmation, the funds will not be released; a very reliable middleman will be holding the funds in escrow. If there were an airdrop, then the receiving party could say they never received the goods. Negotiations at that point could get difficult. We want to avoid problems."

Jim and Christopher looked at each other. Both were thinking the same thought: *Problems like a MiG.*

"I know what you're thinking," Jacques continued. "Why not just shoot both of you in the head and say you never arrived? Simple: the customer will be providing assurance of ten family members until the exchange is complete. Along with tracking and funds in escrow."

"What's so important that they would give that type of assurance?" Christopher asked.

"Come with me." Jacques stood up, leading the men to the back of the hangar, where they saw a stack of metal canisters and a tarp over what looked like boxes.

"Cyrillic letters. Russian-made . . . what?" Jim asked, looking at the writing on one of the canisters.

Jacques pulled off the tarp and moved to the first dull green, coffin-shaped box. Undoing the latches, he fully opened it. Jim and Christopher stepped forward with interest to see what was so important.

"Igla-1 MANPAD," Jacques said. "It's effective to eleven thousand feet, unlike the older Russian Strela-3, which had a ceiling of seventy-five hundred feet. Used to shoot down jets and other aircraft. They can also be used against armor."

Jim looked at the device with Christopher as Jacques stood back. The shoulder-fired rocket launcher and white missile were nestled into purpose-cut foam.

"May I?" Christopher asked.

"Here, let me show you in case there are questions," Jacques said, lifting the end of the launcher and propping it on the edge of the case.

"Like a bazooka, it is loaded from the rear. You then point in the general direction of the aircraft and flip this switch, like so."

Jacques hoisted the launcher to his shoulder and pointed it at the mouth of the hangar.

"Once you flip this switch, you hear the sound."
Jacques flipped the switch, and the men could hear a
tone. "The tone will go up once the launcher has acquired
the target. Then pull the trigger. And if you need to keep
firing, the launcher can be reused."

Jacques replaced the launcher and closed the case.

"We will leave at the end of the week. Until then,
we move all inventory here for loading."

Jack Lyons

Chapter 13

The flight out started bumpy and didn't smooth out until they were crossing the lake between Tanzania and the Congo. Instruments glowed in the cockpit, illuminating their faces. The tension the men felt was high. Neither wanted to experience another run-in with the MiG pilot.

The old C-130 was a solid workhorse of a plane, capable of carrying a lot of cargo. Today it carried hundreds of crated AK-47s, RPGs, grenades, claymores, and ammunition, along with the Igla-1 rockets. Medical supplies cleared from the warehouses around Tanzania were also loaded onto the flight.

Jim navigated the aircraft, wearing a head harness and night-vision goggles to scan the skies. He had some experience with night-vision equipment. He and Christopher both hoped that the equipment would make a difference.

The big propellers thundered the plane through the night air. Flying lower than optimal kept them below the few radar installations in the country, but their progress was slowed in the thicker air close to the ground.

"Come to heading two-seven-six degrees," Jim said as they reached a navigational milestone.

"Two-seven-six degrees," Christopher said as he turned the yoke of the plane to the new heading.

The hours stretched as they flew over the dark

landscape. The relative coolness of the lake air changed to the heat of the jungle below them. What they were attempting was an extremely dangerous maneuver, flying into an unknown rendezvous at night to land on an unlit road in the middle of the Congo jungle, providing weapons to people who wanted to use them on other people. Whether for defense or offense, the arms they were transporting at the end of the day would be used for the purpose designed: taking human life.

Hopefully not theirs.

The overcast sky had hidden most of the stars during the trip. As they neared their destination, the clouds began to fade, removing their cover and reflecting on a sleeping land below them.

"Aircraft, identify yourself." A familiar voice sounded on the radio.

"Fuck!" Christopher said, craning his head to look through the windshield.

The MiG streaked past them in the dark. Its lights were also turned off, so only the roar of its flight revealed its closeness. Jim's heart pounded as he calculated just how vulnerable they were.

"Aircraft, identify yourself," the MiG pilot repeated. "L'avion vous identifie immédiatement."

"See him?" Christopher asked.

"No," Jim said, dropping the night-vision goggles back over his eyes.

Another roar as the MiG again flew past them. Jim followed the quick flash of the jet's afterburner.

"He's using the sky as a backdrop, coming in low and seeing us outlined. He may not have night vision. Give me the aircraft," Jim said.

"Your aircraft."

Jim pushed the yoke forward, diving the plane closer to the ground. The green and black blurs of the instrumentation helped them figure out their position, but they were playing a dangerous game.

"We may buy some time, but we're still sitting ducks," Jim said.

"Maybe not," Christopher replied.

"What?"

"The Iglas. Maybe I can shoot out of the cargo door."

Jim considered the suggestion and couldn't think of anything better. "Do it. Hook up to the intercom and I'll see if I can help you."

Christopher extracted himself from the seat and scrambled to the cargo area. Jim heard the scrabble in the headset as Christopher hooked in.

"Check," Christopher said.

"Read you loud and clear."

"Lowering cargo door."

"Check."

Jim watched the green cargo door light change to red as the large ramp in the aircraft's rear began to lower. The aircraft became harder to control, more sluggish, as the ramp door disrupted the airflow around the plane. Jim was struck by the thought of shooting at road signs from the back of pickups as a kid. He laughed out loud.

"What the hell are you laughing at?" Christopher asked.

"Nothing," Jim said. "You ready?"

"Two loaded. Not turning on until target is in sight."

Off in the distance, Jim could see the red, blinking light of the jet moving through the sky. The pilot, he knew, thought they were unarmed, sitting ducks. He was letting them know of his arrogant assurance that they were not dangerous.

"Aircraft, this is Colonel Transell of the Democratic Republic of the Congo air force. You will respond or be fired upon."

Jim watched the blinking red light dropping down and lining up with his altitude. The attack, most likely guns, was going to come head-on. The other pilot was a real cowboy. Jim knew he only had seconds and that Christopher could not shoot at a plane in front of them.

"I see your door down. Do not drop that cargo!" Colonel Transell ordered.

"We surrender, we surrender," Jim said into the radio. Then, switching the microphone to internal communications, he said, "Christopher, get ready!"

The MiG flew below the C-130 without firing. The tone sounded in Jim's headset as the Igla-1 launcher searched for the MiG in the night sky. The tone went higher, and then Jim heard the rocket launch. Jim watched it streaking toward the MiG as fiery white antimissile flares leapt out of the MiG in the night sky.

"Hold on, Chris!" Jim yelled, pulling back the yoke, willing the plane to climb, remembering what he'd been taught: *Always take the high ground in the fight.*

He watched the MiG turn in desperation to escape as the rocket, lured by an antimissile flare, exploded in the sky. The MiG turned like an angry wasp, its pilot searching for the plane that was now thousands of feet above him. The jet appeared to be heading away. The harmless opponent had almost bit him.

"Chris! Chris!" Jim yelled into the radio headset. "No joy, no joy."

With no response from Christopher, Jim looked rapidly at the sky and could not see any sign of the MiG. He supposed that the jet would return to its base, not wanting to risk being shot down by arms smugglers with effective weapons.

Jim leveled the aircraft, put it on autopilot, and levered out of the seat. He hated to leave the cockpit but had to check on Christopher. Jim had to know if he was hurt or even still in the plane.

Red lights filled the fuselage, casting a pall of scarlet over the cargo, providing enough illumination to see. Rushing, clambering over the webbing-covered pallets, Jim saw Christopher sitting against the aircraft's wall, looking around, dazed, an empty Igla tube in front of him. Another tube was sitting on top of the first pallet, the webbing askew where Christopher had dug out the launchers.

"Chris!" Jim shouted. *The sudden maneuvers must have knocked him around*, he thought.

Chris snapped around, looking at the cockpit in alarm.

"Autopilot is flying!" Jim shouted into his ear. "We missed the MiG. He flew off."

Jim lifted Christopher up to help him get to the cockpit. Sudden sounds of impacts to the fuselage made them both duck. Shattered glass from the windshield cut both men as it was sucked through the plane and out the open cargo door, the interior of the plane becoming a moving wind tunnel. Jim instinctively covered Christopher with his body as the tempest roared around them.

They both looked up, squinting as the air whipped by. The plane was bucking, trying to compensate automatically for the wildly different pressures and whatever mechanical failures had occurred. Jim was knocked to the deck, while Christopher clung to the webbing on the pallets. Jim's feet suddenly touched the cargo bay roof as the plane fell out of the sky and then recovered, lurching back to level.

Jim felt a sharp pain as the loaded Igla-1 rocket launcher flew up into the air and cracked him squarely between the eyes. Stunned, he reached out to grasp the tube to stop it from hitting him again. His ears were ringing loudly as he looked at Christopher reaching out for him, their eyes meeting as time slowed.

Jim reached out for Christopher's hand, taking in the tanned face lighted by the red glow. Deep blue eyes, crinkles and wrinkles, laugh lines and stress lines all made the face of the man who had lived in the world for sixty-odd years sear itself into Jim's brain in a moment of calm.

Then all that was Christopher suddenly exploded, covering the interior of the cargo bay. Jim felt the change in air pressure as the 37mm cannon shells passed in front of his face. He knew they were being fired upon, but could only watch as the rounds impacted the interior of the cargo bay, too stunned to process what had happened: a life ended, snatched away.

The pallets lurched and slipped as more incoming rounds shattered the cargo restraints. In shock, Jim could only sit there and grip the launcher, trying to establish a reference point for the destruction.

The aircraft started to dive. Jim was trying to sit up when his legs were dragged out from under him, tangled in the webbing of the pallet nearest the door. With the loss of gravity from the dive of the doomed plane lifting both him and the pallet, Jim was ripped out of the aircraft into the night sky.

Spinning and tumbling, Jim could only scream incoherently when the pallet suddenly jerked as the cargo parachute deployed, leaving him hanging from the webbing as the bundle of cargo fell through the air. The dark jungle was waiting thousands of feet below. Hanging upside down, legs hopelessly tangled, Jim saw the horizon from an inverted position. Highlighted against the moon was the glow of the MiG's afterburner.

Jim realized the rocket launcher was still in his arms, crushed tightly against his body by the cargo webbing. Its tone was the ringing that Jim had been hearing. Rage filled Jim as he desperately struggled to move the launcher, the MiG retreating. He jerked and swung, swearing into the void, not caring that he fell, only wanting to lash out. To die fighting.

While struggling, Jim realized the tone had changed to the higher frequency indicating the launcher had acquired a target. Desperately sliding his hand down to the trigger, he quickly depressed it. Instantly the rocket streaked from the launcher tube, its flame burning his body as it flew into the sky, searching out the jet in the night.

Jim didn't see whether the rocket impacted. His descent had met with the top of the jungle canopy. Crashing through limbs and trees, Jim was tossed and inverted again, at one moment chasing, then chased by, the pallet of heavy weapons and crates. Jim plummeted, dragged in the darkness toward the jungle floor. The pallets or parachute would catch for a moment, slamming painfully to a stop against tree limbs or webbing. Then gravity would tear, and everything would smash through the thick branches again and again, Jim being both pummeled and crushed by the branches, netting, and cargo.

A final great lurch stopped the fall. Through the blood streaming down his face, Jim saw out of one eye the floor of the jungle below, illuminated in patches by moonlight. His mind judged the drop to be about fifty feet. He contemplated his imminent demise, only hoping that it would be quick.

Jim heard and felt the load above shifting and breaking the tree limbs once more. The final pull to the earth started with near-weightlessness as the branches above him bent and broke, releasing the heavy weight, and it ended with finality, spilling most of the crates onto the ground. The nylon webbing burned Jim's body, neck, and face even as it cradled him. His right arm slipped out of a loop in the net, his slack fingers brushing the moist soil of the jungle floor.

Blood dripped into the dark earth below.

Chapter 14

Jim slowly swayed, trapped in the embrace of the cargo net. No strength remained to free himself. Whatever his injuries, he knew they must be extensive. Consciousness came and went as Jim struggled to breathe, his chest compressed by the webbing and his own body weight. Eventually he ceased to struggle and waited for death.

A rustling sound brought Jim from a dazed stupor. Opening one eye pressed against a hole in the netting, Jim saw a dark shape moving around. Fear of the next unknown gripped his heart. The thick foliage made it hard to ascertain what the form was. Jim heard the crack of twigs as the shape moved out of his line of sight.

Soft steps came closer, smaller crunches of undergrowth. Someone or something was very near. Jim felt weak and vulnerable with his limbs restricted by the webbing and injuries. Completely unable to defend himself, Jim waited for whatever would happen, resigned to his fate.

A noise came again, a sense of movement. A man's face came level with his, a brown face in the dim light. Hair, wild and unruly, stood out around a large forehead and bearded chin. Jim had a sense of large shoulders. But the eyes were the focus for Jim: intelligent eyes framed in shadows, looking at him, into him.

"Are you going to get me down?" Jim gasped

finally.

The man's face was impassive, observing him.

"Well?" Jim croaked, his tongue thick in his dry mouth.

Still the man did not move, only watched. Jim felt fury, then loss, then acceptance while transfixed by those eyes. He and the man stared at each other in the jungle moonlight.

"Help me, please," Jim asked, then repeated it in both Swahili and French: "Nisaidie. Aidez-moi."

The man took a knife from his waist and examined the netting. Choosing a spot, he began cutting the nylon straps. Each cut brought Jim closer to the ground until he rested in the cool dirt. Jim groaned as his injuries protested. The man put away his knife and lifted Jim carefully, moving him away from the netting.

Jim looked up at his savior while trying to process the pain. The man did not look like the Congolese he had seen before. He was tall, broad-shouldered, and, inexplicably, wearing the brown robe of a monk. Wild hair and a full beard with streaks of gray surrounded the dark skin of the continent.

"Who are you?" Jim asked.

"I am Abraham."

The man's deep voice rumbled with a definitive American accent, a touch of education and southern origin wrapped together.

"You're American?" Jim asked incredulously.

"Yes. You?"

"Canadian."

The men regarded each other and considered the odds of meeting fellow North Americans in the middle of the deepest part of the darkest African jungle. Then

Abraham went to one knee at Jim's side.

"I would like to check your injuries," he said.

Jim tried to nod his consent, air whistling through his lips as a sharp pain protested in his neck. The big, strong hands efficiently probed Jim's body, gauging his reactions. When Abraham reached Jim's left leg, his manipulation of the upper shin brought a gasp from Jim's lips, a jerk from his body.

"Probably partially fractured," Abraham said.

Jim nodded grimly, laying his head back.

"That you in the sky, making all that noise?" Abraham asked.

"Half of it. The other guy might be in another tree somewhere else, if you want to check." Jim winced, coughed, and winced again.

Abraham leaned back his head and laughed, a joyous, rumbling sound.

"A warrior fallen from the sky, found by a man of God. Still some piss and vinegar in you," he said.

"Don't know about the vinegar, but the piss is all over myself," Jim said, adding, "I was wondering about the robe."

"I have wondered about it many times myself. What is your name, my son?"

"David," Jim said. "David Somers."

Abraham looked deep into Jim's eyes, calmly taking him in.

"What is your name?" he repeated.

"David Somers."

Moments passed, with Abraham keeping a steady gaze on Jim.

"What is your name?" Abraham asked again, patiently.

Jim stared back into those green eyes, caught in their hold of kindness. Abraham's gaze was so deep and profound you could get lost. Jim had become used to denying his name. Yet, after everything that had happened and the fact that his death would most likely occur in this jungle, he didn't feel a bit of concern about keeping his secrets.

"Jim. Jim Stabbert," Jim said, his birth name falling from bruised lips.

"And where are you from?" Abraham asked.

"America. Kentucky, originally."

Abraham stood. He picked up a wooden staff from the ground; Jim had not noticed it before.

"I thank you for sharing this truth with me. I am Brother Abraham Michael Hunt, a man of God in this wilderness, a wanderer from another place, and your countryman," Abraham said, leaning against his staff. "I would pray for you, Jim, and ask that the power of God, the Holy Spirit, flow through me, an unworthy vessel. There have been times where I have been blessed to be an instrument of the Lord in healing."

"I haven't believed in God in a long time, Abe."

"Abe. I like that name, one from my childhood. As far as God, it does not matter if you believe in that tree. It is there, regardless of your belief. I offer you a chance to be healed through the power of the Holy Spirit."

Jim lay back again, regarding his unlikely savior.

"Whatever, Abe."

Abraham nodded and turned his back on Jim, stretching his arms wide, holding his staff in both hands. His head was bowed in deep contemplation.

"Oh Lord, grant me the peace to be Your instrument. Allow me the grace to heal Your child."

The prayer done, Abraham knelt beside Jim, laying his staff again on the ground. He stretched out his hands above Jim's left knee and closed his eyes. Moments turned to minutes as Abraham whispered too softly to hear. Jim lay back in his pain.

"I am unworthy," Abraham said finally, removing his hands. "I don't feel His grace."

"Welcome to the club," Jim said. "I have a package in my right cargo pocket. It can help."

Abraham gently opened the flap and withdrew a canvas bag. Opening the top, he laid the syringes, spoon, lighter, and baggie of white powder on the ground.

"Is this what I think it is?" Abraham asked.

"If you think it's heroin, then yes," Jim said, wincing with pain.

Abraham looked at the equipment. With Jim's instruction, he deftly made the necessary preparations. Sliding up Jim's sleeve, Abraham stopped and looked at the track marks nestled amongst the cuts and friction burns.

Jim felt shame in having this man look at him and his degradation.

"I—" he began.

Abraham shook his head, quieting Jim. "This will help you for now. You have significant injuries. You could go into shock without it. And it will allow me to transport you more easily."

Abraham wrapped a piece of netting around Jim's arm, then slid the needle into a vein. Jim let out a sigh of relief as the opiate hit his system.

While Jim rested, Abraham gathered and assembled branches in the early morning light, using cargo netting to build a travois, a litter that could be dragged.

"We will travel east while we can," Abraham said, moving Jim onto the contraption. "I have a place carved out not far away, humble as it is. On the way, you can tell me how a hillbilly from Kentucky finds himself in this lonely place, help me understand why God has brought us together."

Abraham turned, sliding his staff between the two loops of netting secured to the travois where Jim lay. Then, setting the staff on broad shoulders, he began pulling Jim along the jungle path.

Jim lay back on the travois and tried to breathe through the pain. The heroin could only do so much.

As they traveled slowly and painfully through the jungle, Jim told Abraham of life growing up in Kentucky, his time split between the city and his family in the countryside, his summers of roaming in the forests and along the trails.

Abraham listened as Jim recounted his acceptance to the naval academy. Jim's story spilled from bruised lips. Abraham's footsteps were steady, slowly pulling the burden along.

The choice of training as a Marine Corps pilot instead of a Navy aviator was the path that had led to Maggie and then to the war. Jim held nothing back. Doubts and failures were laid out along with joys and triumphs. Never before had he opened up to anyone as he did to Abraham that night. The close brush with death made speaking about life meaningful.

Abraham listened to the story for hours before pausing at a small river where the jungle had opened up to a clearing cut by the water's edge. He set down his burden and walked to a small campsite comprising a tarp lean-to and fire pit among some small trees on a rise above the water. Picking up a plastic jug, he returned to Jim.

"Here, drink, Jim. I have boiled the water, and it should be clean."

Jim drank deeply from the gallon jug, the water tasting muddy but delicious. He handed the jug back to Abraham, who consumed the remaining liquid.

"And the rest of your story?" Abraham asked.

Jim was quiet for a moment, taking in this peaceful place. Green and lush plants were on all sides, the small river rippled and gurgled, and a faint roll of thunder sounded in the distance. He fixed his eyes on the horizon of green hills as the rest of the story unfolded.

He told of his marriage and his decision to leave the service, of Maggie's death and the baby's, of the betrayal he felt from the government and country he had served, which had denied him justice. He told of the drive into the desert and of his clarity of purpose in the decision to enact revenge on the man who had killed his family and his friend. He told how the killing of Champos was accomplished.

Then Jim told of his flight from the consequences of his actions: the trek by sea, then the flying of arms and supplies in Africa. He ended by describing the fight with the MiG and Christopher's death. Jim laid bare his life as he had lived it, the words flowing until he was finished.

Abraham calmly listened to the whole story, at one point arranging Jim under the shelter and starting a fire to prepare food. He only paused in the listening to fill a pot with water and set it to boiling.

His story done, Jim was quiet. Darkness had fallen in the valley. Twilight lighted the sky as the two men sat staring at the fire, surrounded by the darkness and sounds of the primordial jungle. Abraham sat in quiet contemplation, then began to tell his own tale.

"My parents were killed in a car crash. My immediate family had no way to take care of me. They were scattered and, anyway, not very helpful," Abraham said. "I was staying with a childhood friend when they died. The police were able to track me down after figuring out that I wasn't home. They had a Jesuit priest with them, an old man, Father Paul. He was very kind to me. He sat with me and told me that my parents had been in an accident and that they were in Heaven. When I asked him who he was, he said he was a friend. Before leaving, he gave me his business card and told me to call if I had any questions or needed help."

Jim watched the large man grow quiet, tears forming on his face as he stared into the fire.

"I was taken by child services to a foster home. I imagine they thought they were doing what was best. I was placed in a house with an older couple and some other boys. One night I was awakened by the old man and abused . . . sexually," Abraham said, breathing deeply. "I was a child who had lost everything and desperately needed something to hold on to and trust. That man used me as an object for twisted gratification. I think back about those moments, being frightened and confused, being hurt. I desperately wanted someone to explain things, to protect and comfort me, and the person who was supposed to do that was the person doing the damage."

Abraham stopped to quietly sob, his hands drawn before him, fingers bent straight, shaking in a supplicant act, surrendering to the horrible memory.

"He left me hurting and confused and then angry. So much rage in such a small body. I cried for a bit, and then the tears just left," Abraham continued. "As small as I was, I knew some things. So I went downstairs as quiet as a mouse, slipped outside, and got the gasoline from the shed. I went back into the house, doused the front of the couple's bedroom with the gasoline, and set it on fire. I went outside and waited to see what would happen. What happened was that the whole house went up, killing the couple and the other three boys inside. It was a miracle I didn't go up as well.

"The fire department and police showed up to find me sitting on the lawn. I was taken into the station and questioned, but I never said a word. They figured it out by the gas I had on my clothing and the blood in my underwear.

"They sent me to a juvenile hall for a few weeks, figuring out what to do. Then one day Father Paul showed up. I still remember sitting outside on a bench when he walked up to me and kneeled to look into my eyes. That made a difference to me; I was always looking up at adults and feeling small."

Abraham stared into the jungle.

"Father Paul asked me if I would like to go to a place where I would be safe. I started crying and just blabbered and begged to be forgiven. He put his hand on my shoulder and said that while what I had done was a great sin, telling him was what was called a confession and was protected, private information. Then he asked if I would like to be absolved of that sin and make up my debt to society. I said yes.

"After that, I went to a school run by the Jesuits. There I did my best to be worthy of the chance to redeem myself. Filled with admiration and love for the men who raised me, I aspired to become, and eventually became, a brother in the order of the Brothers of the Sacred Heart.

"As is one of the missions of the order, I went to be a missionary in Africa, here in the Congo and in Tanzania. I have worked with refugees for the past six years, bringing comfort to the displaced and solace to the broken and unwanted. And, of course, I am always trying to bring the light of Christianity to those souls who choose to embrace it.

"One day I learned that a bishop was coming to the camp, all the way from Rome. The other brothers and I met him and showed him around the camp. He stayed a few weeks. One night, one of the children of the camp came up to me, crying. He said he had been hurt by the bishop but wouldn't tell me how."

Abraham drew a ragged breath, looked down at his clenched hands, and continued.

"I went to the bishop's tent and found him sexually abusing a small boy. I was in shock, to say the least. The bishop tried to explain things—as if there could be any explanation—and I was so dumbfounded I walked away, taking the boy with me to protect him. I thought deep into the night.

"In the morning, the bishop was addressing the people. I wandered into this mass of people surrounding the speaking platform where he was leading a prayer. As I walked through the people to the stage, he smiled from his position above me, looking down on me. A liar's smile, a smile that took instead of giving. A bishop bestowing a blessing and me only a lowly monk, powerless to right the wrong, as weak in my position of the church hierarchy as the child I had once been.

Unfortunately for the bishop, I remembered another smile from the past, another man above me. He also had a liar's smile. The bishop smiled as if he were knowledgeable about my soul, my worth, and that he would not be troubled. His face was so relaxed and beatific.

"That is, until I jumped on the platform and began beating him with my fists.

"I was strong in my rage. My brothers tried to stop me, but I was filled with the Holy Spirit and brushed them off like flies. In my righteous anger, I destroyed that beatific face and everything it represented. Soon I stood over what was left of the bishop. He was convulsing and gurgling, his white robes covered in blood.

"When I turned to the crowd, I could not speak. I just stood there. It wasn't until a woman, the mother of the small boy who had told me about the abuse, came up and took my hand that I snapped out of it. She led me through the crowd. They parted as water before a ship. People handed me the few things I have here, and I walked into the jungle.

"I beat a prince of the Church, to death or coma or what, I don't know. I committed the sin of wrath and took God's judgment into my own hands. I have been out here in the wilderness since then, alone until now. Praying for forgiveness. Praying for another chance to redeem myself."

Jim regarded Abraham's grief-stricken, tear-stained face, framed by the wild hair and beard, all illuminated by the dying flames. Silently, Jim lay back and closed his eyes.

Jack Lyons

Chapter 15

Jim awoke to hear rain falling on the tarp. He gently moved his head from side to side, assessing his injuries. Over the past four days, Abraham had allowed him to rest and brought him food and water.

Abraham had determined that three of Jim's fingers, his left leg, and his right collarbone were broken. He had set and splinted the fingers and leg, having picked up a good deal of medical training in his work. The collarbone was manipulated into place and a figure-eight sling was fashioned to pull Jim's shoulders back and allow the bone to heal. A separate sling supported the right arm. Between the broken bones and the muscle tears and sprains, pain was Jim's constant companion, though injections of the heroin had made it somewhat bearable.

"How is the patient?" Abraham asked, seeing that Jim was awake.

"Dying to piss."

"Right away, monsieur, the piss boy is here," Abraham said, laughing as he picked up a jug and walked to the tarp shelter.

Jim did not care for being an invalid, but even the call of nature was too challenging to accomplish on his own. For some reason, Abraham was able to make it not feel unnatural. His good heart and healing gifts allayed Jim's embarrassment over things that would ordinarily have mortified him.

Abraham walked away with the urine container, emptying it in the brush. He returned with a rag and a pot filled with water.

"Let's see if we can't clean you up. I'm amazed that you haven't gotten at least some infection from the cuts. The *ibonya* appears to be working."

"Is that the plant you rubbed on me?" Jim asked through gritted teeth as Abraham lifted him to a sitting position.

"Yes, it's astringent and antiseptic," Abraham said as he wrung out the rag and began to clean Jim's back. "It grows fairly well here. How are the muscles in your back?"

"Everything is still stiff, but not locked up like it was."

"Probably a good sign," Abraham said as he lay Jim back down on the bed of banana leaves under the tarp and began examining and cleaning other cuts and injuries.

"So, how long have you been out here, Abe?" Jim asked.

"Not really sure; maybe six months."

"You have a plan?"

"Didn't think I needed one," Abraham replied as he wrung out a rag.

"You staying out here forever?"

"For as long as it takes."

Abraham drew a small thermos from his pack and opened it.

"What's in that?" Jim asked.

"A tincture of insight. A balm for the pain of the body and mind. I was about to take it myself, to find some answers, when you crossed my path. Last night I prayed for guidance, and I felt led to share this with you, helping you find your path forward before deciding on my own."

Jim looked dubiously at the thermos.

"Liberty cap psilocybin mushroom tea," Abraham explained.

"Magic mushrooms?"

Abraham nodded.

"They come from Africa?" Jim asked. He'd had no experience with drugs of any sort before heroin made its way into his life.

"They grow everywhere," Abraham said. "Here you just need some cattle dung. It is theorized that our ancestors ate these while following the herds of cattle and that ingesting the mushrooms inspired them to evolve. Though the church is still clinging to the Garden of Eden thing."

"What will it do?"

"For some it is an amusement, a look at the pretty lights, a body high. For others it is medicine from a higher knowledge source. Either way, it is not to be taken lightly."

"What is it for you?" Jim asked, watching as Abraham poured some tea from the thermos into a cup.

"A lesson," Abraham said. "A lesson that only leads to more and more lessons. Fear, hate, love, all wrapped up into one, and at the end, clarity. I think you may require the transparency to let go and go on with your life.

"In listening to your story, I came to believe you are stuck in your past, in the great pain you have endured. Carrying such a heavy load, you became desperate for anything to make the pain bearable, even for a short while. You have been using alcohol and then heroin to hide from that pain. But the heroin you have been taking, have become dependent on, will soon run out. And even if you made your way back to the city and bought more, it would only be a way to separate from the pain, bury it, ignore it for a while. That is, until it took you to your grave. If we were at the refugee camp, then I would use an *iboga*, a ceremony with the community to clear addictions, to release the hold on you. But that would only be the beginning.

"Jim, you have lost your love, faith, purpose. When those are taken away, there is only the pain. In order to find your way back, you must find them again, and in order to do that, you must face your pain. That is, you must face yourself. It is my hope that this tea will help you do that."

Jim considered the words. "Maybe you're right," he said. Then he drank from the cup put to his lips, the earthy taste reminding him of soil and nature.

"It can be a rocket-ship trip, meaning that you will hang on to the tail while it goes where it needs to. Don't resist it, don't fight it. Your ego can be in charge later."

Jim lay back and looked through his right eye at the canopy above him. Just enough moonlight filtered down to make out shapes. Abraham walked away into the night. Jim lay still. After a time, he perceived a diminishment of the pain he had felt, or at least a lessening of the caring about it.

A thought occurred to him that, in his extreme pain, he was weakened and helpless as he had not been since he was an infant. His long explanation to Abraham on the jungle trek, then his forced immobility, were the first time in a long while that he had stopped to think about his unlikely journey. Lying in the clearing, Jim reflected again on his life's path: from a tip-of-the-spear gentleman warrior, a jet pilot, the best of the best, all the way to a banged-up piece of meat in a steaming jungle.

He had always had certainty as his center growing up, civilized structure, a plan to follow to success. His life had followed a direct path until a chance meeting in a bar in Pensacola had moved everything else to second place when Maggie had come into his life.

Once he knew he loved her, life altered. Maggie became the center about which life revolved. She was the core of his attention and sense of well-being. Once she was killed, his life had spun out of control. He thought about his decisions upon her death, the betrayal of his oath to his country, the consuming anger for revenge that had driven him, the killing of Champos, the leap into this new place, away from everything he had known.

Jim felt something—something happening. A different pain began to surface, a spiritual pain from deep in his chest. Feelings of loss, of shame, of betrayal bloomed and filled him, pushing away the physical. Jim felt tears running down his face, hot tears of anger and sorrow. He felt the grief of what could have been, where he could have gone, and the knowledge of the limitations, physically, morally, and spiritually, that had brought him to this place. He could feel the mixture working; he fought against it, trying to maintain control.

A blanket of despair and helplessness covered him for what seemed like hours. Eventually, Jim acknowledged the truth.

He was the architect of his own misery.

He was the one who had left everything behind for

honorable love or faithless ego. The single decision of revenge had brought him to this place.

Jim cried out and surrendered to the medicine, both not wanting to face the truth and desperately wanting to embrace it. He both laughed and called for Maggie and for the life they'd had. Jim cried for the loss of his country and the path of honor left behind. More tears fell for his child, whom he would never hold. Tears came for his parents and the thought of never seeing their faces again, tears for the child he had been and the man he would never be.

Farther and farther he fell, into the pit of emotions, into a hell not of fire and punishment but of cold, stark infinity. He was cut off from the light and facing a void of indifference.

The starlight was becoming difficult to look at—too bright—so he closed his eyes. Then flashes of light, moving formless yet bright and frightening behind his eyelids, began to merge and take shape. Rising panic began to engulf him, his body beginning to react to a danger that could not be quantified.

"Help me," Jim whispered to a jungle that could not hear him.

No help came, only the night sounds of the jungle, the heaviness of the air in his lungs. Sweat poured from his body as Jim struggled to master his emotions, clinging tightly to the control he had always kept, the control he thought had kept him safe.

Breathing, that was the key, he thought. He struggled not to retch up the contents of his stomach. For ages, it seemed, he alternated from eyes closed to eyes open. Each condition held its own challenges.

Jim pulled his arm closer to his stomach. "I'm

fine," he said to the darkness. "This is just a feeling that I must master."

Abraham's face came into view.

"Go deeper, Jim," Abraham said. "Let your ego be in charge later. Go deeper and release the control. You're safe. You can stop fighting."

Abraham again held the thermos cup, and Jim drank deeply.

Jim's breathing became labored. His muscles ached as they struggled to cope with the emotions his mind was throwing at him, fear of the void, of what he would become without that control, of who or what he would end up as. Hours passed.

Closing his eyes to face his fear, Jim saw the colored lights vanishing, and all was darkness. His body began to relax, and his breathing slowed.

"I'm sorry," Jim whispered to the void. "Please help me, please forgive me."

As his muscles slowly unclenched, a flicker in the void behind his eyes, out in infinity, moved and then began to grow. Jim watched the light with trepidation. The object grew until he realized it was not growing bigger. It was getting closer.

Jim squeezed his eyes closed, willing himself to not be afraid, to surrender and let the light swell, brighter and brighter, closer and closer. It raced toward him from the darkness as a shame began to surface, the shame of knowing that he was unworthy, that he was in the presence of the divine. Jim screamed in his mind at not being able to control the speed or direction of the collision. He screamed until he was not just in the light, he *was* the light.

At the last moment, he stopped fighting or

155

resisting, releasing control and responsibility in one moment. And then he and the light were one. How long he stayed there, he could never know or say. Only that he felt whole and loved for the first time in a long time.

Jim wept.

Time traveled past as the day grew lighter and new. His tears had faded. The clutches of hopeless despair had gone with them. Jim had not known how much pain he was in until it was gone. His breath grew even and as steady as his ribs would allow. If this were to be his life, this life of emptiness, he would live it.

"I'm sorry," Jim whispered to the jungle. "I'm sorry. Forgive me. Help me, please."

A glowing light in the clouds broke to a stray beam of sunlight that streamed through the thick overhanging canopy to rest upon his face. Despite the protestations of his body, Jim raised a hand to feel the warmth that had found him. As he felt the sunbeam stream through his fingers, Jim felt another warmth begin to build in him. The energy in his hand felt like a vibration, a thrumming traveling up the arm to the chest and throughout his body. Tears began anew as he dropped his arm to his side and let the beam rest upon his face.

Joy filled him. The emotion, so forgotten and so lost, reached into his soul. Jim felt his body begin to shake. He was filled with love and acceptance, and somehow he knew it was an answer to his plea for help. As he lay wrung out and motionless on the ground, the strangest feeling descended: forgiveness from somewhere else that was also within himself.

Mercifully, finally, he slept.

Chapter 16

T he fire burned before the men, keeping back the darkness surrounding them.

"Nebraska by way of Georgia. Went to school there. That was my last place of living in the land of my birth."

Jim turned his eyes to Abraham as they sat by the fire. The heat of the jungle night soaked him as he lay upon the crude cot Abraham had made to keep him off the ground.

"You have a certain way of talking, Abe."

Abraham smiled. "It's the Geechee. Freshwater Geechee."

"What's a Geechee?"

"Descendants of slaves in Georgia. It's like Creole, but different. The language is Geechee; the people are Gullah," Abraham said, picking up and then handing Jim a steel canteen.

Jim took it and winced as his wounds protested. He was able to hold the canteen now and take a drink, which was an improvement.

"Ribs?" Abraham asked sympathetically.

"Ribs, face, legs, back. You name it. You see my right earlobe?" Jim asked.

Abraham nodded, his shaggy air bouncing as it framed his face, illuminated by the firelight.

"That's probably the only place that doesn't hurt."

The two men stared into the fire, the flames more to keep the night away than for warmth.

The psychedelic journey he had kept to himself when Abraham had returned. He was still processing the event. It had left him somewhat untethered but with a new emotion.

Hope.

Jim had had no experience with recreational drugs of any kind, other than alcohol, before coming to Africa. He had always considered the people who used them to be frivolous, weak. But Jim knew the experience had changed him, helped him. The pain in his soul was gone.

"Where are we headed again?" Jim asked. "You said we would leave today."

"To the east. There is a valley where there are fewer bugs and more clean water. To get there, we will cross some plains that are home to larger predators, but the fire should keep them away. You ready to go?"

Jim nodded his assent.

The pair traveled slowly across the landscape. The dense jungle gradually faded to scrub vegetation, then plains of grass. Jim didn't know where they were heading. The was no conversation; Jim was dealing with his pain the best he could, and Abraham's physical exertion left him with little energy to talk.

The hot sun beat down on the men as they found a small stream to camp by.

"That's it for now," Abraham said, settling down beneath a tree.

"It's been a long one," Jim said.

Abraham sat with his back against the tree, eyes closed. Jim watched the man rest, his brown robe soaked with sweat, salt crystals flaked about his shoulders and chest. Pulling the travois had to have been demanding, but no complaints had come from the stoic brother. Long minutes passed as Jim lay back and closed his eyes, listening to the gurgle of the stream and the buzz of the insects.

"Enough rest for now," Abraham said at last. "I will make the camp. We will need a lot of fire tonight."

"Expecting it to be cool?" Jim asked.

"No," Abraham said, lifting his staff. "There are plenty of tracks: lion, jackal, and hyena. It's why we are stopping early. It may be a long night. We need water, just as they do."

Jim looked at the small clearing they had stopped in. A thick, impenetrable copse of brush and thorns curved to shield them from two sides. A low hill topped with thick thorn bushes sloped down to the streambank, creating a small defensive perimeter with access to water.

As Abraham walked away, Jim steeled himself as he lay back and took stock of his injuries. Besides the multiple minor lacerations on his body, the torn muscles in his back and legs had cramped and tightened up. The splinted fingers on his left hand made it nearly useless. At least three ribs on his right side ached deeply in counterpoint to the broken tibia of his lower leg. The splint placed there by Abraham and secured to his unbroken right leg made both legs unusable.

Jim groaned and breathed deeply, slowly rotating his neck from side to side, the tight muscles resisting him. He also flexed the fingers of his right hand. Carefully moving and assessing his body, Jim was able to determine the current state of his physical limitations and injuries. The sweat poured down his face and body as he flexed and moved the parts he could until he gave up, exhausted by the efforts.

Abraham returned with wood in his arms and arranged it around the campsite. Working steadily, in an hour he had gathered a pile as high as his head. Jim looked at the mound of brush and then at Abraham as he sat to rest.

"Expecting a dark night?" Jim asked.

Abraham sat silently with his head bowed and eyes closed. Jim had become used to the man taking his time when pondering questions.

"A darkness is now coming to us, Jim," Abraham finally said. "A reckoning. I feel it here." He touched his chest, still with his eyes closed, his brushy hair quivering slightly.

Abraham looked up. Jim saw that his eyes were wet. The dark green irises surrounded by white glistened as they looked at Jim. Tears shone on Abraham's dark cheeks.

"It is coming, and I am afraid."

"Afraid?" Jim asked, becoming unsettled with the strength of Abraham's gaze.

"I have premonitions, I always have. A sense of doom followed by . . . well, something. It is not recognized by the church, and they do not condone any mention of it, but it occurs."

Abraham looked away at last and stood, surveying the campsite.

"This humble place will be where we meet this darkness."

He turned back to Jim and knelt, reaching out his large hands.

"I know that you are an invalid at the moment, Jim, and I do not wish to unsettle you. However, I want to ask you a favor."

Jim took the proffered hand, looking up steadily into Abraham's eyes.

"Ask, Abraham."

"I have told you my confession to take on the burden of my past. Tonight we die, as we die every time we grow. Spiritually and physically. Every time we change, that which was us is dead and in the past. But for the most part, we carry the past and live there. The living dead and the dead living. Life is present and being in the moment. When I walked away from the refugee camp, I walked away from all I was, yet not all that I could be. You and I have made the same choice for different reasons. We both went against what we had been taught, what we had believed in. But for the right reasons."

"Why would you think we are going to die?" Jim asked.

"The face of evil is my face, your face. I am a sinner, as are all men. It is the redemption of our souls that shows us God's grace and love for us. As we walked, I felt the sun on my face, the whisper of the wind. I let it flood me, fill me. It is the Holy Spirit. When it filled me, it was because God has a trial. The Bible says, 'I will reveal myself to you in signs.' Never written but on my heart I feel the sign."

"I respect your views, but I have seen little of God's grace."

"You're wrong, Jim. You see it every day but do not know it. You ejected in the middle of the Congo rain forest, to be deposited at the feet of one of the tools of God. I had prayed alone in the wilderness for God to forgive me, to give me a sign of his forgiveness: a task to prove my worthiness, to redeem myself. And you were brought to me. Want to figure the odds of that? The math is well beyond me."

Jim sat quietly for a moment and considered the words. Abraham's hands moved deftly, assembling both a fire pit and a pile of starter brush. Abraham picked up the pot from the travois and walked down to the stream to fill it. After he had set it over the fire, he continued.

"I was ready to die out here. I have seen mutilations, killings, and the results of rapes. People doing horrible things to each other. It is evil, Jim. Evil and darkness is alive and well here in Africa and will be for some time. Tens of thousands of displaced peoples, wanting to go home but having no hope to do so. Organizations that say they will help but then have agendas of their own.

"I was selfish and arrogant in my meekness and goodness—the sin of pride. I committed the sin of apathy in keeping my head down while I tended to those who required it. The sin of wrath was the latest addition to my ledger."

Jim listened, turning his head to sounds from the brush in the deepening darkness. Nocturnal hunters were beginning to stir and roar in the hot night. He shivered from the cold feeling he had despite the humid heat.

Abraham looked at him as he peered into the darkness.

"Every day is a test, Jim, a test and a testament."

Abraham stood and walked over to him.

"Will you allow me again to try and heal you, Jim?"

Jim nodded. Abraham knelt and placed his hands lightly on Jim's chest. Jim's breathing slowed. Abraham closed his eyes and held in silent concentration for many moments.

"His grace still eludes me," Abraham said at last, sitting back and staring into the fire.

The fire had burned down to glowing coals. In that dim light Jim saw the outline of a primordial scene, he and Abraham next to the dying fire, surrounded by memories, darkness closing in about them.

"They are here," Abraham said, rising to his feet.

The wind moved through the leaves of the trees above them. The moisture and the musk of the jungle hung in the air. Jim sat up with difficulty. Noises came from the darkness: bestial, deep, and close. Jim felt his body react to the danger, an ancestral response from within flooding him with fear. The harsh sounds were almost musical, a language of beasts unseen in the blackness. Jim turned his head toward them. The pain was forgotten as a deep fear gripped him. The calls became a chorus.

"Lions," Abraham said, reaching for more wood and placing it on the coals, stirring them back to life.

As the fire flared, Jim saw that Abraham held his staff. Abraham turned the sturdy branch slowly in his hands, staring into the night. At the mouth of the enclosure Abraham had made, a deep growl sounded. Jim didn't bother to look, only crawling to the back of the campsite as fast as possible.

Abraham moved then, jumping over him. Jim rolled in time to see Abraham land a terrific blow to the head of a male lion pushing into the brush. The cat darted to the side, taking some of the brush fence with him. Abraham struck once, then twice more, a wailing, undulating roar coming from deep within him. Jim could make out an occasional word, but most seemed to be just noise and gibberish.

"Oh damn," Jim said, breathing heavily as the brush on the fire dampened, the light failing.

Jim felt the ground around him, scrabbling for more wood. A piece of brush found its way under his hand, the thorns piercing his skin. Ignoring the pain, Jim threw the limb onto the dying fire.

Light erupted as the dry wood and dead leaves were caught by the flames. The growls and roars of the lions were all around. Jim saw shapes and flashing figures at the edge of the darkness. Light reflected from large eyes outside of the brush perimeter.

Abraham moved smoothly, a dervish in the firelight, shouts thrown back at the night and its terrors. Again and again the lions surged forward, snarling at Abraham, who battled back with blows and thrusts from the staff, striking the eyes, ears, and noses of the enormous animals. Jim continued to grab what sticks and branches were in reach and heaped them on the fire to bring more light to the struggle. He was rewarded with a meager rise of flame.

"The fence!" Abraham yelled. "Light the fence!"

Jim looked around him. The high brush fence that Abraham had pulled around their campsite was dry and shot with thorns. The ongoing struggle had moved large chunks of the wall of brush, its protection in disarray. There were more gaps, he saw, than Abraham could cover.

Rolling onto his side, Jim pulled a flaming branch from the fire and tossed it into the brush. As quickly as possible, he threw more lit brands around them and even over the fence.

"There we are," Abraham said, looking at the

suddenly brighter night.

Abraham came to kneel by Jim's side, panting heavily, sweat streaming down his face.

"That should hold us for—" Abraham's words were cut off by a roar and the shape of a giant male lion leaping the fence and flames.

Jim felt the impact of the cat on the ground. Flames leaping up behind it, the lion roared, a primordial terror outlined in fire. The overpowering, rancid smell of the beast filled the space around them.

Abraham screamed back and thrust at the lion's face, driving the beast back into the flaming brush. A swipe of the lion's massive paw caught Abraham and threw him to the ground, away from Jim. The lion surged sideways for a better angle on the prone Abraham, its hindquarters to Jim.

Jim stared at the tawny tail as it rotated up over his head, the lion preparing to spring. Desperately Jim scrabbled with his left hand and grabbed a flaming branch from the fire. With his right hand, he seized the tail. The stench of the beast was overwhelming. Lifting the thick tail, he thrust the pointed, burning stick up the lion's backside as hard as possible.

The lion's fierce roar changed to an unearthly scream. The lion simultaneously kicked out with its rear legs, spun, and leaped over the fire-engulfed fence. Jim was thrown to the ground near Abraham.

Both men lay panting as the roars of pain from the lion faded into the distance. The night became quiet. Jim and Abraham struggled up, helping each other closer to the firelight, and waited for morning.

Jack Lyons

Chapter 17

It had been months since the night of the lions, and Abraham had been quiet for a long time. Jim was equally reserved, lost in his thoughts. The confrontation with their own mortality had deeply affected them both. Jim had bound the deep scratch across Abraham's chest from the lion's claws raking him. With no stitches available, the only medical assistance he could give was the mixture of plants that Abraham had gathered. As time had passed, Jim had begun to be able to walk, first with a staff, then unaided. Jim had sweated out the sickness from the heroin withdrawal long before.

"I want to go back to the refugee camp," Abraham said. "I am needed. I know it."

Jim agreed readily. The two men had become closer in their mutual healing, and after what Abraham had done for him, Jim was prepared to follow him anywhere.

The men gathered their small things and set out. Their progress was slow but steady, with as many breaks as they needed. The trip took ten days, walking across the sparse landscape, then back into the coastal jungle to arrive on the shores of Lake Tanganyika. A friendly fisherman gave them a lift across the massive lake in exchange for a blessing from Abraham. Another two days of walking brought them to the beginning of a widespread clearing, the earth denuded of trees.

Soon they were standing on a slight rise, the camp below them, spread out on the valley clearing. Stretching a mile wide and four miles long, the teeming mass of humanity nestled into the red landscape mostly slept in the pre-day gloom. People were just beginning to stir within the shanty construction, which had tarps and branches where other materials stopped and was crisscrossed with trash-strewn dirt paths.

"Is this what you saw, Abe?" Jim asked.

"Yes," Abraham said. "Why, I couldn't tell you, but it was clear to me that I needed to be here. I prayed for guidance, for where I needed to be."

Wordlessly the men began walking slowly into the clearing and toward the refugee camp. At the edge of the makeshift buildings, Jim saw more people moving around, some starting fires to prepare a meager breakfast. Abraham began to outpace him. The path between the huts meandered but kept in one direction, and Abraham walked with purpose.

People were beginning to look at the two of them, sticking their heads into structures, murmuring to those inside. A stream of people started to fall in behind Abraham, with Jim limping along with them. Some gave Jim curious looks, but Abraham was the center of their attention.

Jim made his way to a clearing between buildings, with Abraham standing in the middle of a growing crowd of people. Smiling, the whites of their eyes flashing in dark faces, they reached out to touch Abraham. Abraham spoke to the people, answering questions and firing back his own.

Leaning against a hut with a bench attached to it, Jim rested in the shade from the roof. His wounds were mostly healed, but the last few days had been rough on his knees. He observed Abraham standing in the middle of the crowd. The two men made a curious sight, even here in the squalor and deprivation of the camp. Their clothes had deteriorated almost to rags, and they both now had shaggy hair and unruly beards. Neither man had washed other than by dipping rags in streams in the bush.

Jim's face had lost any roundness it might once have had. The injuries mostly healed, his body had become leaner and harder. His deeply tanned face was punctuated by white scars. The time in the jungle had been a trial, and it showed. But it had also been a balm.

Abraham continued to speak with the crowd. His face lit up as different persons came to speak and be spoken to. Soon an ancient man approached him, his gnarled hand on a young boy's shoulder. The crowd parted, allowing the elder to come forward. The voices and sounds ceased at his appearance.

Standing in front of Abraham, the man looked him up and down, his puckered mouth gumming and sucking. He reached out a stick-thin arm to the ragged brother, who took his hand in greeting. The young child was waved away and merged with the crowd. The old man took Abraham's head in his hands, turning and examining it. The inspection complete, the old man shuffled back, letting one hand drop to Abraham's chest. He pulled back the ragged robe to reveal four long, parallel scars standing out red from the dark skin. The old man spoke to Abraham and nodded at his answer. Then, turning to the crowd, he spoke, his voice surprisingly deep and robust.

"Un père nous a quitté. Un lion est revenu. Père Lion."

Motioning for the boy, the old man went his way, shuffling off into the camp. Abraham watched him go, pulling his robe together. The crowd of people milled around Abraham again, touching him and calling out to him, adoring looks on their faces.

"Père Lion," some in the crowd murmured.

They followed Abraham over to where Jim rested.

"Happy homecoming?" Jim asked. "What did he say in that last part?"

"The elder's name is Musimba Kabeya," Abraham said, looking down at Jim. "He said that I had left as a father—a priest—but come back as a lion. He called me Father Lion. Because of these," Abraham said, motioning to his chest and the scars.

"Is he a chief or something?" Jim asked.

"Or something," Abraham replied. "People listen to him."

"This is my friend Jim," Abraham said to the people behind him. "And, Jim, these are my friends Tatame, Gautier, Prudence, and Father Michael."

Jim nodded at the three men and one woman.

"Jim, is it?" Father Michael asked. He was a short, chubby, balding, middle-aged white man with a French accent, dressed in a white cotton shirt and black pants.

"Yes," Jim replied.

"Let us get you cleaned up and fed. Can you walk?"

Jim started to rise, and Prudence stepped forward. A thin, dark woman with a bright smile and happy face, she slipped under Jim's arm and helped him up. She peered at him with a bright smile.

"Penchez-vous sur moi, monsieur," she said.

Jim looked to Abraham.

"She said to lean on her," Abraham explained. "She is training to be a nurse."

Prudence's slim frame was surprisingly strong. She half-helped, half-carried Jim, her arm around his waist. The group went to a nearby Quonset structure.

"De la nourriture puis un bain, monsieur," Prudence said, gently lowering Jim to a bench beside a table.

Jim looked around at the small, square eating area under the shade. Prudence snapped orders at the men Tatame and Gautier. Obviously she held some sort of superior position to the two young men, who went to their tasks.

"Food, then a bath," Abraham said. "I agree. What has happened since I've been gone, Michael?"

Abraham and Michael took seats across from Jim at the table. Father Michael poured glasses of water.

"The camp runs as it did before you left. More people coming, as usual, and very little assistance from outside. Though without the international food aid it would become dire very quickly." Father Michael toyed with his glass, not meeting Abraham's eyes.

"What else, Michael?"

"A militia came about a month after you left, though 'militia' is a stretch. They have been coming and taking people."

"Where are they taking them?"

"I believe it is to work as slave labor for coltan, cobalt, and tin mines in the Congo. The war killings have decimated the mining labor force, so a need has developed."

"Tin I know," Abraham said. "What are coltan and cobalt used for?"

"As I understand it, cobalt is a primary component of lithium batteries. A byproduct of saving the world from global warming, it seems, is enslaving people. Coltan is an electronics necessity, mainly for cell phones."

"So modern advances are driving age-old misery," Abraham said.

Father Michael shrugged.

"How many have been taken?" Abraham asked.

"In the months since you have been gone? Five hundred at least, men and boys."

Abraham stared into a distance only he could see.

"No one will help?"

"Who is to help? Tanzania has some soldiers, but not enough to guard refugees. If the international aid communities did not pay the government, they would probably turn them all back. As it is, they allow the camps to exist. The land is not being used for anything else, so besides the trees, it costs them nothing." Michael leaned back into his chair.

"So they are on their own."

"What of you, Abraham, where have you been? When you left after the—"

"Sin?" Abraham supplied, picking up his water. Michael nodded. Abraham took a long drink, then set down his glass.

"How is the bishop?" he asked.

"Gone," Father Michael said. "Medically evacuated. Your reprimand was severe. Multiple broken bones, teeth knocked out. I seriously doubt that he will ever be sent anywhere again."

Abraham nodded.

"Abraham," Michael began, "what you did—as a

Christian, I . . . I can't condone it. As a man, though, I'm glad the bastard found his judgment on the earth."

"I'm ready to face punishment, Michael," Abraham said.

"Punishment?" Michael said. "I think that your time in the wilderness and your trials there should suffice."

"I attacked a bishop."

"You attacked a pedophile bishop who was on his last chance. And what's more, you fought for people whom no one has fought for in a long time." Michael accepted a cup of tea from Tatame, who then left and returned with Gautier, the two men bearing bowls of food and a loaf of bread.

"Look at them, Abraham." Father Michael gestured to the crowd watching the men. People came and went, all chattering happily. "They are happy you're here. It's given them hope to see you, and hope has been in very short supply lately."

Jim dug into the bowl of food. The spicy meat, rice, and vegetable mixture was heavenly. The bowl was empty in seconds. Having had minimal food for so long, he could feel his body responding to the nourishment.

"Plus de nourriture, monsieur?" Tatame asked, gesturing to the bowl.

Jim nodded and returned the young man's smile. Tatame took the bowl and returned with it heaping.

"Thank you," Jim said.

"De rien," Tatame said.

"And where did your companion come from, Abraham?" Father Michael asked.

"From God, as most things," Abraham said. "So, what else is happening? You said more people are coming?"

"Mostly Congolese. The government is pushing into more land again, fighting the rebels as well as other forces. It's bad and getting worse."

"How much worse?"

"Entire villages wiped out. It's a genocidal terror campaign now, although the world isn't calling it that. Mutilations, rapes, murders of all sorts."

Abraham put down his spoon and stared out, taking in the crowd of people surrounding the hut. A long moment passed with Jim and Michael regarding the ragged figure before them.

"Something comes," Abraham said.

"What . . ." Michael said, turning to look at Abraham.

Abraham rose, walking out into the sunlight, again staring off into the distance. The noise of vehicles could be heard, growing louder.

"It's the militia, coming to gather workers," Father Michael said. "They haven't been back for a few months. The rain was slowing operations."

Michael headed outside. Jim sighed and finished his food. The crowd of people had dispersed. He sensed that the camp was moving around and that this was not the normal flow. Heading outside, Jim saw a convoy of six army trucks and two jeeps. Camouflage-clad soldiers were around the trucks, with rifles slung.

Jim walked to within earshot of the crowd gathered around the lead jeep. A soldier, more elaborately uniformed than the rest and wearing a beret, stood talking with Father Michael. Abraham was a few feet back from the two men, surrounded by people from the camp. Jim figured the uniformed man for an officer. He certainly pointed like one.

Father Michael and the officer were exchanging loud words. Jim eased around a hut and got closer to listen. The soldiers seemed agitated and were beginning to unsling their rifles.

"These people do not wish to go with you," Father Michael said.

"They are Congolese, yes? We are the New Congolese Defense Forces," the man in the beret replied.

"Whatever you call yourself, these people are refugees. They have no part in your rebellion."

"These people must work to fund the rebellion!"

"Who says this? There is no government backing for you. Where are the men who left with you before? I don't see any of them with you, and none have come back. None have even communicated with their families. What is your name?"

"Colonel Keneyusu is my name, Father."

"Colonel, there is nothing for you here. I suggest you take your men and go." With that said, Father Michael turned and walked away from the jeep.

The colonel turned to his men, laughed, and motioned to them to mount up. The soldiers clambered back onto the trucks, and the entire convoy started up. Jim eased well out of sight as the trucks rolled away. After they departed, Jim walked to where Abraham and Father Michael were speaking.

"What was that about?" Jim asked.

"Politics and money," Abraham said.

"Yes, I am afraid so," Father Michael said, taking off his hat and wiping his face. "There are many different groups armed to the teeth; that one is just exploiting people to get money. They raid over the border and wipe out villages. They will be back."

"Back into a fire, Abraham?" Jim asked as they watched Father Michael walk away.

"So it seems. Let's get cleaned up and rest. We can talk about it in the morning."

The bath and rest made Jim feel like a new man. Prudence had trimmed his and Abraham's shaggy hair and beards, then directed them to a tub of clean water. Father Michael had provided a bar of soap. The men sloughed off dirt and grime. Clean clothes for Jim, including shoes and socks, were a welcome relief. Abraham kept his monk's robe but allowed Prudence to mend and clean it.

The men were shown to sleeping mats in a hut and fell exhaustedly asleep.

Chapter 18

Weeks of proper food and rest in the camp returned Jim's strength. He had clarity of mind now. He helped with food preparation, talked to the people. In earlier times, Jim would not have known how to relate to people who had lost so much. Now he did, and being a part of their day-to-day lives made him a part of them, one of them.

Breakfast was rice, fruit, and water, prepared by Prudence, who seemed to have adopted Jim and Abraham as sons. Jim listened contentedly as she sang softly in the kitchen. When he was finished eating, he put up his dishes to stroll about the camp.

"Good morning, Mr. Jim," Tatame said as Jim walked into the morning sunlight.

"Tatame," Jim said as the two men fell into step with each other. "I thought I'd have a look around."

"I am to do my rounds. You can accompany me if you like," the young man replied.

"I would like that very much. Where are you from, Tatame? You speak English very well."

"A village outside of Kazumba, in the Katanga Province in Congo." The young man's English was spoken with a lilt that Jim found pleasing. "My brothers and I were raised by the Sisters of Charity at a church orphanage in Ndekesha."

"Your provinces are like states in the US?"

"More like your counties, I think."

"And it was a school as well?"

Tatame was waving to persons moving about the camp: children running by in play, a troop of women walking by with firewood. The smell of cooking fires and meals filled the air, always with the heavy, humid smell of vegetation and the lake.

"Yes, a school. The sisters were very strict about learning. It was planned that I might be able to attend the Christian Bilingual University in Beni, but . . ."

"Fighting?" Jim asked.

"Yes, always fighting."

"How big is this camp?"

"About one hundred hectares, built for two thousand people."

Jim looked around at the sprawl and everyone milling around. "This looks a bit more than two thousand."

"Yes. The fighting pushes people where it will. I was traveling from the orphanage on the train when the war broke out. The militias raided the orphanage. I received word when I got to Beni. So I returned, buried my brothers and the Sisters of Charity who were left."

The calm manner in which Tatame explained the death of his home and family was something that Jim was becoming used to in Africa. Sudden violence and turmoil were for some daily events amid the multinational, multiparty official and unofficial wars in the Congo.

"Zaire is where I was born. The Democratic Republic of Congo is where I was raised. I am a Tutsi, as are most in the camp."

Tatame stopped to chat to an older woman

preparing a meal in her hut. Jim waited and thought about the conflicts that had made camps like these necessary. Father Michael had filled him in over morning coffee one day. A child born into a country at war, Tatame had never known a time without conflict.

"Zaire was under Mobutu?" Jim asked when Tatame emerged from the hut.

"Mobutu's Zaire lasted for almost thirty years until the current uprising with the AFDL. Rwanda had invaded, backing the rebel leader Kabila, and the breakdown of a country already in turmoil had begun. The Tutsi and Hutu peoples were just factions in the ongoing struggle. First the Tutsi peoples were killed by the hundreds of thousands by the Hutus, then the Tutsis, in turn, killed many Hutus. I heard that over a million refugees streamed across Lake Tanganyika for a chance to live," Tatame said. "We go now, Mr. Jim. Brother Abraham is waiting for us."

The two men walked back to the center of the camp, where Father Michael and Abraham were standing in a crowd of people. Voices were raised, and people excitedly spoke with gestures and animation.

"What's going on?" Jim asked.

Abraham turned to him.

"These men were out hunting for food. They say the soldiers are camped about five kilometers from here."

"The same soldiers from the day we arrived?" Jim asked.

"Yes, they were breaking camp an hour ago," Father Michael said.

"Not soldier, militia," Tatame said.

"Not official?" Jim asked.

"Basically outlaws at this point," Father Michael

replied. "Colonel Keneyusu is a bandit warlord. He is coming either to take workers or to kill them if they don't go. They are Mai-Mai. Modern slavers."

"I've heard about Mai-Mai before, but I don't quite understand who they are," Jim said.

"Mai-Mai are bandit groups. They are used by different parties for disruption of the peoples, killing, raping, stealing. As long as it's not their peoples, anyone is open game," Father Michael said.

"Would they attack here?" Jim asked. "This camp is larger than most; does that make it safer?"

Father Michael shrugged. "Perhaps. Better funding. They can afford the guards—or bribes—necessary for safety."

"You think they're coming to attack?" Jim asked.

"Possibly. Something has shifted in the plans of the military or the rebels. The Mai-Mai need men, money, and supplies. By attacking some camps, they can start to group more and more people in smaller areas. Then they can control the flow of supplies, basically stealing the aid."

"Just bandits in uniforms, grabbing what they can get," Tatame said, nodding. "Or this may be a terror raid, driving people throughout the country to disrupt the environment in preparation for war."

Jim saw the news begin to travel from person to person. Children began crying, and women and men started to gather their things, preparing to flee yet again.

"I will stay," Abraham said.

"Why do you want to stay, Abraham?" Father Michael asked.

Abraham stood silently, looking out at the people moving about the camp. In a place where some sense of normalcy had been found, once again war and violence had come to these people.

"This is where God wants me," he said. "Here among His children. To give strength to the weak, comfort to the strong."

Father Michael and Jim stared at Abraham, Father Michael in disbelief, Jim in resigned acceptance. Abraham raised his hands and spoke to the camp.

"People, people, listen to me. Calmer les gens." Abraham's deep voice was powerful, and people began to take notice. "Tatame, translate what I am about to say. My French is not adequate."

Abraham began speaking to the crowd of people, which started to swell. Tatame translated the stories that wove into more stories. Jim looked at the group being spellbound by Abraham, the man telling people without hope to have hope, telling them that the weak would be strong together. He would stand with the people if they would stand with him.

"He's mad," Father Michael said to Jim. "These people need to flee."

"What about the ones who can't?" Jim asked.

"No one is interested in old or crippled workers."

As Jim watched, the crowd of frightened, demoralized people became calmer; their energy began to shift. The tone of Abraham's speech was building and uniting individuals into a group.

"Show me where the trucks may arrive," Jim said to Father Michael.

Father Michael merely waved in a direction. He was too astounded at what was happening between Abraham and the people to leave. Jim walked in the direction indicated.

The camp was a vast collection of huts, shanties, and a few small, temporary buildings. As he walked between them, Jim noted that at least the majority of the camp was twists and turns. Very few straight lines existed except in the originally planned area, which the camp had quickly outgrown, sprawling in every direction. Roads and pathways wound throughout, and even the main road snaked through the center. While the thin material of most of the structures could not be depended on to stop bullets, he thought, the structures would at least cut down on the straight lines of fire.

He wondered why he was thinking in the manner of conflict. His infantry training was kicking in. Was it the crowd? Whatever was going to happen, he would stand by his friend.

The sound of trucks broke his thoughts. Slipping around the corner of a hut, he saw trucks pulling into the camp with a jeep in front. Abraham was approaching the jeep, standing in the middle of the road, the crowd behind him.

The jeep stopped and Colonel Keneyusu stepped out. Soldiers poured from the trucks, fanning out. Their rifles were not held casually as before. Instead, their faces were excited, their eyes searching. Abraham turned to the crowd and held up his hands. A simple gesture of moving his hands apart split the crowd off the road.

"Et qui etes-vous?" the colonel asked, taking in Abraham and the crowd.

"I am Brother Abraham, and you are not welcome," Abraham said, turning back toward the colonel and standing with his arms crossed, a powerful expression on his face.

"Like the Bible, I think," the colonel said, his tone

mocking. "Are these your flock, Brother?" A tall man in his green uniform, his red beret displaying a golden crest, he began striding up to the robed figure.

"Go back from where you came," Abraham said.

His broad face displaying arrogance, the colonel smiled. He walked closer to Abraham and the crowd.

"A hundred today, no more. For the liberation of Congo," the colonel said, then pointed to some of the men in the crowd. "You and you, get over there." He gestured to the trucks.

"They will stay," Abraham said.

"So you say." The colonel spoke as he was turning, his hand dropping to his pistol. He drew it and leveled it at Abraham.

"Now, Brother. Now our little game is over. My patience is ended." The colonel stood fifteen feet from Abraham.

Abraham was unmoved. He stood still and glared at the colonel and his pistol. Jim began to angle his way nearer to the scene, desperate to get closer to his friend. A soldier walked from behind the colonel, his AK-47 pointed at Abraham. The colonel laughed and pulled the trigger of his pistol. The gunshot shuddered the crowd as it whined down the road harmlessly. The bullet had missed and was gone. Jim increased his pace until he was at the hut closest to the three figures. The colonel looked at his pistol, then back to the robed figure. Once more, he raised the pistol.

"Bon prêtre!" the colonel roared as he began firing, walking toward the still-unmoving figure of Abraham. Three shots rang out, with no apparent effect.

"No!" Jim yelled as he rushed the colonel.

The colonel turned and looked, quickly bringing

the pistol to align with Jim as he shot. Jim tripped and fell. The bullet went over his head and impacted the corrugated hut behind him. Jim looked up to see Abraham grab the colonel by the throat and crotch, lift him into the air, and bring him crashing down into the soldier behind. The heads of the colonel and the soldier made a dull cracking sound, and both men fell senseless to the ground.

Jim scrambled along the ground as fast as he could to the two men, grabbing up the soldier's rifle. He quickly turned, aimed, and shot the astonished machine gunner and driver of the jeep.

"Tuez-les tous!" a soldier by the first truck shouted.

The green-clad figures remembered their rifles and began bringing them up. Jim immediately ran to the front of the jeep for cover. Without hesitation, he took aim and began firing bursts down the line of trucks, hitting multiple soldiers. Ducking back down behind the jeep, Jim looked at the limp figures lying on the ground. He knew he would be out of ammunition in moments. He had to get to the full magazines on the prone soldier who had been standing behind the colonel. Standing against the front of the jeep, Jim fired another burst down each side of the convoy, then ran to the soldier on the ground. People had vanished from the lanes to between the huts on either side of the fight.

Abraham was slowly walking toward him as Jim knelt and grabbed a magazine from the ammunition pouch on the soldier's chest. He rolled on his back, the bodies of the colonel and the soldier providing a small amount of cover from the bullets he heard cracking around him. Jim knocked the spent magazine from his rifle and inserted a fresh one. Rolling back into position, using the prone figures as support for the gun, Jim shot at two soldiers approaching down the left side of the vehicles. One went down, clutching his leg and screaming, while his companion darted behind the jeep.

"Are you injured?" Abraham asked, standing above Jim. Jim looked up at the robed man, outlined by the sun, a calm expression on his face.

"Get the fuck down, Abe," Jim said, looking for a target. He heard gunfire but wasn't sure what the soldiers were shooting at.

"God is with us, Jim. I feel His grace," Abraham said and began to walk toward the vehicles.

Jim scrambled to his feet with the rifle pointed toward the line of vehicles. Abraham had already reached the side of the jeep. A soldier popped out from behind a truck and took aim.

"Brother, lay down your arms. We are together," Abraham said as he walked toward the trucks.

Jim saw the muzzle flashes of the rifle and heard the bullets as they flew by. Desperately he moved forward to get a clear shot around Abraham. Another gun was fired, and Jim saw bullets pluck at Abraham's robe. Reaching the jeep, Jim aimed quickly and fired a burst, knocking the young soldier back.

"Abe!" Jim screamed desperately, reaching for Abraham's shoulder.

A clanking sound to his left made him turn with his rifle raised. A soldier trying to raise his own gun had caught its tip on the wheel well of the jeep. He looked at Jim with wide eyes. Jim pulled the trigger, and nothing happened. The gun had run out of bullets. Jim's fist caught the young soldier on the chin instead, knocking him down and out.

Jim moved to the left side of the jeep, swapped in a new magazine, and fired a long burst at the three men who were attempting to move up. All three fell, two squirming and one lying still.

He plucked a fresh magazine from the body at his feet, knocked the old magazine out, and replaced it, at the same time scrambling backward to gain cover. He then advanced around the jeep and went forward. Abraham was walking two trucks farther up, his hands by his sides, palms forward. Jim was aware of faces poking out from the gaps in the huts on both sides of the roadway.

Jim saw movement from the corner of his eye and hit the ground. A soldier hiding between the jeep and the truck had fired. Jim rolled left, bringing his rifle up and firing, but missed. Belly-crawling to the jeep's rear tire, Jim swept the rifle under a truck but could see nothing.

A soldier suddenly darted out of the gap between the trucks in front of him, screaming and firing toward Abraham's back at almost point-blank range. Jim, prone on his belly, aimed and fired a burst, taking the man low in the legs. Looking up at hearing a noise, he saw the soldier who had been hiding on the bumper of the jeep leap toward him, bayonet extended. Jim rolled to the side and the blade buried itself in the ground.

Desperately clinging to the man's rifle with one hand, Jim struggled to bring his own rifle to bear. The soldier kicked Jim hard in the head, stunning him. Jim lost his grip on the gun, and the soldier pulled it out of the ground and aimed it at him. Jim saw mud and grass clogging the barrel of the rifle as it pointed toward the center of his chest. Twisting away, he desperately grabbed the barrel with both hands, pushed it hard to one side, then drove it back into the man's face, knocking him to the ground unconscious.

Picking up his rifle and another spare magazine from the now-still body, Jim turned to look for Abraham. Now three trucks up from Jim, he appeared to be pleading with the heavens and the soldiers. Even though his ears were ringing, Jim could hear Abraham proclaiming.

"Dear God, spare them! Let them know their lives are worth more."

I don't know what sort of religious hallucination he's having, Jim thought, *but I need to get him down before his luck runs out.*

Jim advanced up the line of trucks with his rifle at the ready. Scanning for other soldiers, he made his way to Abraham, who was still standing with his hands extended to the sky. Desperately looking around, Jim reached for his friend. Abraham spun to face him. Jim saw two soldiers run from behind the trucks and take a kneeling position to aim at both of them.

"Abe, watch out!" Jim yelled as he darted left, trying to pull his friend to cover between the trucks.

Time slowed as the strong brother shook him off and advanced to the men. Jim desperately raised his rifle as the muzzle flashes began to pulse from the ends of the soldiers' machine guns. Frozen in place, Jim could almost see the bullets as they tore through Abraham's robe, plucked at his hair.

A sharp impact struck the rifle in Jim's hands and drove it into his sternum, knocking him over and driving the air from his lungs. Lying on the ground, he looked up to see Abraham standing, arms outstretched toward the two soldiers, who were looking at him with confusion.

One man looked at his rifle, then at Abraham, and dropped the gun on the ground. Kneeling, he covered his head with his arms.

His companion cursed, fumbling for another magazine. He pulled it free of its pouch, knocked the used magazine away, and slotted it into the rifle. A practiced hand motion pulled back then released the rifle's slide.

"Put down the rifle, my son. There has been enough violence this day," Abraham said.

Jim struggled to a seated position, a hand pressed to his bruised sternum. He tried to get a breath. Abraham stood to the left and in front of him. The soldier looked feverishly from Abraham to Jim.

"Surrender!" the soldier's accented voice said.

Jim looked at the ruined rifle on the ground in front of him, its wooden buttstock splintered and destroyed. The gun could probably still fire, he thought, but his body did not feel as if it could react at any pace fast enough to not get shot. It seemed impossible that both he and Abraham were still alive.

"Put the gun down, my son. Detends, mons fils. Personne ne te fera de mal. No one will harm you." Abraham, speaking softly in French and English to the panicked soldier, took a slight step forward. The other soldier remained with his hands on his head, rocking slightly and whimpering.

"Leve-toi, fou!" the soldier said to his comrade.

Other soldiers were coming up behind the one with the gun. Jim still could barely move. It was unusually quiet, he thought, after so much noise, though his ears were ringing from the gunshots.

"Get down! Get—"

The soldier could not finish his command. A roar drowned it out. Jim looked up to see people erupting from between the huts, washing over the soldiers in a blur of violence. Shots rang out from the other side of the trucks as well, and then there was only shouting. Jim imagined that any soldiers there had met the same fate as the ones in front of him. They had been bludgeoned so quickly, by so many people, that their living bodies had been reduced to pulp in moments.

"Stop! Stop!" Abraham shouted to the crowds, but it was no use.

Jim struggled to his feet and was then aided by solid hands. He looked up to see Tatame and Prudence standing beside him.

"You are well, Mr. Jim?" Tatame asked. "Are you shot?"

Jim looked down at his chest and legs. He shook his head. His body ached, but he was unharmed. He could feel the adrenaline ebbing out of his system and the queasiness it brought.

The crowds of people were now dancing and singing, swarming around the trucks and Abraham. Many people were dancing around Jim, touching him. Father Michael walked up to Jim and put his hand on his shoulder.

"Are you all right, Jim?" The short man peered up into Jim's face, a concerned look in his eyes.

Jim nodded, finally able to get a full breath. He walked over to Abraham, who was surrounded by happy, dancing people. Abraham looked at Jim, tears streaming down his face and wetting his beard. Jim touched him on his shoulders, arms, chest, and legs. His robe was full of bullet holes, but no wound was visible.

"They didn't have to die," Abraham said. "I could have protected them."

"You protected *them*," Jim said, gesturing to the people of the camp. "But how we are not dead, I'll never know."

"God was with me. I felt Him fill me and guide me." Abraham looked at the crowd surrounding him. "I wish things had gone differently, but I think we just started people believing. Believing in God . . . and perhaps in themselves."

"I think we just started a war," Jim said.

Chapter 19

Twenty-two soldiers had been killed, along with twelve of the people from the camp. All the bodies had been gathered up and lay side by side. The soldiers' boots and uniforms had been stripped to be better used by people without clothing or shoes.

Colonel Keneyusu, concussed but alive, had been shielded from the violence by Abraham when the camp fought back. Abraham had convinced them through force of will that the colonel and one surviving soldier, named Bibuwa, should be spared. Jim and Abraham went into the guarded hut where they were being held.

"Bonjour, Colonel," Abraham addressed the man, now stripped of his uniform—he and Bibuwa were wearing only pants—but not his arrogance.

"Bonjour, prophet," the colonel said. "You would have been better off to kill me, I think."

"There has been enough killing, Colonel," Abraham said as he sat upon a stool and regarded the pair of men. The colonel returned his gaze with amused hostility; Bibuwa kept his eyes on the ground and his mouth shut.

"Killing is like the swallows. It always returns." Colonel Keneyusu flexed his arms against the ropes that bound him. "And now, Brother? What do we do now?"

"Why are you here?" Abraham countered. "Where did you come from?"

Colonel Keneyusu laughed: a deep, braying rumble. "You have the lion in your den and you don't know what to do with him, is that it?"

"God will tell me what to do," Abraham replied calmly.

"And who is the mzungu warrior?" Colonel Keneyusu asked, looking at Jim. "British, Australian?"

"It's none of your concern," Abraham said.

"None of my concern? He killed my men, and you say it's none of my concern?"

"Your men attempted to kill peaceful refugees," Abraham replied.

"They are the people of the Congo. They must work to bring peace to the Congo."

"Mining?"

"We use what we have to use."

Abraham looked to Jim.

"Where are the people you took earlier?" Jim asked the colonel.

"Ah, an American," the colonel replied. "Where they are needed, of course."

Jim motioned to Abraham, and they left the hut. Jim felt the colonel's calculating eyes upon him as they went.

"Well?" Jim asked when they were far enough away to not be heard.

"The colonel is playing with us. Surprising when you realize that his men are lying dead over there."

"He's probably pretty good at figuring out the angles. And he's right. We do have a lion in the den," Jim said, looking at the bodies on the ground. A few men and women were moving them over to a truck to take them somewhere to be buried. Prudence, that tiny but forceful woman, was organizing the work and chiding people along.

"Let's separate them," Abraham said. "The soldier Bibuwa might let on something if he isn't in front of the colonel."

"Tatame, come here, please," Jim said.

The thin young man came over, wearing a combat harness and holding an AK-47 liberated from one of the soldiers. Jim had placed him in charge of a group of men to guard the prisoners.

"Bring the man Bibuwa to the center hut," Abraham said to Tatame. "Feed him and wait for us."

Tatame signaled to two men, who went inside to drag out the soldier. Bibuwa, apparently thinking he was headed for execution, began to shout and struggle. An additional two men grabbed on to him and started helping to drag him away. When he continued to struggle, Tatame smacked him in the head with the butt of his rifle, which immediately fired a burst of gunfire into the air.

Everyone in the immediate area crouched, looking around. Tatame looked sheepish as the other men dragged Bibuwa away. Jim walked to him, reached out, and moved the safety on the rifle to the safe position.

"I'll give you some training later, Tatame. Be careful."

Tatame nodded and walked after the men dragging Bibuwa. The crowd of people, not seeing any more danger, went back to their business.

Jim looked back at Abraham. "Bibuwa first, then back to the colonel."

Abraham looked at the hut containing the colonel. "He might want to hear about his man."

"Yeah," Jim said. "Let him sweat a bit."

Jim and Abraham entered the dining hall to see Bibuwa holding a rice bowl and surrounded by Tatame and four other men. All were pointing their rifles at his head. Bibuwa was wide-eyed and clearly terrified and confused. Abraham motioned for the men to lower their rifles.

"Thank you, gentlemen. We will take it from here. Tatame, stay, if you would."

Abraham crossed to a chair opposite the soldier. Bibuwa regarded him with wary eyes.

"Where are you from?" Abraham asked. "D'ou estes-vous?"

Bibuwa sat mute, holding his bowl, watching Abraham. Abraham regarded him for a minute, then stood again and walked over to the man. Standing, Abraham stretched out his arms and raised his face to the ceiling, speaking in a loud, deep voice.

"Oh Lord, God of Heaven, let this man know he is among Your children. Let him speak the truth to Your glory."

Cringing in his chair, Bibuwa stared wide-eyed at the robed brother.

"Let Your fire of righteousness fill his soul!" Abraham said, his tone and volume becoming louder and sterner. Abraham reached out and grabbed Bibuwa's head with one hand, his other raised above. Bibuwa began to shake, dropping his bowl, the rice spilling on the floor.

"Let Your love and judgment be upon him," Abraham said, suddenly dropping to one knee and staring into Bibuwa's wide eyes. "Bring peace to my land and to my brother here. Let him know no fear."

Jim watched the drama play out as Abraham nodded and then released Bibuwa, who shook and trembled at the power of Abraham's prayer and presence. Abraham rose and spoke to Bibuwa.

"Where are you from?"

The man responded in chatter that Abraham obviously couldn't understand. Finally he looked to Tatame for help.

"It's Lingala," Tatame said, then asked Bibuwa, "Français? English?"

Bibuwa shook his head and rattled some words back at Tatame.

"He's a Bantu from Uganda," Tatame said.

"Ask him how long he's been a soldier," Jim said.

Tatame asked, then translated the response. "Fifteen years . . . since he was a child."

"Where are the men who were taken before?" Abraham asked. "Where were the people taken today going to go, and why?"

Tatame asked and received a series of answers. Jim could not follow the strange dialect, which bounced back and forth.

"He says they were to gather people to mine in the north. It was supposed to be peaceful work. Instead, there has been more fighting and killing, the mineworkers' numbers are depleted, and new workers are needed. The colonel gets paid for every worker he brings in."

"What happened to the people taken before?" Abraham repeated.

Tatame spoke briefly with Bibuwa.

"They were sent north, like others. Probably died."

"How many people have been sent to the mines, and how many was he supposed to get?" Jim asked.

Tatame relayed the question. "He's not sure how many have been sent. The fighting has been terrible. A few hundred, maybe. Disease is rampant in the camps— Ebola. They have been taking as many strong women and men as they could. Once they gather them in the trucks, they drive them to the coast to some boats that transport them over the lake."

Jim and Abraham looked at each other, Jim motioned with his head to the door, and both men stood.

Then Bibuwa said to Tatame, "Generale . . . Generale Kosoa . . ."

The two exchanged words for some time as Jim and Abraham waited.

"He says that General Kosoa is expecting the first people by this evening," Tatame related at last. "He and his soldiers are waiting at the boats. Men are out in other camps as well, and if they do not return by morning, Kosoa will send more soldiers."

"How many soldiers does he have?" Jim asked Tatame.

"Two hundred or so," Tatame responded after consulting Bibuwa. "Forty left at the boats, and the rest in three other groups."

"Why is he telling us this?" Abraham spoke up.

Tatame exchanged words with Bibuwa, who was chattering with excitement.

"He is happy you did not kill him, and he thinks you must be strong with God. The bullets could not hurt you," Tatame said. "He said it must be a miracle. He has seen much shooting and has never seen a man face two rifles at that range—rifles wielded by trained soldiers— and not be harmed. He recognizes that the hand of God must be upon you. That is why he dropped his weapon."

Abraham looked long at Bibuwa. The soldier looked back for a moment, then dropped his eyes reverently.

"If we released him, would he show us where these boats are?" Jim asked.

"Why are you asking that?" Abraham asked Jim before Tatame could translate the question.

Jim held up his hand and looked to Tatame. Tatame spoke to Bibuwa, who hesitated, then looked at Abraham. After holding Abraham's gaze for a moment, he spoke back to Tatame.

"He will go for Abraham, if Abraham will bless him," Tatame translated.

Jim looked to Abraham, who was staring intently at Bibuwa. Then Jim walked out of the building and motioned to the men waiting outside. Abraham came out as the other men went in.

"What do you think, Jim?" he asked.

"What do I think?" Jim looked around at the trucks and the pile of bodies. "I think that there will be more soldiers here by tomorrow morning when these trucks don't turn up where they're supposed to be. Two hundred soldiers this time. We can't fight so many and win."

Abraham nodded, then bowed his head in thought for a moment.

"What if they do turn up where they're supposed to be?" he asked.

"What do you mean?"

"We put our people in the soldiers' uniforms, load into the trucks, go to the river, and get back the people who were stolen."

Jim looked at his friend, stunned. "With untrained people? Limited weapons and ammunition? What chance do we have to accomplish a rescue?"

"What chance do the people who are already taken have in slavery? What chance do we have if the soldiers come here? How many will die fighting? Some might run away, but look around: the children, the old people, they can't flee into the jungle. And even those who might manage it would likely starve before long."

Jim thought about the predicament as Father Michael came up to the pair.

"I spoke via radio to the camp north of us," Father Michael said. "Unfortunately, they were also hit this morning. Thirty people killed, including a doctor, and a hundred taken."

"How long ago did they leave?" Jim asked.

"Two hours."

"What about the Tanzanian army? What about the peacekeepers?" Abraham asked.

"Ten of the peacekeepers were killed in the first assault. The rest ran off into the jungle. The army might get involved, but it will take time, time the people don't have."

Jim looked at the camp and the milling people. The adrenaline dump from the fight had left him shaken and queasy. The rifle in his hands felt very heavy, a burden. He wanted to lie down and sleep, to awaken in a different place, a different world.

"Let's do it," Jim said.

Jim held a brief training period while the soldiers' uniforms were washed clean of blood. A surprising number of men from the camp, some of them former soldiers, already had knowledge of the rifles, but most were unfamiliar. Jim taught them the basics as best he could and then divided the more experienced evenly between the vehicles. Energy had blossomed in the hastily assembled force as the camp inhabitants saw their chance to strike back.

Soon the trucks were growling along the dirt road, pushing through vegetation as the day turned into night. Jim was in the lead truck as Bibuwa drove, Tatame in the middle. Abraham was in the second truck. The rest of the camp's men, and some women, were in the other trucks as they made their way to the lake rendezvous point. Colonel Keneyusu's bullet-riddled jeep had been left behind, as had the colonel himself, who was still under guard in the hut, now watched by Father Michael and two older men.

Bibuwa pointed to the road and slowed, then stopped, the truck.

"What is he saying?" Jim asked.

"There is another kilometer to the sentries. The lake is very near them," Tatame said. The colonel's uniform hung on his thin frame.

Jim nodded, scanning the trees and bushes as the light faded. Opening the door of the truck, Jim then stepped out. Holding a rifle and wearing the combat webbing from a dead soldier, loaded with magazines and grenades, Jim felt the old familiarity of his infantry training from the academy taking hold. Abraham walked up from the convoy along with the ten men Jim had selected as the most experienced with weapons and combat.

"Is this the point?" Abraham asked.

"We are about a kilometer away. My team will cut over that ridge toward the lake. Give us forty-five minutes, then go in. Have the men capture the sentries, then head toward the boats. We will set up an ambush point to flank the forces. If we can't get them to surrender, then at least we can have a tactical advantage. If a fight starts, just go right at them."

Abraham nodded, then embraced Jim, saying, "Go with God, my friend." He then placed his hands on the heads of each of the ten men, who smiled at the blessing.

Jim signaled to the men and sent the two aged but experienced soldiers in the group ahead. The rest of the team moved out with Jim. He had already explained the plan to them in camp, drawing on the information provided by Bibuwa. Along with instructions for silence and keeping the weapons' safeties on, he had explained that their only advantages were surprise and the darkness with which the night would cloak them.

Through the light brush, the men moved quickly. In twenty minutes they had reached a hill where the assembled trucks and boats could be viewed. The landing craft, capable of carrying trucks, equipment, or people as needed, looked about seventy feet long.

"Shit," Jim said under his breath. The campfires showed about fifty soldiers. He could see no captives. Perhaps they had already been transported.

Jim felt a touch on his arm and looked to see one of the scouts, Henda, his deep eyes hidden in shadows. Henda pointed at a clump of trees thirty yards from the boats. Jim nodded and moved his hand flat along the ground, side to side, to mimic a snake.

Henda moved off quietly and smoothly. The other men followed, moving through the shadows until they reached the trees. There was no indication that they were noticed in the full dark of night.

The men spread out and looked at the scene before them. A few fires showed the soldiers lounging, eating, and drinking; some even appeared asleep on the ground. Sounds drifted up of drunken men singing. The boats had their ramps down on the shore, but whatever was inside was hidden in darkness. Jim, approaching from behind, pointed to Henda and one other man to come with him to scout the craft. He motioned for the other men to stay concealed in place and watch the camp.

They moved out slowly toward the lake and the boats. The smell of fresh water and diesel fuel reminded Jim of summer trips a world away in his youth. Peeking into the first boat, Jim saw and heard men sleeping. He ducked back down. Motioning a man whose name he did not remember to stay, he led Henda under the lowered ramp, both men on their bellies.

The two other boats held at least twenty sleeping men each. Jim thought quickly. Time was running out. He now knew that they faced at least a hundred men. His party of ten and the convoy made only fifty. They were at a severe disadvantage, and at any moment the party would start.

Jim shook his head in wonder. It was absurd what they were about to do. If he'd had communications with the convoy, he would have called the operation off. It was madness to think that they could triumph. But there was no choice. Abraham and the convoy would arrive and be decimated if he did nothing.

Slipping two grenades from pouches, he handed them to Henda. Through hand motions, he was able to indicate to the older man what he wanted him to do when the time came: slip both pins out and throw them into the farthest boat. Henda smiled and nodded, his gapped white teeth catching the firelight.

Jim crawled back to the second boat under the ramp, readying his own grenades. He could barely see the man he had left by the ramp of the first boat. He waited for the trucks to arrive.

The sound of a footstep on the ramp above Jim made him freeze. He was holding two live grenades, one in each hand, the pins already removed. There was no way he could find the pins in the darkness.

A stream of urine began to splash on the ground by Jim's feet.

Moving quietly, he crawled out the other side of the ramp and came into a crouch. The man on the ramp was still taking the world's longest, loudest piss, his back to Jim.

Jim moved up on the ramp behind the man and swung his right hand as hard as possible. The grenade took the man behind the ear, dropping him unconscious to the ground. Jim crouched again and waited, listening.

Suddenly shouting and gunfire erupted from where his team was concealed. Jim turned to see the outline of a soldier, illuminated by muzzle flashes, between him and the trees.

"Damn!" Jim said. The plan had gone to hell. There was no sign of Abraham and the trucks.

Jim threw one grenade toward the group of soldiers by the fire. His right hand now free, he pointed to Henda to throw his grenades as well. Then, turning, he tossed his second grenade into the darkness of the landing craft and jumped down onto the ground beside his rifle.

The first grenade's ten-second timer burned down to ignite the explosives within, spraying shrapnel in a muted explosion. Jim crouched down, waiting for the rest of the grenades to explode, not knowing precisely where they were and therefore unable to judge the path the deadly shrapnel might take.

Two more explosions were followed by screams and shouting. One more blast from above Jim's head in the boat was followed by more screaming. Henda crawled up to Jim, his snaggled smile outlined by the moonlight.

"Fuck ces salauds," Henda exclaimed, sighting down his rifle.

Jim didn't know what *salauds* meant, but he got the general meaning. He nudged Henda and motioned to the other man by the first boat. He intended to flank the main group of soldiers as quickly as possible to attain a tactical advantage in the confusion.

When the three were together, with Jim leading, they moved swiftly into the brush behind the camp. Crawling forward, Jim could see a group of soldiers behind tree trunks and rocks, wildly firing back at the original attackers.

He held up three fingers to Henda. The other man then counted down, removing a finger at a time. They came up together, aimed their rifles, and shot at the clump of ten men with a sustained burst.

Just as quickly, Jim brought them down and crawled off in another direction, going counterclockwise around the collection of enemy soldiers, who were now firing in all directions. Automatic rifle fire echoed through the night. Reaching some cover behind a small pile of earth, Jim switched to a fresh magazine. The men with him did the same.

Peeking over the dirt berm, Jim could see across

the camp to where his other men were. Only the soldiers' confusion about where they were being attacked from had kept the ambushers from being overrun.

Where the fuck is Abraham? Jim thought. He knew he had to get back to the men from the convoy as soon as he could. They were brave but untrained. They should have retreated or at least moved. Instead, in the few minutes that had passed, it was very likely that they had shot most if not all of their bullets.

Looking again, Jim spotted a heavy machine gun mounted on a pole in the back of a pickup truck. In the dying firelight, he could just see an ammunition belt hanging from the weapon. The machine gun could be a significant force multiplier. Thinking quickly, Jim motioned his plan to the men. Henda nodded and quietly spoke to the other man.

Jim moved out in a crouch, rifle at the ready, the other men close by his side. No one was between him and the machine gun. As he reached the truck, Jim realized that the night sky was becoming lighter. As the other two men took positions near the truck with their rifles pointed into the camp, Jim climbed up into the truck's bed to grasp the gun.

About fifty enemy soldiers were slowly moving toward their position, looking toward the boats and the clump of trees concealing the men from the convoy. Jim looked up at the gun, recognizing the charging handle and trigger, working out in his mind how it functioned. Then, moving upward, he racked back and released the charging handle and swung the gun toward the advancing soldiers. Before he could fire, Henda opened up behind him. Jim saw two enemy soldiers who had been creeping up go down. Henda smiled his snaggled grin and returned to watching Jim's back.

Jim began to fire in the swinging transverse burst method he had learned in his infantry training. The heavy rounds swept into the large group of soldiers spread out before him. As he swept the gun slowly from side to side, the rounds laid waste to the opposing force. The loud explosions and flashing fire from the end of the muzzle were both blinding and deafening.

When he could see no more movement in front of him, he swung to the left, moving around the center point of the gun mount. Jim felt impacts to the pickup. Quickly searching, he located another group of soldiers, who had taken cover behind the third boat. Depressing the trigger, he walked the heavy rounds up to the metal landing craft until they decimated its sides and interior. Screaming as he did so, Jim held the trigger until the gun stopped its bucking, its ammunition belt finished.

Jim released the machine gun, picked up his rifle, and jumped down to the ground beside Henda. The thin old man looked at him in awe and fear, disbelief evident on his face. Jim pulled his last grenades and threw one toward the middle boat and one toward the area from which they had received the previous fire. He waited for them to explode, then turned to his men.

"Let's go!" Jim said as he pointed to where the ambush point had been.

They moved fast, grabbing magazines from the dead bodies on the ground as they went. They scanned around, seeing no resistance. Soon they were beside the clump of trees. Jim looked down on the group of fighters he had brought with him. They were lying down, clutching their rifles, all of which appeared to be empty. They had shot their last rounds and then waited to die.

And yet, incredibly, not one of them seemed to be dead or even wounded.

Jim couldn't have known it, but he was now framed in the first light of dawn breaking over the lake. Beams of sunlight breaking through the smoke lit him up from behind. The men on the ground saw a figure outlined by the smoke and light. The smell of charring wood and gunpowder punctuated the scene of carnage and destruction. As the men climbed up, they surrounded Jim.

Jim turned to look at the camp. Nothing moved. Bodies littered the ground everywhere. The light of the new day lay upon death and silence. Jim sat on the ground with his ears ringing, suddenly exhausted. He wrapped his arms around his head, rocking back and forth.

The sound of trucks approaching made him look up. Tatame and Abraham walked over to him, their eyes concerned.

"Jim, are you all right?" Abraham asked, kneeling down to look at his friend.

"Yes, just tired. Help me up."

Abraham put his arm under Jim's and raised him up onto shaky legs. Jim noticed Henda speaking with Tatame and the other men in animated and excited tones. Then, with Abraham beside him, he walked to the group.

"Ange, ange," Henda said, walking up to clasp Jim's arm.

Jim was confused but was more concerned with the group being attacked. "Where are the soldiers? The captives?"

"L'Ange de la Mort," Henda said, smiling his snaggled grin at Jim. Turning to the other men, he announced, "Père Lion et l'Ange de la Mort!"

Abraham translated as Jim looked at him quizzically.

"Father Lion and the Angel of Death," he said. "All of the soldiers are either dead or run off. We lost no one. The captives were up the road. They had four guards and were herded up against a cliff under the guns."

Jim looked out across the scene of the battle. The men from the camp, under Tatame's direction, were stripping the bodies of any useful items and moving the weapons and material to a separate pile.

"When the firing started, we were getting the sentries tied up and moving in. Then we ran into the captive people. We couldn't get by easily. We came on foot."

Jim nodded; he motioned at Henda to load the trucks with the weapons and supplies. Abraham continued talking.

"You have made a huge difference today, Jim. You set people free. You're a hero. And none of our people got killed."

"I don't feel much like a hero. 'Angel of Death' doesn't much sound like a hero," Jim said, turning to face his friend. "You could tell me that it may have been necessary, and maybe I would agree, but I carry the blood on my hands. So what now? Back to the camp? Back to the jungle?"

Abraham was silent, bowing his head to think. Then he began to walk toward the landing craft. One was sinking into the mud from damage from the fight, but the others floated where they were. Three men from the camp guarded a group of five huddled and miserable crewmen.

"Où sont ces bateaux de?" Abraham asked. "Combien de personnes ont été prises?"

"The boats are kept at Île Kavala, an island north of here on the Congo side. The people are transported there, then sold."

The speaker, a middle-aged man with sharp features, was dressed only in shorts. Abraham motioned him over. The man stood up and followed Abraham to where Jim and Tatame stood.

"What is your name?" Abraham asked. "How do you know so much? Are you a soldier?"

"Gérard," the man said. "No, I grew up on Île Kavala. My family has been there for generations."

"You sound educated," Tatame said, assessing the man. "Why are you here with these soldiers?"

"The soldiers came to the island about two years ago. They wanted an isolated place to do their trade. There are small settlements on Kavala, but we could not resist them. I had just returned from teaching school in Burundi and was visiting my parents."

"What are you doing on the boats?"

"I grew up on the lake. It is my home. We have always been fishermen. The soldiers needed people skilled with boats, people who could get them where they needed to go. These men and I were recruited at gunpoint."

"What do you teach?" Jim asked.

The man drew himself up. His posture was straight. "I teach up until secondary school. I travel a circuit to some of the more rural villages, teaching mathematics and languages."

"How many taken persons are on Kavala, and how many soldiers?" Abraham asked.

"The last time I was there, about a hundred persons were kept in the old village. The majority of the soldiers came on the raid, but there are about fifty soldiers still on the island."

"How do they communicate with buyers and the boats?" Jim asked.

"By cell phone, usually, from what I can see," Gérard said. "Many of the soldiers who ran off will probably call as soon as they can to report this attack."

Abraham thanked Gérard and motioned for him to return to the group.

"So they have been there for most of a year, off and on, carrying on a modern slave trade, basically," Tatame said. "Does anyone else know? Does anyone care? Probably not. We care, though. And today we have made a difference."

"But there is more work to do, and soon," Abraham said. "Jim, what do you think?"

"I think we got lucky, a lot luckier than we deserve," Jim said. "Those soldiers will notify the island, and they'll send reinforcements."

"We need to rest, recover, and plan," Abraham said. "What about those?" He pointed at the landing craft.

Jim considered the options. Whatever path Abraham had started, he would follow, but even had that not been the case, he knew he would have gone after the slavers. He had been watching the captives being loaded onto the truck. Many showed signs of beatings and other cruel treatment. Some people's utter brokenness showed in their blank eyes, but in some the light of hope could be seen. When he looked over them, they cast their eyes down, but once his gaze had passed, they shyly looked up.

Finally, a child, not more than eleven or twelve, walked alone toward the trucks. Jim's eyes followed the young man as he searched the faces of the people around him, asking, "Brother, sister?" That made up Jim's mind. He walked back to where Gérard was seated.

"How long to get to the island?" Jim asked.

"Three hours," Gérard replied confidently.

"How many places are there to land on the island? Are there fortifications or bunkers? Do you think the soldiers will fight?"

Gérard considered his questions. "Most of their leadership was here. A few sergeants are left, and a couple of officers. There are multiple places to land. What are your plans?"

Jim wasn't sure how to respond to that question. What were his plans? The battle had left him shaken and tired, but new energy filled him now. He walked back to Abraham and Tatame.

"We have to keep going," he told them. "They're on their heels and don't know what to expect. We started this thing, and either we'll end it or it will end us."

"The men are tired, Jim," Abraham said. "This was a great thing we did here, but more? We cannot continue the killing like this. These were men; bad men, perhaps, but all can be redeemed. We cannot become them, take on that evil. How can we do that?"

"We need to do more," Jim insisted. "The slavers are off balance. We have an opportunity to knock them out. We need to keep going."

Jim saw the indecision on Abraham's face and the resolve in Tatame's.

"If we continue," Abraham said, "we have to let those who would surrender do so, only taking life when absolutely necessary. God understands warriors, not butchers."

"Agreed. We will learn from this, do better. I don't know exactly what we've started here, but we can free more, more like them," Jim said, pointing at the former captives. "And they'll make us stronger. We'll take the ones who can fight and are willing to fight, and we'll send the rest back to the refugee camp."

"We can do it, Brother," Tatame said pleadingly. "The light of God is with us now. We have food and water gathered and can rest while in the passage there."

Abraham breathed in deeply, looking at the tired but eager faces of the men. He tilted his head at Jim, one eyebrow raised.

Jim nodded.

Jack Lyons

Chapter 20

After Jim had spoken with Gérard, twenty-five men boarded each of the two functioning landing craft. Gérard and the other boatmen had agreed to help rescue the captives on their island. Jim would lead one team, with Tatame and Abraham in the other boat. As the boats pulled away from the shore, those freed persons who were not on the boats waved from the shore.

His strength recovering, Jim felt voracious and began to eat from the pots of rice and meat taken from the soldiers. As he ate, he looked at the ample supply of arms and ammunition. He was painfully aware that they could very easily be some that he had flown into spots around the country.

After his meal, the drone of the diesel engine and the rocking motion of the boat lulled him to sleep, reminding him somehow of the aircraft carrier from so far in the past.

How long he was asleep, he wasn't sure. A change in the engine's tone brought him around. He stood up and looked at Gérard, who was at the controls.

"Kavala," Gérard said, pointing at a giant green blur about a mile in front of them. The sun had moved. It was late afternoon.

Jim looked at the island in the middle of the vast lake. Blue freshwater stretched out to the horizon, to the slightest blur of land. A few smaller islands could be seen to the east, and Jim pointed to them.

"There, those small islands. Can we hide there until night?"

"The larger one has a village, relatives of mine. We can hide on the side away from Kavala. No soldiers go there."

Jim nodded and stepped up onto the rail around the interior of the cargo well so that he could see over the high side of the landing craft. Catching Tatame's eye on the next boat, he motioned to follow them to one of the smaller islands. Tatame made it clear that he understood.

The approach was uneventful, and soon the two landing crafts nudged the beach surrounded by dense jungle. Jim went down the boarding ramp to meet with Abraham and Tatame.

"Gérard, could you draw a map of Kavala, showing us how it's covered and the best approaches?"

The lake man nodded and set to work with a stick in the wet, sandy mud. He quickly sketched out the island's outline and set about marking buildings and landscape features.

"There are numerous beaches we can land on," Gérard said, then pointed with his stick. "This is the main village, and the captives will be in buildings here and here."

"Are the soldiers all dressed in uniforms?" Tatame asked.

"Usually it is the only clothing they have," Gérard replied.

"Where do the soldiers stay?" Jim asked.

"Here and here, with a command area here in the meeting hall," Gérard said, indicating the structure.

"So there are no real bunkers or fortifications?"

Jim asked, rolling his head to loosen his neck muscles.

"No, but the beach becomes steep and is open only between these buildings."

"How long would it take to hike from this side to the village side? Is there a place we could land without being seen?" Jim asked.

"Yes, there are hills on this side and trails you could use if you were guided. Say, maybe an hour or so?"

Jim regarded the drawing and thought about their options. Then a noise made him look up as Gérard got to his feet. Jim could see nothing but palm trees and brush, but Gérard was looking intently into the jungle.

"Hactu! Hactu!" Gérard said, waving his arms. Jim picked up his rifle and held it ready.

"No, sir," Gérard said, waving his hands, palms down. "They are relatives."

Jim pointed his rifle down and watched as Gérard walked to the edge of the beach. Six men came from the underbrush and walked down to meet him. The group conferred with Gérard, who was waving his arms and pointing at the men on the landing craft. The discussion complete, Gérard walked back to where Jim and Abraham stood. He was smiling.

"They are my cousins. I told them about you and what happened, as well as what we are doing here. They want to help."

"How can they help?" Abraham asked.

"Many of them were in the army and militias. They can also land in other places on the island and scout for us. They have gone back now to gather more men to get rid of the slavers."

"Why would they want to do that?" Jim asked.

"You have extra weapons. They have extra hands

that know how to use them," Gérard said. "The slavers have taken children from this village and others. This is to ensure that food and supplies are brought and to keep the people in line."

"Well, we have about forty extra AKs if they can use them. Would they be willing to be a distraction while the main party attacks the camp from the rear?" Jim said.

"These men are from these islands," Gérard replied. "This is their home. Their people, their families, their children are being held by the militia. They will help all they can."

Gérard hurried off to the jungle, where one man had waited for him. Jim turned to Abraham and Tatame.

"What do you think, Jim?" Abraham asked.

"I would like to send Henda and Tatame along with the fishermen to scout out the landing area today. We'll rest here until, say, nine or ten, then the main force will unload on this part of the island, about here," Jim said, pointing to the map in the sand. "After the landing party has made its way across the island and gotten into position, the boats will come in close and open fire, drawing attention enough to wake the soldiers and bring them out from the village onto the beach, where they'll be trapped."

"So you want me to stay on the boat?"

"Yes. Gérard will be with me, along with Tatame and Henda and the other men."

"Remember, Jim," Abraham said, grasping his shoulders, "we show mercy when we can."

Jim watched Tatame relay the information to the men, then lay down in the landing craft to rest. The night would be busy, and he wanted to save his strength. After the events of the day, he felt overcome by exhaustion.

Closing his eyes brought immediate sleep.

"Jim, Jim."

Jim came awake with a start to see Abraham standing near, regarding him with his green eyes.

"How long have I been out?" Jim asked.

"Six hours. I thought it was important to let you rest." Abraham held out food and a canteen. Jim took them and began to eat.

"Did the scouts return?" Jim asked between bites of food.

"Yes. Apparently the landing zones are empty. The soldiers appear to be back in the camp. And there is more."

"Oh?" Jim asked, finishing his food and drinking from his canteen.

"Come see," Abraham said, standing up and walking out of the landing craft.

Jim followed to see about a hundred men on the beach, scattered in groups, resting and eating. Most were dressed in shorts and T-shirts.

"Who are they?"

"Islanders. Men who want to fight." Jim turned to see Gérard standing behind him.

"Tell them to try their best to take the soldiers unaware and use clubs or hands," Jim said. "If possible, we want to take them alive. If they need to use the rifles, tell them to use the single fire option. It's the second position down from safe. It will be easier to aim, and it will conserve bullets."

Gérard moved off to the groups to pass the word along. Jim looked around and figured that he had done all he could do. He spotted Abraham, who had a group of men kneeling before him. Jim waited until the men dispersed and then walked up.

"Communion?" Jim asked.

"Conversion, communion. There seems to be a thought that those blessed cannot be hurt."

"Blessed by Father Lion?"

"Blessed by God the Father. I am merely the instrument. Are we ready?"

"Ready to begin, anyway. It feels more like we are being carried along rather than going somewhere."

"It feels correct, as if by God's will," Abraham said.

"We will see," Jim said. Then, spying Tatame, he called out, "Mount up. Let's get going."

The men started climbing into the landing craft. Most islander men climbed into the large canoes on the beach, which had outboard motors.

"Do they know where to go?" Jim asked Gérard, who stood at the controls of the landing craft.

"They were born here. They know what to do and where to go."

Gérard started the engines and signaled to his men to raise the ramp. Adjusting the throttles, he steered the craft as it backed out into the lake waters. The other craft repeated the maneuver. The expedition was off and motoring into the night toward the island of Kavala.

The trip was short. The boats, guided by islanders already there, made landing on an isolated beach. Small fires on either side of the beach allowed the two craft to be signaled in. After the front ramps dropped, men walked into the night and assembled in two groups at the edge of the scrub vegetation. The ramps were raised, and the landing craft pulled back out into the dark lake.

Jambi, a lean islander in shorts and a T-shirt,

waited for Jim and his group. Tatame and Abraham would go with the other group. Jim looked around to make sure everyone was ready and then motioned to Jambi to set off.

The groups moved slowly along a trail. There was just enough moonlight for each man to see the person in front of him. Strict orders had been given to not speak. Rifles' firing switches were in the safe position; an accidental shot would alert the enemy soldiers that they were about to have visitors. Despite the precautions, the men moving along the trail made a horrible amount of noise: canteens sloshing, bits of metal clanking, and the heavy breathing of untrained and unconditioned men.

As they moved through the dark, Jim heard birds and ground-dwelling animals in the trees and bushes around them. They had started on reasonably level ground, but soon the trail began to climb up into the hills they would have to cross to get to the camp on the other side. Finally, after an hour of steady walking, Jambi stopped and held up his hand to Jim.

"We should stop, sir. We have reached the top and will be dropping down from here. More islanders will meet us and let us know about the camp," Jambi said.

Jim nodded, grateful he could catch his breath and drink some water. Although his body had healed much in the weeks after crashing to the earth, there were still aches from the hill climb and from carrying the equipment and weapons he would need.

As the men sat quietly drinking water and recovering from the climb, Jim sat beside Jambi, who watched the darkness. Looking down, Jim could make out pinpoints of light from the village below. Dawn was still at least four hours away, and the cloudless sky was filled to bursting with stars. He knew that out there in the darkness, the other team was making its way to the village's west side, while his team would approach from the east.

A new and different bird whistle came from the darkness. He felt Jambi tense up beside him. Then Jambi relaxed and gave the same whistle. Two men came from the darkness and knelt beside Jambi.

"There are no sentries around the village," Jambi said after conferring.

"They didn't post anyone?" Jim asked.

"They posted men. But the island can be dangerous," Jambi said, smiling as he drew a finger across his throat. "The last watch change has occurred, so we have about four more hours. We have no choice but to go forward now."

"How many soldiers are left?"

Jambi conferred with the men and nodded. "Around thirty are left, but that includes about four who are sick or injured. Some of the men from the previous fight have returned."

"Do you think they know we're here?"

"No," Jambi said. "They couldn't believe that they were attacked in the first place. No one had ever put up resistance before. At least not an effective one."

One of the men said some words to Jambi that Jim couldn't make out. Jambi spoke rapidly back and forth with the man.

"It seems that reinforcements are coming, more men from an additional camp somewhere," he said. "The general arrived yesterday; there was much shouting and promises of revenge. It was a big speech he made. He called somewhere, and more men will be here sometime today."

"Do you know how many?" Jim asked.

Jambi conferred with the men. "No, only that they are expected."

The timeline still held, but Jim knew they must not get caught between the two forces.

"Let's move out to be in place on time," Jim said.

Jambi and the other men rose with Jim, and the group moved out down the hill trail toward the village. There was tension in the group as they approached the outskirts. Jim halted the men while he surveyed the village. Long, rectangular grass-thatched huts were arranged in orderly rows. Cleared fields surrounded the settlement.

Jim sent men in small groups left and right along the perimeter. Islanders were with each group to guide the men quickly through the buildings. A group of ten men, older but still willing, was kept as a reserve force and to keep soldiers from fleeing into the hills. All of these plans had been discussed during the night.

Moving up in small groups, the men went to the edge of the village and stopped. Jim made his way from one group to the next.

"Safeties off, single fire, pick your targets, and don't kill villagers or captives," Jim said to each group. "If possible, use the butts of your rifles to disable the soldiers, not to kill."

The men who understood English passed on his orders to the others. The group waited while Jambi and three other men moved off to wake what villagers they could and clear them out of the way. Jim peeked around the corner of a hut and saw people stumbling out of their homes toward his group. Three young women in various states of dress were dragging a young boy between them.

If the plan was going correctly, Tatame's group was beginning the same process on the west side. They also knew that getting the villagers out of the fire zone was the priority, eliminating the soldiers only when necessary.

The sky was getting lighter with the oncoming dawn, but still no soldiers were seen. People continued to filter out of the village and head toward the trees. Finally, Jambi came back to the group and motioned to them. Jim waved to the groups of men who moved up house by house.

"The soldiers are waking. We hit them now," Jambi said. "Follow me. I will spot them for you."

Jambi turned and began threading his way past the first huts. Jim and his men followed. Jambi raised his hand, stopping their advance.

"Careful, careful," Jim said, his rifle ready but pointed downward.

Jambi motioned with his hand for them to stay in position. Jim watched as Jambi picked up a log from beside a hut and hid it behind his arm as he approached a table with two soldiers sitting at it. They looked barely awake, and in two efficient blows from Jambi's makeshift club, they were knocked cold.

Jim moved up with the rest of his men, only to be halted again by a signal from Jambi. Jambi walked up to a hut and called out.

"You girls, you come now and prepare food for the soldiers. They are hungry."

The sound of waking from inside the huts was followed by four girls stumbling out from the darkness within. The first girl was rubbing her eyes when she caught sight of the unconscious soldiers. Her eyes widened and she took a breath to scream. Jambi covered her mouth roughly with his hand and pointed to Jim and the other armed men. Jambi spoke in her ear and pushed her away toward the trees.

"Qu'est-ce que c'est ça?"

The voice came from a man dressed in fatigue pants, standing in the doorway to the hut. Jim raised his rifle to sight on the man's chest, but before he could pull the trigger, Jambi leaped forward and rammed the club into the soldier's stomach.

Shouting erupted from the hut, and a chatter of automatic gunfire followed. Jambi dove out of the way, scrambling to get away from the bullets tearing through the doorway and walls.

Jim fired a burst through the door, and his men opened up as well. Splinters and fragments flew from the hut's walls. Dust boiled inside and from the door.

"Cease fire, cease fire," Jim said as he waved his arm at his men.

The shooting stopped—eventually. Jim wasn't sure how many rounds the men had fired, but firing discipline was certainly gone.

"Single fire, one bullet," Jim yelled. He heard gunfire from the west. The other team had started their part. He heard the flat crack of bullets passing overhead and the sound of bullet ricochets whining off.

"Get down, get down on your bellies!" Jim shouted. He demonstrated and began crawling forward. "Fingers off the triggers." He pantomimed the motion. For the moment, Jim was more concerned about getting shot by his own people than by the soldiers.

He began crawling forward again. Two soldiers

rushed out of the hut across the clearing from him. One he was able to shoot in the leg and bring down. The other darted around the corner of a hut and disappeared.

Jim looked at the men spread about, excitement in their faces, rifles pointed in every direction, eyes wide with fear. *If we'd had a few weeks of training,* he thought, *just for the basics. Hell, I'd have been grateful for a few days! Oh well, gotta go with what you got.*

Trying to control his breathing, Jim wiped the sweat from his eyes with his shoulder. The volume of fire from the other side was increasing. As he belly-crawled forward again, he glanced back to see the men moving with him. They were glancing into huts to try and see if any soldiers were within.

Jim found himself at a small open space and waited as he motioned the other men up. He turned to see Jambi at his shoulder, a rifle held ready.

"You okay?" Jim asked.

"Fine, fine, I fine," Jambi replied, smiling. "More soldiers up ahead. They are scattered and scared now, I think."

"Jambi, tell six of the men to stay here and cover this path. Soldiers may come up from behind, trying to flank us. Tell them to conceal themselves and watch and listen closely. The rest of us will continue around and link up."

Jambi went to tell the six men, who broke off on either side of the path and ducked behind crates and corners as well as they could. Once they were concealed, Jim advanced, rifle at the ready.

"Okay, everybody else spread out. Tell them to seek cover when they can," Jim said to Jambi.

Advancing slowly, Jim reached the corner of a hut.

Peering around the corner, he saw three soldiers huddled behind baskets, nervously looking around. They did not see him. Jim turned back to Jambi and the men. He held up three fingers.

Before they could respond, a soldier came running around a hut behind them, a pistol in his hand. His eyes widened when he saw the group of armed strangers. Jim reversed his rifle and drove the butt into the soldier's forehead. The man lay still on the ground.

"Tie him," Jim said.

Immediately, gunfire came ripping through the walls around Jim, who dropped to the ground. He saw one of the men get hit, doing a half spin before dropping.

Jim crawled around the back of the hut to the opposite side, where a narrow passage between two shacks gave him a line of sight on two soldiers. He aimed his rifle and sent a burst that took both of them in the legs.

Jim backed up from the side of the hut, then stood and carefully moved closer to the next hut. The firing had stopped. Moving back to his men, he saw that one had fallen and was staring in shock at the blood from his leg. One of Jim's men was standing there, and Jim grabbed his hand and pulled it down to the wounded man's leg, pushing on the wound.

"Keep pressure on it!" Jim yelled. The man might not have understood his words, but he seemed to follow the actions.

They needed to keep moving, to keep the momentum and link up with the other group. Jim raised his rifle and went around the corner. He replaced the magazine and scanned for the next threat. Then, motioning to the group, he began to move toward the sound of gunfire..

Peeking around a shack, Jim saw a group of about ten soldiers firing at what he assumed was Abraham's team. There was no choice. He motioned his team forward, and when they were in place, they fired. The barrage of bullets dropped all of the soldiers.

"Move up," Jim said as he walked past the bodies, some still twitching on the ground.

One soldier was crawling, his arm hanging uselessly where a round had shattered it. Jambi stepped up and swung with his club to the back of the soldier's neck. Jim pushed down the revulsion that rose in his throat and kept to the task at hand. They had to get to where they could support the other team.

Moving toward the shouting and shots fired, the group emerged from the village to a broad beach lined with fish-drying sheds. To their left, they could see Abraham and his group, firing toward the sheds, around which the remaining soldiers were clustered. Abraham spotted them and waved in greeting from his concealment point behind a low mud wall.

The soldiers stopped firing and put their heads low when Jim's group added to the bullets flying toward them. Soon the bodies of at least twenty enemy soldiers were grouped around the sheds.

The roar of the gunfire faded, smoke drifting over the grass and bodies. A tense moment held, followed by movement from behind one of the sheds as a dirty white flag tied around the barrel of an AK-47 was waved back and forth.

"Cease fire! Cessez le feu!" Abraham yelled.

The shooting stopped. Men peered around the walls and huts where they were concealed. Dust and gun smoke floated in the air as an eerie stillness settled on the village.

"Jambi, tell the men to hold their fire, not to shoot unless shooting starts again," Jim said.

From cover point to cover point, Jim began to make his way over to where Abraham was crouching. He saw the brother begin to rise.

"Stay down!" Jim yelled. Abraham complied.

Jim rushed the last few yards to the wall concealing Abraham. He looked over to see soldiers peeking around the sheds and bodies. No one had come out yet.

"Anyone hurt?" Jim asked.

"A broken arm, some bumps and bruises. You?"

"One man shot, but in the leg, and it didn't look serious."

Abraham snapped his head around to look at Jim. "Where is he? We must go to him." Again he made to rise. Jim pushed him down.

"Back there, in the village." Jim motioned with his head. "Wait, though. What kind of resistance did you meet? Did you find the captives?"

"Thirty or so soldiers were killed, most in their sleep, in the barracks, by the local men. It looks like four or so sentries were eliminated as well. We found and freed sixty captives who were being held in huts under guard. We sent them up into the hills with the villagers."

"How many up there?" Jim asked, indicating the sheds.

"Ten, maybe?" Abraham said. "And, I believe, the general."

Jim looked over the wall. There was no movement from the soldiers.

"Looks like they're stalling," he said. "Those reinforcements could be here soon."

"Talk to Jambi and see if any of the villagers can help our wounded man. We may have other wounded as well, from the soldiers. I will attempt to speak to them," Abraham said, nodding at the sheds.

"All right, but stay under cover until I get into position," Jim ordered.

"Will do," Abraham replied. Noticing Tatame nearby, he acknowledged the young man, whose face was tight but determined. "Tatame, you good?" He gave him the thumbs-up sign. The young man gave a weak smile in return.

Jim turned and made his way back to his position. When he was beside Jambi, he waved to Abraham to go ahead and speak. Then he asked Jambi, "Do you have any doctors or healers in your village? We need to help our man who was shot."

Jambi nodded. "Some of the women can help him. I will send a man to find them."

"Send three men in case there are more soldiers in the village. We have these pinned down."

Jim turned his attention to the drying sheds. Abraham was just beginning to speak to the soldiers hidden there.

"Hello! English? Français?" Abraham's baritone voice carried across the beach clearing.

A moment passed. Then a voice answered, mature and with authority, in slightly accented English.

"Who are you? Why have you attacked us?"

"To whom am I speaking?" Abraham replied.

"General Kosoa, commander of the New Congolese Defense Forces. You have illegally killed soldiers of the liberation of the Democratic Republic of Congo! Therefore you are a criminal."

This guy is stalling, Jim thought, watching Abraham digest what the man had said. Then he turned to Jambi.

"Jambi, send more men to look out for boats coming in. I think this general is stalling for time. What do you think?"

"Yes, Jim. I think that as well. I will send men to watch. If they see boats, they will fire two shots."

As the men Jambi had picked went in opposite directions, Jim looked to the drying sheds. The soldiers were keeping themselves hidden as much as they could.

"Throw out your weapons," Abraham said. "You will not be harmed."

"You are a criminal who has committed murder! Surrender *your* weapons," the voice of General Kosoa said from one of the sheds.

Jim began to work his way around the huts to get a better view of the sheds. The exchange continued.

"You are surrounded, with nowhere to go, General. There does not need to be more bloodshed," Abraham said. "Surrender, and you and your men can live."

Jim peered around the corner of the hut farthest down the beach. Across the clearing, he saw a man he assumed was the general, crouched down, looking in Abraham's direction. He was talking to a soldier who had a cell phone up to his ear.

"Damn it," Jim said under his breath.

Two shots rang out from the hill behind Jim. The sentry must have seen a boat or boats approaching. As Jim watched, the general looked around, searching for something. The general had been playing for time. Even now, the relief force could be landing, ready to come up behind them.

"You will surrender now! The forces of the Congo will be merciful," the general shouted, a triumphant look on his face. He had picked up an RPG, a shoulder-fired rocket, and was aiming it at Abraham.

Those were his last words. Jim aimed and fired at the general. This action triggered the rest of the men to fire as well. The drying sheds were reduced to splinters.

The roar of the rifles subsided, and Jim could see only shattered wood and shattered men.

Before Jim could speak to Jambi, Abraham strode over, a furious look on his face.

"Why did you fire? I could have gotten those men to surrender. They didn't have to die! Jim, life—all life—is precious. You threw it away," Abraham said, pointing at the ruin of the sheds, anger and anguish clear on his face.

Jim got to his feet, grabbed Abraham by the sleeve with one hand, and gave him a shake.

"Listen to me!" he said. "Those two shots were the spotters I sent to watch for the relief force. By talking with you, the general and his men were stalling for time—time to land their other soldiers. The general was communicating by cell phone to coordinate the landing. He wasn't going to surrender. And he had an RPG pointed straight at you, Abe. That's why I shot him. He would have killed you!"

Jim released Abraham and continued, "They could be coming here to kill us all right now. This isn't a movie or a book, damn it. If you want to get us killed, then keep acting like there's a choice. Sometimes we kill them or they kill us. It's that simple."

Realization dawned on Abraham's face. He looked around, searching for the new threat.

"I'm sorry, Jim. I didn't . . . I should have . . ."

"There's no time, Abe," Jim said. He turned to Jambi and also Tatame, who had walked over to the group. "Separate the men into four teams of ten and reload—get magazines from the bodies if you need to. Securely tie the soldiers who surrendered or are wounded. Put three men on them."

They rushed to carry out his orders. Jim turned to see one of the men he'd sent to watch for reinforcements come up to Jambi and speak. Jambi sent him to Jim and Abraham.

"Les hommes arrivent, beaucoup d'hommes," the man said, pointing at the hill behind the village. "Soldats, soldats."

"What did he say?" Jim asked.

"He said many men are coming," Abraham translated, then turned back to the man. "Combien d'hommes?" Abraham listened to the man's response and turned back to Jim.

"Well?" Jim asked.

"Thirty or more men in one boat. They landed over the hill on a small beach, using an old fishing boat that they ran aground. They're moving slowly toward the village, and they will be here soon."

Jim thought quickly, sizing up the situation and his resources. He looked at the men around him, who were all waiting on him for answers, for a decision. It struck him that he had once again become a leader of men. And they were good men, better than he had known when they'd set off from the camp. Jambi and some of the senior men of the village, in particular, understood Jim's tactics and took his orders without questions, and they were quick and courageous.

"This is what we're going to do," Jim said and began to explain his plan.

Chapter 21

Colonel Keneyusu let his men take the lead to thread their way through the brush toward the village. The cell phone call from the general had been abruptly cut off as they were arranging the relief force's entry into the fight. A few soldiers had been found hiding in the forest and had told them about the attack, at least as much as they could tell, having run away: villagers and other men had attacked at dawn, and a man in brown robes had been with them.

The colonel told the fleeing men to fall in. He might need their guns in a moment. Their cowardice would be dealt with later.

Palm trees and scrub brush began to thin out as they approached the village. His men spread out, as concealed as they could be, before the cleared area. It had taken time to loop around and come from the opposite side from where they had landed. The colonel took out his small binoculars and scanned the village. He could see nothing moving.

In many raids before, he had preferred to hit ruthlessly, fast and hard, bringing surprise and ferocity to bear on unsuspecting people. It was much better to overwhelm resistance before it started. Unfortunately, that could not be the case now. Whoever had attacked the village knew that they were coming.

The colonel watched the village and tried to

perceive the best route to take. After escaping from the refugee camp following the humiliating defeat by ragged refugees and the terrible warrior with the brown-robed brother, he had to be cautious. He wouldn't get another chance. Men don't follow leaders who get them killed. Only by lying and saying that it was the Tanzanian army that had defeated the refugee camp raiding party had he been able to retain the slightest bit of dignity and obedience.

The escape had been easy, but the task ahead would be arduous. The quiet village was a lie. The colonel knew that what he was looking at could not be true. Though the peaceful scene before him did not look it, danger was in the air.

If he'd had more men, he would have split them to attack in two directions at once. But since his force was limited, he would try different tactics. He knew he was likely facing an ambush, so he needed the defenders to reveal themselves. He would have a few soldiers make their way to the opposite side of the village, open fire, and wait for a response. When the response came, he would have the defenders flanked and bring concentrated firepower to bear.

Watching and waiting as the soldiers moved to their positions, Colonel Keneyusu strained his senses. The heat of the day was rising, and he and the men began to sweat. No sound or shots came from the soldiers sent to draw out the defenders. The colonel was aware that the time allotted for the diversion had passed.

***

"I will go out to them," Abraham said, "and

entreat them to surrender or leave."

"Just sit tight, Abe," Jim said. "Any minute they are going to cross into the kill zone, and then this thing is over. We will have no more casualties of our people."

They watched from concealment in one of the thatch-walled huts that were raised from the earth on posts. Having seen the three soldiers detach from the main force, Jambi and Henda had slipped up and captured them. Jim appreciated the impressive stealth of the men who had been raised as hunters in the African bush. Others had quickly ushered the villagers and liberated captives up into the hills and small caves that only the villagers knew about, putting them out of harm's way.

"No," Abe said. "I can save them. It doesn't need to be this way. They don't know what they are walking into."

"That's the point, Abe," Jim said, exasperated. "It's called a tactical advantage. Now sit down and shut up."

Jim could feel the brother fuming beside him, wanting to avoid more bloodshed, but after the conflict on the beach, Jim knew that to do so might cost them lives. Whoever was in charge out there in the brush was waiting too. It had come down to a chess game. Would they withdraw or advance? The first one to move would lose.

The colonel had waited too long. The men had not fired the shots to start the operation. Had they been captured or killed? Had they run off? There was no way off the island, except by the number that only he could call. He was the only one who knew the cell number of the captain of the boat. But frightened men may run, even knowing they cannot escape.

He could sense the unease of the men. They were feeling the same way he was. So he had to make a decision. *Leaders lead*, he thought. *Right decision or wrong, just make a decision.*

"We will advance in groups of three to the edge of the village, spreading out and moving to the interior. Quickly!" he said to the sergeant, casting the die.

Jim saw movement from the trees and brush as three men rushed forward to the edge of the village, followed by three more men after the first group had crossed the open ground. He had expected this tactic, and as with the distraction force, he had told the men not to fire. If the reinforcements had advanced as a group, the concealed men would have opened fire, catching them when they were most vulnerable. Since the attackers had chosen to distribute their advance, the men in place would stay put, not moving until the group had passed or they were discovered.

The group of soldiers passed into the village, searching but finding nobody. They did find the places where bodies had fallen when soldiers were killed. Bloodstains and shell casings littered the ground.

The group made its way through the village to the beach where the gun battle at the fish-drying sheds had occurred. Colonel Keneyusu motioned two soldiers to go investigate the pile of bodies there, then turned the others back toward the village. The quiet was eerie and the stillness enveloping.

"Don't relax. It could be a trap," the colonel said, thinking, *Is it possible that the raiders have left?*

The men grasped their rifles and scanned the apparently empty village. Behind them, the men at the pile of bodies waved the all-clear.

What next? the colonel thought. *Did they all leave?*

The men were looking to him for guidance, guidance that he was expected to give them. He ordered them to advance to the drying huts. Looking down at the soldiers and former comrades who had been killed, one of them reached down and pulled a rifle from the pile of bodies.

An enormous explosion followed from the grenades that had been wired and buried under the sand.

The hot grains blinded the men. Living soldiers wrenched and dropped to the ground beside their brothers, desperately clawing at their eyes and screaming. Immediately, gunfire erupted from underneath every hut ringing the beach clearing, bathing the ground in a lethal onslaught that decimated the soldiers blindly trapped in the open.

Jim rushed forward with the five men from the outer perimeter to engage the soldiers from behind. The explosion had been their signal to attack while the opposing force was stunned.

The booby-trapped bodies had been a quick job with the grenades found in the weapons cache in the village. All the time the bodies were being moved and the grenades hidden, Jim had thought the relief force would arrive at any moment.

Abraham had expressed his displeasure and distaste for the act through his body language and glowering look. Still, Jim was the combat leader who so far had kept all of the men alive.

Firing and maneuvering, the men were able to quickly overwhelm the bewildered soldiers. What was once a peaceful morning on the island had been turned into a killing ground.

"Move right!" Jim shouted to Tatame, motioning at a knot of soldiers trying to hide behind a hut.

Jim grabbed Henda and Jambi to follow him in a flanking maneuver. A soldier peered around the corner of a hut and was shot by Henda. Then, working their way opposite Tatame, they cleared three more soldiers trying to hide.

Once they had reached the edge of the clearing, Jim looked back. The firing had slowed to sporadic pops. Gun smoke and dust floated across the beach. Two battles in one day had been fought on these sands, and the toll on the slaver soldiers had been terrible. Bodies lay strewn about, men moaning in surrender, blood soaking into the sand.

Jim moved to Jambi's side.

"We work our way back along the huts," Jim said. "Tell the men in those positions to reload and remain where they are. We will start searching the village for surviving soldiers."

They moved from cover to cover. Wide-eyed stares greeted them from the men in the firing positions, men who had never been able to fight back but had now found that they could—and that they could win.

"Tu vas bien, mon ange? You good, angel?" Jambi asked each man as he and Jim stopped and explained the instructions. Smiles and thumbs-up signs came from the men, and they began to chant: "Anges! Anges Destructeurs!"

Anges Destructeurs.

Jim needed no translation.

Destroying Angels.

Why did he want to name them that? Jim thought, then answered himself. *To give them something, anything to hang their confidence on. Something to fight for.*

Again, miraculously, no one was killed on the side of the Angels. Two men had lost fingers and one an ear from the fight; however, they seemed unconcerned with the small injuries. At least in comparison to dying, they were small. The soldiers were not so lucky. The ones who had not died immediately in the explosion or firefight were being searched over by Henda and Jambi and some other men.

Finally Jim sat down on the stoop of a hut facing the beach, completely exhausted. The area had been made reasonably secure. Two teams of ten men each had been sent out to search the village and scour the island for any survivors not already accounted for. Word had been taken to the villagers and the former captives that it was safe enough to come back. The wounded soldiers had been rounded up and were receiving what medical care Abraham could provide.

The Angels had begun to sing in their triumph over death and fear and oppression. They had won a victory over being powerless and small in a place where to be helpless and small was to be prey.

"Anges! Anges! Anges!" the men chanted, holding their rifles in the air.

Jim smiled. He knew he should get up to restore

order and make sure no counterattack occurred, however unlikely. Pushing through his exhaustion, he stood, leaning against the hut as he was light-headed for a moment.

"Stop, stop!" Jim heard Abraham's voice shout. "Stop them, save them!"

Jim looked to see Abraham running up to the beach. He was yelling at Jambi and Henda, who were about to put the wounded soldiers there out of their misery. The two men looked up in confusion. Jim sighed and made his body pick up his rifle and trot over to where Abraham stood amid the bodies.

"Stop, Henda!" Jim said. "Tie them. We will deal with them soon."

Tears were in Abraham's eyes as he looked at the destruction and death around him. The smell of smoke, fire, blood, and shit was in the air, a battlefield smell as old as time.

"What have we done, Jim?" Abraham's deep voice was quivering with emotion. "This is what we wrought? This, this death?"

Jim looked at his friend, confused; then clarity began to sink in. It was all well and good to free people and help people in need without knowing the cost. The past days had been a whirlwind: first the attack on the camp, then the counterattack that had freed the first captives, then the dogged pursuit to the island. It was overwhelming, and the toll on his body that Jim had pushed down, pushed away, began creeping back in.

Little sleep, little food, and the constant adrenaline dump were making Jim's brain burn. He couldn't rest, though, and he certainly didn't have energy to spare for grieving dead slavers. All that could be done to preserve life had been done.

"Abe, we still need to make sure we are secure."

"Oh God, forgive us. Forgive us sinners upon this earth. Let us be saved by Your grace." Abraham's deep powerful voice rose, tinged with sorrow, as he raised his hands to the sky. People began gathering around the brother as he preached. Then the crowd began to swell. *It must be the captives and the villagers*, Jim realized. Quickly he and Abraham were surrounded by at least two hundred people.

Abraham went on, beseeching God to take the dead slavers into His forgiveness, into His holy heart. The crowd murmured and swayed, the voice of Abraham touching them even if they did not understand some of the words.

Jim watched as his friend worked himself up into an emotional state. In the months they had shared together, he had only seen Abraham this agitated on the night of the lions. If Abraham was even aware of the crowd, he did not show it. Copious tears ran down his face. Then his eyes flashed from intense concentration to dissociated blankness.

"Oh God," he said, bowing his head, and then fell silent. A moment passed, then another. Jim felt the weight of the silence.

"Oh God, we who are Your children reach out to You," Abraham said at last, raising his arms, facing the center of the crowd. "We thank You for Your mercy and Your guidance, for keeping our Angels alive, for leading us into a righteous battle. *But is this Your will, Oh Lord? This necessary destruction?*" Abraham was now shouting at the sky. The crowd took a collective breath at the volume and power in his voice.

Jim's eyes lost focus and he felt light-headed again. Feeling himself swoon, he took a knee, his rifle butt to the ground. Vaguely, from the corner of his eye, he saw Henda, Jambi, Tatame, and other Angels kneel beside him.

"Did we do right, oh Lord? Did we do enough? Did we do Your will?" Abraham continued.

Jim felt the restful pose start to relax him. His eyes drooped. If he could only rest them for a moment, he thought, he would be all right. He leaned his forehead against his hand on his rifle. The stress of combat was calling for its due. His body desperately wanted to rest as the last of the adrenaline and energy washed out of him.

"What is Your will now, oh Lord? What would You have us do?" Abraham prayed.

A slight cough in front of Jim brought his eyes open in an instant. A soldier lying in front of Jim, at Abraham's feet, was stirring. Instantly Henda and Jambi were on their feet, alert to the danger the soldier represented to them as well as Abraham. Jambi drew his club and moved forward but was halted by Abraham.

"Stop!" Abraham said, his voice strong and sure. Jambi stepped back but still held his log at the ready.

Abraham knelt by the soldier, who moaned as his head was taken gently in Abraham's hand.

"L'eau, l'eau," the man groaned.

Jim thought that the man was just babbling, but apparently he was asking for water, because Abraham reached out his hand to Henda, who gave him his canteen after unscrewing the cap. Abraham brought the canteen to the soldier's lips and dribbled water onto his mouth. The soldier's mouth was slack, then moved as he began to drink.

Jim looked at Abraham, whose face was a mask of concentration and concern as he kept giving the soldier sips of water until the soldier's head sank back into Abraham's hand. The man's dark skin was pale from blood loss, his breathing shallow. His camouflage uniform shirt was torn and soaked with blood. Open wounds were weeping. His death was not far.

"Merci," the man whispered, his eyes open but distant.

Abraham nodded and breathed deeply, closing his eyes. He raised his free hand to the sky, fingers outstretched. Jim and the crowd around him were silent. Then, after a long moment, Abraham set his large hand upon the man's chest and began to whisper.

"Dear God in Heaven, use me, Your servant, as Your vessel. Accept my humble being to do Your work. Fill me with Your divine power and blessing. Heal this man and make him whole. Show Your forgiveness to those who have done evil and turned their faces away from You."

Jim watched the scene, riveted by the faith and solemnness of his friend. The hairs on his arms stood up, and he felt a chill go down his back despite the heat.

"Let love win in this place of evil and death. Let Your light fill me with the Holy Spirit. Pass through me to this man and make him whole."

The man in Abraham's hands was stirring. His breathing appeared to become deeper and more vital. Abraham's body was trembling. Jim watched the man's wounds as they seemed to slow their weeping of blood. The man's color was improving, from a pale bluish tinge to a darker, more robust color.

No way! Jim thought. *I am not seeing what I am*

seeing.

The crowd was seeing it too. As Jim watched, people wept and held their hands up to the sky, whispering in different languages.

"My son, you are healed by the grace of God," Abraham said, his voice shaking.

This is not happening, Jim thought.

Abraham took the man's forearm and helped him to stand, supporting him as he looked around at the crowd of people, many now on their knees.

"I live," the man said, then fell to his knees as well, raising his hands to Abraham.

Chapter 22

Jim slept soundly through the night. Carrying his rifle, he stepped out into the morning. The bodies had been cleared away from the beach and village, presumably to be buried in the hills. The soldiers who had surrendered were confined to a stone building. After witnessing the miracle of the soldier, many had asked to be baptized, and Abraham was happy to oblige.

Children were about, running and playing. The absence of the soldiers had allowed for the start of normalcy. It was amazing how fast the children went back to childhood, and Jim wondered at their resilience.

As he walked through the village, people waved and came up to him. Some seemed to want to touch him, be near him. Some appeared frightened, and Jim couldn't blame them. The day before had been a terrible day.

"Merci, ange," Gérard said, handing him a banana leaf of rice.

"Thank you, thank you," others said.

Jim continued walking as he ate, not knowing how to deal with either the happy looks or the frightened ones. He saw Tatame and Jambi together, talking and looking around. He went to them.

"Tatame, Jambi, how are things?"

"There are no more soldiers in the village," Jambi said.

"Two parties went to the hills and found three

soldiers," Tatame said. "Father Lion instructed us to take them alive."

"Any make it back?"

Jambi shrugged. "They are where they need to be. They are no longer a problem. They are confined with the others."

"Where is Abraham?" Jim asked.

"He retired to a hut," Tatame said. "I believe he is resting now."

"Where are the soldiers' bodies?" Jim asked.

"Buried," Jambi replied.

"The equipment, weapons, ammunition?"

"We have gathered all we could find. We also have moved it, along with the other supplies, to a hut for storage. The medical supplies we are using for wounded persons. There also was a good deal of money. It is under guard too," Tatame said. "The soldiers will be tried and their punishment determined. It has been decided by the people of the island. Please do not interfere. We are capable of both mercy and justice."

"Show me where Abraham is, please," Jim said.

Jim followed Tatame to a hut on the outskirts of the village, thanked him, and went into the small structure. He found Abraham seated on the floor. His eyes were closed, but he did not seem to be asleep.

"Knock, knock," Jim said to announce himself.

"Come in, Jim," Abraham said without opening his eyes. "Have a seat."

"You feel all right?" Jim asked, sitting on the hut floor.

"As well as can be expected," Abraham said, his eyes opening.

"That was quite something last night."

"Yes, it was. I felt filled as I never have before. I felt God working through me."

"Was it a miracle?"

"To the man it was, and to the people who watched."

"What now?" Jim asked. "You know the islanders are going to try the soldiers?"

Abraham paused before answering.

"Yes. They are the authority here. Justice must be served. As to what happens now, I have been sitting here thinking of that same question," Abraham said. "We have accomplished more than I ever would have thought possible. I was acting from instinct, to protect. I did not know it would lead here."

Jim waited as Abraham gathered his thoughts.

"What would you do so that people could protect themselves when we have gone?" Abraham asked.

"Train them, I guess. Give them weapons and supplies. Teach them to fight. To survive."

"That has been the way of the past, I suppose: either protect them or teach them to protect themselves. Gérard says that the slavers we encountered are not isolated. Miners are needed for all types of minerals. There are large and small operations all over the countryside. The oppressors and the oppressed are everywhere."

"Is it our fight?"

"Apparently it is now, if we pick up the quest."

"Is that what you want to do?" Jim asked.

"Is it what *you* want to do?" Abraham countered. "Do you want to stay here? Go home? Go back to flying? What?"

Jim considered where his life had taken him. There

wasn't really anything to go back to. That choice had been made.

"You could start over, you know," Abraham said finally.

"What do you mean?"

"This doesn't have to be your fight. You have skills that others need. You could disappear. The world is a big place."

"You trying to get rid of me?"

"I'm trying to give you a chance, maybe your last one. I have decided I will help the people I can until I can't help them anymore. These people, the people I will encounter."

"You plan on fighting to do that? This isn't a place where you can go halfway. You've seen what it looks like, how it's most likely to be: ruthless, dirty, and tough."

"I understand what the fighting will involve, Jim. The question is, are you willing to stay or do you want to go?"

Jim considered the question as he looked at his friend, his savior.

"That was decided when you saved me, Abe. I was dead, and you brought me back. For me, you were a miracle that I had absolutely no right to. I should have died a hundred ways in the jungle, and I didn't. I'm not going anywhere. If you'll have me, then I'll stay with you till the end. I won't say that I believe in everything you do, but I believe in you."

Abraham smiled. "Well, let's figure out what it is that we are going to do and how we are going to do it. Some of the men, if not most, will want to go back to their families. So we should return to the camp, if only to see what is happening there."

"Why don't you talk with Tatame and see what we need to do to move?" Jim suggested.

In a dusty government office in Kinshasa, the capital city of Congo, a telephone rang on an uncluttered desk. A trim man with wire-rimmed glasses answered.

"Bonjour, Bureau de L'Agriculture. Sous-Ministre Tomas," the man said in a pleasant tone.

"Tomas, we have a problem." Colonel Keneyusu's voice came through the line. He was weary from his escape. His luck had held when the soldiers around him had surrendered. Evading capture in the forest, he had waited until nightfall, then swum the two miles to shore.

"Colonel, how are you? Is the general well?"

"The general is dead."

"Terrible news," the colonel said, adding with a grin, "Was it someone he ate?"

"The issue is more dire than that. We were attacked twice: once at a camp while gathering new recruits and once at our processing center."

"Attacked, you say? Who attacked you?"

"A well-trained and well-supplied force of overwhelming numbers. Revolutionaries."

"Revolutionaries? There are so many of those now. What do they call themselves?"

There was a pause as Colonel Keneyusu considered this.

"Angels. Angels of Revolution of the Democratic Republic of Congo."

"Angels? Like religious angels? Like Michael, Raphael?" Tomas's tone was calm and unconcerned.

"Like avenging angels. They are led by a priest—a foreign priest—and a foreign soldier who is called the Angel of Death," Colonel Keneyusu replied, suppressing the anger he felt.

The colonel could not admit to Tomas or anyone else that barely trained refugees, led by an unknown foreigner and a religious zealot newly walked out of the jungle, had decimated his force of more than three hundred trained soldiers.

"Do these leaders have actual names or just noms de guerre?"

"The priest was referred to as Père Lion. He has scars on his chest that look to be from a lion. The foreign soldier was referred to as Jim. He sounded American."

"Really? How many men did you lose to this Father Lion and the Angels? Sounds like a pop group from Nigeria."

"Tomas, they eliminated almost all of the men!"

"All of them? Three hundred men?" Tomas replied, losing his humorous tone.

"Yes. You see now? This is serious."

"How were you able to survive?"

"Superior tactics."

"Are they Special Forces? These Americans? These Angels?"

"Maybe, I don't know. They worked with Congolese men."

"Hmmm," Tomas said, considering the colonel's news in a new light. "Very well, I will investigate. Where are you now?"

"Kabinda, the Grand Hotel."

"Stay there until I call you," Tomas said, ending the call.

Tomas hung up the telephone and sat back in his chair. He swiveled around, looking out the small, dirty window of his office at the dusty streets of Kinshasa. The loss of the soldiers was a setback but could be overcome. Soldiers were everywhere in Congo. The loss of the workers at the various mines around the countryside was more critical. He had contracts with the owners to deliver workers, lucrative contracts from businessmen both local and foreign. They would be unsympathetic to the new developments. They only wanted results.

Tomas rifled through his desk and withdrew a small book. He perused the notations, picked up the telephone, and made a call.

Surprisingly few men went back with Abraham. Those who did took messages to the families and friends of those who stayed behind. The islanders were more than happy to have more men on the island in case more soldiers showed up.

One early morning, Jim went with the remaining men on a run around the island to assess their fitness level and resolve. He himself felt winded occasionally but did his best not to show it. He knew that being in shape would come back. Jim threw himself into the training. His body became more fit as the days and weeks went by. The days consisted of running and calisthenics in the morning, followed by weapons and hand-to-hand combat training in the afternoon. He also taught basic soldiering skills such as shooting and mission discipline, first aid, and keeping a camp sanitary. The experienced soldiers helped bring the others along, and Jim, while he had never been a drill sergeant, turned out to have a natural ability to shape the men into a fighting unit. The men began to communicate with Jim through a patois of the English they had learned and the French Jim was picking up.

Fifty-two men and sixteen women were training. Tatame and Henda were each the leader of a squad. Henda was a natural, an old soldier full of tricks after a lifetime of fighting one way or another across the continent of Africa; Tatame, though younger, showed his intelligence and discipline and quickly gained his men's respect.

Abraham returned to find the units shaping up. He arrived by motorized canoe, driven by Gérard. Striding up the beach, he grabbed Jim in a bear hug.

"How goes it, Abraham?" Jim asked.

The men were doing maneuvers on the island. Tatame's squad was tracking and finding Henda's. The new leaders needed to learn how to operate without direct oversight by solving the myriad problems of moving through the countryside by themselves.

"You will never believe it, Jim."

"What?"

"A church is being built."

"What church? Where?"

"The people of the camp were so inspired, they have decided to build a church: L'Église des Anges et des Lions, the Church of Angels and Lions. They are filled with the love of God," Abraham said, smiling at Jim.

"Father Michael? How is he?"

"He is well, happy for the church and the hope it gives people."

"You know that our streak of not taking any losses

won't continue," Jim said. "It's been amazing that we haven't lost anyone yet."

"I am aware—more than aware—of the risks of combat. We have definitely been blessed so far," Abraham replied.

Jim turned away to look out to the village. People were going about their day, children playing. The scene was from another time, red dirt paths winding through thatch huts. The deep blue of the lake in the distance was peaceful.

"It's a nice place here, but we can't stay, not for very long, anyway. Sooner or later, someone will be missing the soldiers who got killed," Jim stated.

"I agree. The soldiers were either working for someone or working for themselves. Either means that someone's money got disrupted. Father Michael was explaining that usually these groups have some sort of connection to or protection from the government, maybe not officially, but someone who can pull strings."

"We need to do what we can to get them ready to protect themselves if necessary. We have enough weapons, and they can set up sentries to watch for other soldiers. With cell phones, we can keep in touch. We will need to get some more of those," Jim said.

"It's a new world: cell phones in the rural African countryside." Abraham stood and stretched his back. "Father Michael told me more news. There is another rebel camp, inland from here. I propose I go investigate and see what I can find out while you continue with the training. I can move through the land more quickly than the group and can move among the people more discreetly."

"Abraham," Jim said, looking at his friend, "where

does this end?"
"Where it has to, Jim. Where it has to."

Chapter 23

The target camp was based some twenty miles inland from Lake Tanganyika, in Congo. The groups of armed men and women moved slowly after being put ashore well south of Kalemie, a small town on the banks of the lake. Henda and Jambi functioned as scouts, making sure trails and roads were clear while the main column moved carefully behind. Henda's knowledge of routes and water sources was proving invaluable as they moved through the countryside.

They numbered a hundred fighters, split into two bands currently moving as one. The weeks of training had hardened them and brought them closer together.

Avoiding the small settlements and farms that dotted the countryside was easier than Jim would have thought, with Henda and Tatame leading them. However, he was not so naive as to believe that their passing would go completely unnoticed. So when the hottest part of the day started in midmorning, Jim called a halt and secluded the group in a copse of vegetation and trees that Henda led them to.

"Tatame, find out what Henda says about the distance to the camp," Jim said, looking over the group, quietly relaxing after the arduous march. With no ready source of clean water, he needed to ensure they did not become dehydrated and start losing people.

"About six kilometers more," Tatame translated,

pointing in the direction of the green hills west of them.

"How many soldiers?" Jim asked.

"There are about a hundred, with very little discipline. They are young. Some are only boys," Tatame said, taking a drink from his canteen.

"Do you think we can surprise them? Make them surrender?" Jim asked. He did not like the idea of fighting children, even lethal ones.

"Maybe. I don't know, but maybe," Tatame continued. "They are Mai-Mai. Most of the boys were probably taken from their homes by force. They are ruled by fear and dulled by drugs."

"Where are we supposed to meet Father Abraham?" Jambi asked.

"We are where we are supposed to be. He should have been here waiting for us," Tatame said. "We are south of a small village, Kindagu. He was supposed to meet us there."

The meeting had been arranged before Abraham had left on his scouting mission, but he had not been in contact since, though he had promised to send word when he could.

"All right, everyone: rest up, be quiet, and put out a perimeter guard. No talking," Jim said. "We will wait for him to get back, and then I will go with him."

Jim approached the village cautiously. Henda was a shadow through the trees. Jim had quickly learned to appreciate the older man's skill at moving through the landscape.

The village was nestled between hills. A small, single-track dirt road wound down one hillside and up another, passing through the town. A small brick shack with a thatched roof appeared to be a store. About ten structures nestled in the small valley made up the village. Small plots of gardens were alongside each house. Jim smelled woodsmoke and meat cooking but did not see any movement.

Jim looked to Henda for his opinion. The older man's gaze was steady, and he didn't move a muscle as he regarded the village. Jim drew a breath, preparing to speak.

"Sssss," Henda quietly hissed as he held up a warning hand to the younger man.

Jim followed the motion of Henda's hand as it slowly moved to point at the village. Jim saw what looked like a trash bonfire, but the pieces smoldering on it didn't look like wood.

Henda motioned for Jim to follow him as he made his way into the vegetation around the village until coming to a concealed spot a couple of hundred yards from the village store. They saw two men, dressed in fatigues, sitting at a plastic table on white plastic chairs, drinking beer. Their rifles were leaned up against the table. They appeared to be somewhat drunk and dozing in the afternoon sun. Jim didn't like the scene and sensed that Henda felt the same.

Jim waited, concealed in the brush, and watched the two soldiers drowse. The combination of the beer and the sunshine seemed to have overcome any training they'd had.

Jim heard faint crying coming from the store. He and Henda looked at each other. They both had heard the noise. After checking to see that the soldiers were still asleep, they made their way to the back of the hut, being careful to keep themselves concealed. Walking to the side of the shack, Jim looked in. An old woman sat holding her head and softly weeping.

"Grandmother," Henda said softly when he was beside her. "Grandmother, what has happened here?"

The woman looked up, rapidly drawing in a breath. She glanced at Jim, his webbing gear with ammunition, his rifle.

"No, soldier, don't hurt me," the woman pleaded with Henda, her voice quiet. "I'm not young. Don't hurt me."

"Grandmother, I will not hurt you. I am not one of the soldiers," Henda said, placing his hand on the woman's shoulder.

"No? Why not? You look like a soldier," the woman said, regarding him with her deep-set dark brown eyes.

"I'm looking for my friend, a brother in robes."

"The brother?" the woman asked. "Abraham?"

"Yes," Jim said. "Do you know him?"

"He was here," she said. "He was here when the soldiers came. They rounded everyone up, everyone who could work. They took them away. Brother Abraham protested, and they beat him."

"Did they kill him?" Jim asked, feeling dread. He wondered suddenly about the fire.

"No. He prayed at them, and it made them angry, but they didn't kill him. They took him with the others. The men from the radio."

"What men from the radio?"

"From the radio station. They were doing a story about farm communities. They hid their equipment before they were taken."

"What about the soldiers at the store?"

"They were supposed to wait and see if any of the villagers came back from hiding in the hills. They decided to drink beer."

"Are they going to be picked up or walk back?"

"I heard the other soldier say they would pick them up tonight, along with any villagers who might have come back and been captured."

"How many were taken?"

"Around twenty-five adults and fifteen children. I'm not sure. Some people ran off and hid in the hills. My feet won't let me run."

"You have done well, Grandmother," Henda said.

Jim took the sleeping soldiers' rifles and then woke the men with the butt of his own rifle while Henda stood guard. The men lay dazed as their uniforms were stripped off, their hands tied securely behind their backs, and sacks placed over their heads. Henda and Jim then dragged them into the back of the store.

Once this was accomplished, Jim took off, running into the brush, leaving Henda to watch the village. It did not take very long to come upon where the group was waiting. Jim relayed what had happened and described the beginnings of a plan.

"How long ago did this happen?" Tatame asked.

"Earlier today. The soldiers came early in the morning and were in the village before many people were up," Jim replied, keeping his eyes lowered.

"How many villagers did she say?" Tatame asked.

"About twenty-five adults and fifteen children. Plus the radio men."

"Radio men? Like reporters, news people?" Tatame asked.

"Yes," Jim said. "She said they were doing a story. We will have to move quickly and free the villagers tonight. It seems strange that the soldiers would take people from a village close to them. It has to be because there is a shortage of workers and captives. No force can exist comfortably in an area where the local populace opposes them." Jim was thinking out loud.

"What should we do?" Tatame asked.

"If we knew more about the camp, we could plan more efficiently," Jim said. "A basic combat tenet is not to split your forces unless you gain a tactical advantage. But they will send a vehicle for the soldiers this evening, and if that vehicle doesn't return, they will send someone to look for it. This reduces their men. If they send out a large force, then that leaves a smaller force at the camp. Both could work in our favor."

"So we split our force, then?" Tatame asked.

"Yes, I think so. You and Henda will take your groups to observe the camp. When you arrive, you will call me and describe the layout. You are not to engage. My group will go back to the village, capture the vehicle and soldiers, and hold them. You will then call me to let me know what the camp does and how many of the forces are sent out. Understood?"

Both Henda and Tatame nodded.

"Keep your main force out of sight. Only let a couple of observers watch. There's less chance of detection that way. No fires, no talking, and no smoking. It all hinges on surprise."

Jim stood, motioned to his group of men, and headed off in the direction of the village at a quick pace. Henda and Tatame briefed their troops.

***

Jim observed the village; it appeared deserted. He could see no people, and nothing was moving. He wondered if they were too late. Concealing themselves in the brush at the edge where the trees gave way to cleared land, they waited. For twenty minutes they observed, looking for any indication that troops were hiding.

As Jim turned to speak with Jambi to tell him to get ready to move, a slight noise made him turn back to the village. Henda, who had returned to guide them, was standing less than four feet behind him, smiling. Jim jumped, startled by the silent approach of the old hunter, and then shook his head, smiling. Henda turned and walked to the village, and the rest of the men followed.

"Which direction will they come from?" Jim asked Henda. "We need to conceal ourselves and engage with overwhelming force. If we can make them surrender, it's better."

"Less blood on the uniforms," Jambi said, nodding.

"Well, there is that," Jim said.

Jim reached into his pocket and retrieved a vibrating cell phone. He glanced to where the team had concealed themselves, to make sure they were ready.

"Yes," Jim said into the phone.

"Two vehicles, six men. Twenty minutes away," Tatame said. "Approximately forty soldiers were left in camp. It's in a valley with two approach points, two concealment points. Light guard, tents in the middle."

"Stay put," Jim said, then shut off the cell to end the call.

Jim caught Henda's eye and nodded at him. They

were set to take the vehicles and men once they were stopped.

The soldiers in the truck and jeep were easy to take. They were all high and reeking of marijuana. As the truck pulled to a stop in the middle of the village, they were suddenly surrounded by fifty-two men pointing rifles at their heads. Some of the Angels pulled the men roughly from the vehicles and forced them to lie facedown in a row. One soldier started to argue and protest, but after Jambi laid the razor-sharp edge of his machete on the back of the soldier's neck, he calmed down.

The men were quickly stripped to their underclothes and tied securely. Lifelong fishermen, they might not have been able to march in perfect formation, but they knew their knots. Securely trussed, the soldiers were left under guard in a hut. Their cell phones, confiscated, were placed in a bag.

Jim called Tatame's cell phone and arranged to meet two kilometers from the camp.

Ten of the Angels would be left to stay with the prisoners in the village. Donning their mishmash of uniforms, the rest headed out, some in the jeep with Jambi and Henda, some in the back of the truck. The vehicles growled and bounced on the rough dirt road. Though it was dusk, following the tracks of the truck back to the camp was a simple task.

A figure stepped out from the woods near the road and waved the convoy down. Jim stepped out to see Tatame walking toward the jeep.

"No problems?" Tatame asked Jim.

"No, they were fairly high, no casualties or

injuries. Have you located Abraham?"

"I haven't seen him yet, but there is a wooden structure in the middle of the camp. It appears to be where the captives are."

"Take me to an overlook to see the camp. Is Henda in position?"

"He and his troops are moving into position after making a large loop around the camp. When we attack, we plan on having a strike force move in as close as possible and set off a distraction. They will attack from that side, from concealment. He has a cell phone. And they will wait until we initiate the attack."

"You're starting to think like a soldier," Jim said. "Let's take a look. Henda, Jambi, with me. The rest stay and wait. Be quiet."

The men worked their way through small hills until arriving at the overlook. A bright moon had risen and gave enough light to see the general layout of the camp. Jim considered his options.

"Jambi," Jim said, turning to him, "you, Henda, and I will work our way as close as we can to the center hut. You two lead the way. I want to get as close to the prisoners as possible before we attack. If we can get them out without being discovered, great. If not, we need to protect them."

"What about the distraction?"

"You'll take two men with you. Have one drive the truck and one drive the jeep. Find a narrow point in the road and leave the truck. Wait an hour, then drive in, fire a few shots, then drive away. When the soldiers follow you, leave the truck behind blocking the road so you can get away. The more soldiers you can pull out of position, the easier it will be for us when we attack."

The men nodded their understanding. After putting the others in position, they worked their way quietly toward the camp.

The air was heavy and still in the darkness. Jim felt his shirt become soaked as they moved through the brush and grass toward the camp. There was no movement and no indication of any sentries.

At the edge of the camp, they stopped. Jim motioned to Henda to scout the path to the center huts. The old hunter slipped away. Jim and Jambi waited in the darkness and the heat, their ears and eyes searching for anything that would give them away.

A hissing sound pulled Jim's attention, and he turned to see Henda motioning from the shadow of a hut. Jim and Jambi crept, following the man who moved like a shadow. As they passed into the camp, Jim wondered at the lack of basic discipline. He couldn't see any sentries or guards. He could hear murmurs and snores from the tents lining the path they were on.

It was a short walk. Here a sentry was at the door, but he was sleeping and was quickly dispatched by Jambi with the butt of his rifle. Jim made his way to the door and lifted the latch and lock mechanism.

"Abe," he said quietly to the darkness within. "Abe."

"Where have you been, my friend?" Abraham's voice came from the shadows.

Jim turned to the voice and reached out his hand. Abraham grasped and squeezed it.

"Are you hurt? Can you move?" Jim asked, concerned. He could see the outline of his friend, but a thorough examination would need more light.

"Bumps and bruises. Seems I'm better at avoiding

bullets than rifle butts. Yourself?"

"I'm fine. Multiple strike teams are in position. How many people are here?"

"About sixty, in different buildings. Twenty or so men from the village are in this enclosure."

Jim looked to the darkness. He could see the shapes of men but not their faces. Some were waking up and moving. He knew he had to get them out before the camp became aware of their infiltration.

"We only have about twenty minutes left until a distraction will happen and wake everyone up," he said. "Is everyone able to move from here?"

"I think so. How far do we need to go?"

"About half a mile should do, just to get them out. Where are the others?"

"I'm not sure. The women are held somewhere else. They—they are being abused, I think," Abraham said, then indicated the man beside him. "Joshua here is a reporter. You see, Joshua, I told you God would provide."

"Get these men ready to go," Jim said quietly. "Henda and Jambi will lead them out. I will search for the women. Is there a man from the village who can go with me to find them?"

"I don't know . . ." Abraham was hesitant. "They're pretty scared and beat up."

"I can go with him," Joshua said from the darkness. "I was taken with the other villagers and met many of them."

"You're from the village?" Jim asked Joshua.

"He's a reporter who was in the village," Abraham said.

"A reporter?" Jim asked. "For television?"

"Radio," Joshua replied. "Radio reaches everywhere. People don't have to have a TV."

"Then you're with me. Abraham, explain to the men what's happening. I'll tell Henda and Jambi. We leave in one minute."

Followed by Joshua, Jim exited the hut and spoke with Henda and Jambi. He then moved off farther into the camp. Moving slowly, he scanned the remaining structures. A small hut caught his notice, and he began moving toward it. He was uncomfortably aware of Joshua bumping around behind him. The man was not used to moving quietly.

Maybe I should have left him, Jim thought.

Approaching the hut, Jim realized he had moved through the camp and was on the other side. Moments ticked by as Jim tried to estimate how much time was left before the trucks rolled up and woke everyone.

"Ten more minutes," Jim said under his breath.

"What?" Joshua asked at his shoulder.

"I only need ten more minutes or so, and I don't have it," Jim said.

"Can you call?" Joshua asked.

"Oh, I'm so stupid," Jim said. The cell phone was in his pocket, and he dug it out, trying to shield the glow that seemed so bright. Jim dialed the number for Tatame, hoping he would pick up. One ring was followed by two more.

"Hello." Tatame's voice in his ear.

"Tatame, stop the trucks if you can. We need more time. Do it now. Wait for firing or for my next call," Jim whispered into the telephone.

Jim pushed the button to disconnect the call.

"Hang back here and wait for me to move you up,"

he said to Joshua. "I'm going to scout and see if they have a sentry on that door."

Jim moved, scanning for any sign of life. At that moment, his luck ran out. Firing erupted from the road in front of the camp.

"Damn," he said under his breath.

Two sentries moved out of the shadows in front of the hut. Both stared at Jim. He was completely exposed in the moonlight. Jim dropped to one knee, bringing his rifle up to his shoulder. As the soldiers began to raise their rifles, he fired two bursts, catching them in their chests. Jim made sure the men were down and then waved to Joshua to come up.

He hated that he'd had to kill the sentries, but he'd had no choice.

He and Joshua moved to the door of the hut and peered in. The sound of women crying and moaning in fear came from the darkness within as Jim pushed open the door and went inside.

"Joshua, speak to them. Let them know we will not hurt them but that they are in danger. Keep them quiet!" Jim delivered the instructions rapidly while he took position near the door to watch for other soldiers.

Joshua hurried inside and began to speak in calming French and English to the women. Jim heard them quiet down as shouts and sounds of rifle fire came from the camp. No one seemed to be investigating the shots he had fired. The men he saw in the moonlight were rushing to the front of the camp.

"They remember me," Joshua said at his side.

"We will move out and get away from here. Do you know how to fire one of those?" Jim asked, indicating the guard's rifle on the ground.

"No, not really," Joshua said.

"I do," said a woman's voice behind them.

Both men turned to see a thin woman dressed in a torn cotton blouse and shorts. She wore no shoes. She passed the men and picked up one of the rifles. With apparent experience, she slid back the bolt to see that a round was chambered and clicked off the safety.

"What's your name?" Jim asked the woman.

"Beautiful," she said, the grim look on her face belying the name.

"Okay, Beautiful, stay in the back and help the women keep up. If you see anyone try to stop us, fire on them. Try and make sure they are the soldiers and not my men, though."

Beautiful nodded and went back inside the hut to get the women moving.

"Joshua, pick up the other rifle and some magazines. Help move the women along. Don't point the rifle at anything or anyone you don't want to kill."

The brief instructions were all Jim could spare. They had to keep moving and get clear of the camp. He didn't want to get caught in a crossfire or shot by mistake.

"We are ready," Beautiful said to Jim, holding her rifle in a practiced manner.

Without further words, Jim moved out of the hut, rifle ready, scanning for danger. Twenty feet away, he took a knee and signaled for the women to move out. As they began to leave the hut, Jim saw women in various degrees of dress moving through the shadows. He began to move toward the edge of the camp. The brush and trees were only a few hundred yards away.

"Stop! Halt!" came shouts from Jim's left.

"Down!" Jim shouted as he raised his rifle toward the new arrivals.

Two figures were running at them from the night, carrying rifles. Jim took aim at the closest one and had just begun to squeeze the trigger when their faces in the moonlight made him hesitate. They were young, basically boys. The two boy soldiers stopped and pointed their rifles at Jim and the women.

"Surrender!" one of the boys shouted, his young voice cracking as he pointed his rifle.

Jim was frozen. He should already have killed them if he was going to. The same youth who had made him hesitate was now delaying the young soldiers who should have killed him outright.

A long burst of gunfire behind him made him instinctively duck. The boys were dropped as the bullets impacted their bodies. Jim turned, expecting to see Joshua having fired, but Joshua was crouched on the ground with his arms over his head. Beautiful was standing behind the group of women with her rifle at her shoulder and smoke coming from the barrel.

"Get up. We need to go," Beautiful said. "And don't mourn those. They raped women like men. They die like men."

Jim turned back, sparing one glance down at the bodies, and stood up.

"Pick up their rifles," Jim heard Beautiful say to the women behind him.

They moved into the brush. No other soldiers tried to stop them. After Jim had motioned the last of the women out of the camp, he took position covering the way from where they had come. Joshua was helping one woman, and Beautiful came to kneel beside him. The sound of breaking sticks and movement came from the brush behind them. Beautiful turned and raised her rifle as other women shrieked and yelled. Jim grabbed Beautiful's rifle and forced it into the air.

"No!" Jim said to the woman, who was struggling to wrest the rifle back. "They're ours."

They both turned to see figures rush out of the darkness, led by Henda.

"We almost shot you, Jim," Henda said, his face dirty and sweat-covered, as his squad took position around them and toward the camp.

"She almost returned the favor," Jim said, indicating Beautiful.

Henda regarded Beautiful with a curious look. He noted the rifle held in her hands and the determined look on her face.

"You were a captive?" Henda asked the woman.

Beautiful turned her eyes to Henda and gripped her rifle.

"No longer," she said.

"Henda, pick three men to escort the women to safety," Jim said, then turned to Beautiful. "You should go with them."

He saw the woman stiffen.

"They will need protection while we find the other captives and free them," Jim explained.

"No," Beautiful said. "My sister is in the camp somewhere. I must find her first."

"Your sister is here?"

"Yes. She was taken by soldiers from the rest of us hours ago."

"We will find her," Henda said.

"I will find her. She's my sister," Beautiful said

and turned to walk away.

Jim grabbed her arm to stop her. The woman turned and gave him a look of complete rage.

"Don't you ever touch me again!" Beautiful growled in a menacing voice, her eyes blazing.

Jim released his hold on her arm.

"You stay with Henda's squad. Do what he says. I'll look for your sister. You can't help her if you get shot by soldiers . . . or my people, by mistake."

Beautiful considered his words, then nodded. Jim turned his attention back to the camp and the sounds of firing that suddenly intensified from farther away.

"Henda, take your squad there," Jim said, pointing to the camp. "Use cover and move. Be careful, as the Angels are already in the camp. That was the ambush you just heard. I'll move through the camp and try and link up."

Jim moved off after receiving Henda's look of understanding. He heard him designating men to protect the captives and ordering the rest to move out.

Jim spotted three soldiers in front of a group of tents. The soldiers were firing at two trucks about fifty feet away. Jim could see that his own men were pinned down there by the sustained gunfire. Quickly bringing his rifle to his shoulder, he first pushed the safety lever to semi-auto mode, then took careful sight on the soldier firing.

Pulling the trigger at the figure illuminated by the moonlight, he saw the soldier fall, gripping his arm. He then took sight of the other two. Both looked at him dumbfounded and then back to their fallen comrade. Jim shot the one to the left in the leg. The remaining man threw away his rifle and put up his hands.

"Jim, Jim!" Tatame's voice pulled his attention back to the truck.

"Tatame, are you hurt?" Jim asked, moving to the truck.

"No, but two of my men are wounded," Tatame said.

Two Angels were lying on the ground. Two others were holding bandages to an arm and a leg, applying direct pressure as Jim had taught them in basic first aid training.

"Let me see," Jim said.

Both wounds, while bloody, seemed superficial, although the men looked shaken. Jim gave each man a thumbs-up, and each returned one back to him.

"You two stay here," Jim said, indicating the men tending the wounded. "The rest of you with me. Henda's squad is on the other side of the camp looking for captives."

Firing in semi-auto mode erupted from the other side of the camp. It was answered by fully automatic fire. Since Jim had insisted that his fighters conserve their ammunition by not firing on full auto, the return fire was most likely from the enemy.

"Sounds like they found some soldiers," Tatame said.

"Let's move carefully," Jim said. "Let's try not to get shot by our own side."

The group of men moved out, keeping their spacing so as not to all get caught by a burst of automatic fire. The men moved from cover to cover, reducing the amount of time they were exposed. Jim noted that the rear two men kept checking to ensure they did not have enemies coming from behind.

Soon a row of small tents was in front of them.

"Set these tents on fire. Be sure it's a soldier who runs out," Jim said to Tatame, who began ordering men to fire the tents and others to provide cover for those men.

The tents caught quickly, fire jumping from one to another, illuminating the sky. Soldiers began running out and were quickly cut down. Jim moved on, leading the way. Tatame and his men fanned out to peer over a pile of logs. There were fifteen or so enemy soldiers behind and inside the hut, firing at someone Jim could not see. Jim assumed it was Henda and his squad.

Turning to look at Tatame, whose eyes were scared but excited, Jim considered the options. Ducking back down, he knew he didn't want the men firing and hitting Henda and his squad.

"Fix bayonets," Jim said, sliding the blade from its sheath on his waist and clicking it into place. He'd had very little bayonet training, but he thought it was the best tactic now. The work would be close and difficult. By using bayonets, they could avoid firing past the men to Henda's group. And they had the element of surprise on their side.

The men looked at each other disbelievingly, then fumbled for the knives at their waists. Jim pulled out his cell phone and called Henda. Jambi answered.

"Hello?"

Jim winced as rifles fired close to the phone.

"Are you pinned down?" he asked. "From the group of men by a hut in the center of the camp?"

"Yes," Jambi shouted. "We have wounded. I mean, some of us are wounded, and so are some captives."

"We are attacking them from behind. Cease firing!" Jim yelled into the phone to be heard over the rifle fire.

"Understood," Jambi said, then ended the call.

"Ready?" Jim yelled, putting the cell phone back into his pocket. "Go!"

Jim stood up and started toward the men firing from the hut. Running toward the men, the Angels let out a ferocious yell just feet away. The thirty Angels hit the soldiers like a threshing machine. Whatever they lacked in technique, they made up in bloody-minded determination.

The soldiers never had a chance.

Chapter 24

T he Angels were relentless. Few soldiers had remained after the bayonet charge. Within an hour, the surviving soldiers had been killed or captured. Jim couldn't help but be sickened at the slaughter, but he hadn't tried to stop it. No soldiers would be killing his men after that attack.

Jim spotted Abraham near Henda, tending to the wounded. He went to his friend and kneeled beside him.

"Are you all right?" Jim asked.

Abraham looked up with tears in his eyes.

"Again the slaughter of children of God," Abraham said before turning back to the young girl lying on the ground in front of him, awash in blood.

The young girl was the spitting image of Beautiful: the long hair, the pretty face.

"Is your sister named Beautiful?" Jim asked her.

Abraham looked curiously at Jim, his tears drying on his cheeks. The young woman didn't answer.

"Can she speak?" Jim asked. "One of the captives we freed was a woman named Beautiful. She said she had a sister. There's a resemblance."

"She is delirious. She has been brutally raped. It appears she resisted and paid the price," Abraham said. "She has been stabbed in the stomach and is in and out of consciousness."

Whatever hesitation Jim had felt at the fighting and

killing of the soldiers quickly seeped out of him. Burning anger started to fill his chest.

"They are animals," Jim said, looking at this girl who could not be more than eleven or twelve. Even though the blossoming of womanhood could be seen, she was still very much a child.

"Even animals are God's creations," Abraham said quietly, then poured water from a canteen onto a cloth and wiped the girl's bruised and bloody face.

"Enisi!" A yell from behind the men made them turn.

Beautiful came running up, threw down her rifle, and knelt by her sister's side.

"Careful, she is very badly hurt," Abraham said.

Beautiful turned to him, tears in her eyes.

"How hurt, Father?" Beautiful asked.

"She has been beaten and sexually abused. Her ribs appear to be broken, and she has been stabbed."

Beautiful keened, her hand to her mouth, as she rocked and cried. Then, reaching out for her sister's hand, she cradled the bloody fingers.

"Can you help her, Father?"

Abraham bowed his head and raised his hands to the sky. Other wounded looked over at the scene. Angels who had been milling around started to walk to where they were.

"Oh Lord, grant me, Your servant, to act as Your conduit to this child. Let me lessen her pain and suffering. Allow me to heal her so that the world may heal a bit more. I ask this in Your Son's name, oh Lord."

Jim felt his hairs stand up as the deep, rolling tones of Abraham's speech washed over him. He watched as Abraham laid his hands upon the girl's chest and stomach. The crowd surrounding them was quiet and solemn.

A long moment went by, and the girl's eyes fluttered.

"Beautiful," Enisi whispered, looking at her sister.

"Yes, sister, yes. I am here," Beautiful said, leaning close to her sister's face.

"It doesn't hurt anymore. It did before—the men hurt me—but it doesn't hurt now."

"Shhh, little sister. You rest. You'll get better."

"I don't think so, my sister. I don't think so. I see people near me."

Beautiful looked around at the crowd.

"The people who rescued us," she said. "These people came here to help us, to help you."

"No, I see a white woman and her black baby. They are shining. She says she is here for me. And for another man."

Jim looked around. There was no one matching that description standing there, no woman, no baby.

"I need the last words, the last words from the father. I want them. I heard of them."

"What?" Beautiful said, confused.

"I know what she wants," Abraham said, moving to the other side of the girl. "My name is Father Abraham. Have you been baptized, Enisi?"

"No, Father," Enisi said, her voice calm.

"Do you wish to be?"

"Yes, I want the words."

Abraham began to speak. "Beloved in the Lord, when the Savior sent out His apostles, He said unto them, 'Go ye, and teach all nations, baptizing them in the name of the Father, and of the Son, and of the Holy Spirit:

teaching them to observe all things whatsoever I have commanded you.'

"He who believeth and is baptized shall be saved. Through baptism men are cleansed from their sins, made partakers in the meritorious redemption of Jesus Christ, taken into the society of the faithful and into the church of Christ, fitted to obtain a share in all the treasuries of grace, with the management and administration of which Christ has entrusted *His* church."

One by one, the men and women began to kneel around them.

Abraham continued. "When an adult is to be baptized, he must be first instructed in the doctrine of Christ, and profess his faith in it, and declare himself ready to observe all that Christ hath commanded, and to renounce all that is in opposition to the doctrine and commandments of Christ. But it is in accordance with the intention of the Lord, who lovingly called little children to come unto Him, that the infant children of Christian parents should be taken up into the company of the faithful by baptism, and soon after their natural birth should be born again of water and the Holy Spirit. And now I ask thee, Enisi. Dost thou desire to obtain eternal life in the church of God through faith in Jesus Christ?"

"Yes, Father," Enisi said.

Abraham leaned forward and breathed three times on Enisi's face.

"May the powers of darkness, which the divine Redeemer hath vanquished by His cross, retire before thee, that thou mayest see to what hope, and to what an exceedingly glorious inheritance among the saints, thou art called. Receive on thy forehead the sign of the holy cross, to remind thee that thou openly profess thy faith in

Christ crucified, and glory not, save only in the cross of Jesus Christ our Lord."

Abraham made the sign of the cross on Enisi's forehead.

"I sign thee on the breast with the sign of the holy cross, to remind thee that thou love from thy heart Him who hath died on the cross for thee, and that as He bids thee, thou shouldest take up thy cross and follow Him."

Abraham made the sign of the cross on Enisi's chest.

"Let us pray. We beseech thee, oh Lord, graciously to hear our prayer, and evermore by Thy power to protect this Thy handmaiden Enisi, whom we have signed with the sign of the holy cross, that *she* may continue in the faith of the doctrines and in the obedience of the commandments of *Him* who gave up *His* life for us on the tree of the cross, Christ our Lord. *Amen.*"

Abraham reached forward and said to Enisi, "I have no salt, but the salt of my tears, let them be enough for Him."

He wiped his eye, which was streaming tears, with his knuckle and touched his knuckle to Enisi's mouth in the sign of the cross.

"Receive this salt as an emblem of wisdom; the Lord grant it thee unto everlasting life. *Amen.*"

Abraham laid his hands upon Enisi's chest.

"O God, Thou author of all wisdom, look graciously down on this Thy servant, and preserve *her* ever in Thy fear, which is the beginning of wisdom, through Christ our Lord. *Amen.*"

Abraham looked down at Enisi's face.

"And now I ask thee, Enisi, before I administer to thee the sacrament of baptism: Dost thou renounce the devil?"

"I do."

"And all his works?"

"I do."

"Dost thou believe in God the Father Almighty, maker of Heaven and Earth?"

"I do."

"Dost thou believe in Jesus Christ, His only begotten Son our Lord, who was born and hath suffered for us?"

"I do."

"Dost thou believe in the Holy Spirit, the Holy Catholic Church, the communion of saints, the forgiveness of sins, the resurrection of the flesh, and life everlasting?"

"I do," Enisi said.

Abraham took the canteen and spoke as he began to pour a trickle of water on Enisi's forehead.

"I baptize thee in the name of the Father, and of the Son, and of the Holy Spirit." At the mention of each branch of the divine Trinity, Abraham made the sign of the cross on Enisi's forehead. Enisi smiled as the water rolled from her forehead, splitting into four parts as it poured, resembling a cross.

"Are those the words? Am I baptized, Father?" Enisi asked.

"Yes, my child, you are forgiven. You are without sin."

"I must go now. I'm so happy. The woman with the baby says I must go."

"You see a woman and a baby, my child? Is it Mary and Jesus?" Abraham asked.

Enisi hesitated; she looked as if she were listening.

"No, not Mary," Enisi said as she closed her eyes. "I love you, my sister."

Beautiful gripped Enisi's hand, tears running down her face.

"Not Mary," Enisi said, her voice growing softer. "Her name is Maggie."

Beautiful cried as her sister's body relaxed and grew still.

Jim sat alone quietly, trying to digest powerful emotions that had risen up at the mention of Maggie's name by Enisi. *There is simply no way she could have known that*, he thought. *None, zero, nada.*

And again he thought, *This is not happening.*

He watched as the Angels dug graves for the dead soldiers. Twenty-six bodies had been laid out, stripped, and left in a line. Abraham had insisted that they be given a proper burial. There had been reluctance to touch the bodies, but when Abraham had started, the teams had pitched in. The wounded and surrendered soldiers were again tied and confined. Their former captives would be their jury.

In his heart, Jim knew that they should have left with the villagers. It wasn't safe staying in the camp, as other soldiers and reinforcements could show up. They had found radio gear and cell phones on the soldiers. Jim had had them load the equipment and a large cache of weapons and supplies on the trucks, then posted teams of four on the approaches to the camp. They would warn if anyone approached.

While the graves were dug, Abraham was baptizing Angels and villagers. A long line of the newly faithful waited to hear the words Enisi had received before she died.

Beautiful had stayed with her sister. She had found a tub and washed her body, then had found a white sheet to use as Enisi's shroud. Jim watched as four of the Angels carried the body to one of the trucks and placed it there. Beautiful would bury her baby sister in their village.

Beautiful looked around as if lost; then her eyes fell on Jim in his seat away from the workers. Watching her walk toward him, he was struck by how much she embodied her name. If her face had any lack of symmetry, Jim couldn't see it.

Beautiful sat down on the ground a few feet from him. The pair sat watching Abraham baptize those who wished it.

"The name my sister spoke. You knew it?" Beautiful asked, skipping any small talk.

Jim turned to look at her. She had spoken to him without looking at him. She was watching the proceedings without facing him. Jim turned his gaze to watch as well.

"I saw your face when Enisi spoke her name, the name of the angel who came for her," Beautiful said.

Jim maintained his silence while he thought about how to respond. Finally he said, "I know . . . well, I knew a person who had that name."

Beautiful turned again and regarded him with a steady gaze. After a moment, she went on, "She was special to you, this Maggie?"

Jim kept watching the scene. *Why is she asking this?* he thought.

"Was she your sister? Your friend? Your lover?"

A long moment stretched as Jim looked over at Beautiful.

"She was someone I cared about," he said.

"I fear I might have HIV now," Beautiful said in a sudden shift of direction. "After the rapes, I mean. So many people have HIV, and they die of AIDS here."

Jim was surprised at the different subject but grateful not to talk about Maggie anymore.

"I was a prostitute," Beautiful went on. "In Kinshasa, I was very popular. Executives, government officials. But always I insisted on the condoms. Always I was safe and tested."

Beautiful paused for a moment and plucked at a tuft of grass.

"My virginity was taken by an older man. I was fourteen, a schoolgirl. He was very handsome and gave me gifts; he was a supplier for the store in the village. My mother knew what he was about, but I couldn't hear her. I refused his gifts for a while, and then he became more insistent and generous. Clothing, money, candies. He called me his blossom."

Beautiful fell quiet for a while, choosing another tuft of grass once she had exhausted the blades on the first.

"I moved with him to Kinshasa after running away at seventeen. He placed me in an apartment, our little love nest. Me, his country blossom. There was so much time then, for loving, for shopping and bars and dancing. He traveled for work, so I had time to myself. I worked in a bar in a hotel. I would go out with girlfriends and dance and drink. I was a very naughty girl, but I was living.

"Then, one day, another man came to the apartment and told me I had to leave. He said my handsome man had been killed and the rent was coming due. I was lost and panicked. I called my handsome man's house looking for him. I talked to his wife. She knew who I was, but she was not angry. On the contrary, she loved her husband and said that she was happy that I made him happy. But yes, he had been killed in an auto accident, and I must now make my own way.

"The man gave me three days to come up with the money. I went to my job at the bar, and the second night a man asked me to go with him, to be with him for money. So I did. I kept my apartment and lived my life.

"That was three years ago, and soon I did not work at the hotel anymore. I lived, I worked. And then my mother got sick and got word to me. I came home to gather my sister and take her with me after my mother died. That was last week. I buried my mother last week, and my sister will be buried today."

Beautiful turned to look Jim in the eyes.

"I don't know why you are here. You seem like those men, the foreign men, the men who would pay to be with me. Like them, but different. I don't know why you would be here to help us. We are not your people. Those men I was with, they would not be here. They would not help people here. So I ask: why?"

Jim thought about it.

"Him, I suppose," Jim said, indicating Abraham. "I was lost, then I was found."

Beautiful considered his answer.

"It is good to be found," she said at last.

The two people from vastly different worlds sat there, watching the stars come out above the grassland.

Chapter 25

J im cleaned is rifle while he sat under a tree. The group surrounding him was his regular choice of fighters: Henda, Tatame, and the original men who went with him to free the captives by the lakeshore. More than eight months had passed since the rescues. While their numbers were small, the two independent bands roamed the Congo. Tatame led one group, Jim led the other.

They were smart, tough, and effective fighters. After only a few months, they had progressed by leaps and bounds in their skills. Scouring the back roads and trails of the countryside of Western Congo, they had made a difference in the activities of the militias and the bandit groups. It was easier for the militias to leave the area than to stay awake at night wondering whether they would be attacked. The Mai-Mais were collapsing. Some disappeared and some combined into larger forces for protection against the Angels.

Abraham's reputation was growing by word of mouth as well as by the radio broadcasts. Many of the soldiers who had surrendered to the Angels had now joined them. The ones who had not participated in rapes or torture were taken in. The ones who had participated faced the justice of their victims.

The villagers the Angels encountered welcomed them. They were happy to have protectors. Jim and the Angels had trained many villagers in the use of confiscated weaponry. A small show of force was still a show of force. Soldiers were more careful when they thought they might get a bullet for trying to brutalize villages.

Jim reassembled his rifle and loaded it. The men watching him did the same. They moved out, seventy men disappearing into the hills as if they were never there, heading for a rendezvous with Tatame and Abraham at a village. The men had been marching for two days, stopping into villages briefly to ensure no soldiers were around. They appeared without warning and took a heavy toll on any soldiers or militia that were bothering the people.

They would arrive at their destination before nightfall.

Jim held up a hand to the column when he saw Henda beckoning from the grassland. After a brief discussion, Jim determined that there was no opposing force in the village, so he waved the men in. Upon arrival, the men took positions around the perimeter while Jim went in to meet with Tatame and Abraham. He spotted them with a group of the villagers. Abraham was baptizing them, as had become his habit in each place he visited. Tatame sat away from the group. Jim walked over and sat down.

"How are things up in the north?" Jim asked, smiling. He had come to like the smart young man.

"We chased the few small groups we could, hitting them on different nights and then pulling back," Tatame said. "We set ambushes and circled around as they tried to chase us. No losses for us. Gérard took us by boat down the lake, then we marched back and hit them again. The larger groups are getting more cautious and moving out. The threat of being tied to a tree and whipped seems to have worked. The guns we captured we turned over to villages to help them defend themselves. Yourself?"

"A villager reported that he had heard of us on the radio, calling you Destroying Angels. Since Joshua put out the story of the rescue, it's been moving throughout the country."

Abraham had finished his business with the villagers and came over to the pair. He opened his arms to Jim, who stood up and gave him a hug.

"My friend, how are you?"

"Good, Abraham. And yourself? You have been supplying Joshua with stories."

"My purpose grows clearer with each day. I spoke to Father Michael, and he sends his regards but also a warning. The government is aware of our crusade and is taking steps to quell it. By supplying Joshua with our actual stories, we can help ourselves not be lumped in with the Mai-Mai. He has to use pirate radio tactics, but they are working."

"Crusade?" Jim asked. "I heard you preaching on the radio."

"We are spreading religion and hope to the people. Our gains in security for the villages are being noticed. God is bringing the villagers together, and the government is not interested in a united people."

"Father Michael say anything else?" Tatame asked.

"Elections are coming up, and he believes that the government has a choice: side with us or not. If it is in the government's interest and they can hold on to power, well, they might. If not, then they will have to discredit us and take action."

"When does he think they will act?" Jim asked.

"'Soon' was all he said," Abraham replied.

"Will the people return to their homes now?" Jim asked.

"Possibly. There is movement from the camps. People hear about the gains we made and want to settle back where there is home and hearth. Hundreds of thousands of people are potentially returning to their homeland, but therein lies the problem."

"How so?" Jim asked.

"Voters," Tatame said. "Hundreds of thousands of potential voters."

"Or fighters," Jim said.

Abraham nodded in agreement.

"Additionally, information that I have received suggests that different factions in the government would go different ways. For example, a new military head was recently installed after the last one was executed for failing to please the president. Others might see that we are making a positive difference, but the newest head general has to make a name for himself, and we may be the target."

"Where are you getting this information? It seems pretty detailed," Jim asked.

"A person close to the sources," Abraham replied.

"Who? Father Michael?" Tatame asked.

"No, a child of God who wishes to aid us and who sacrifices herself for the betterment of the cause. Beautiful, the woman we—well, you—freed. She has returned to Kinshasa and is sending messages to me. Father Michael collects them and sends them by messenger. It has been very helpful."

"You know what she is doing to get close to these

men?" Jim asked.

"I didn't question her. She is sending information, not a confession."

"She's tough and seemed smart, grateful for the attempt to rescue her sister and for the baptism. I think her information is worth listening to," Jim said.

"Beautiful is also baptized," Abraham said. "After returning home, she told me what she planned to do. I tried to dissuade her, but her mind was made up. I began receiving messages soon after. Her latest one warns of a government squad sent to collect what the militia couldn't. Forty miles north of here is a village that they are going to attack."

"And take the people?" Jim asked.

"No, I believe that they are going to terrorize or kill the people and blame it on us," Abraham said.

"When?" Tatame asked.

"Three days."

"We'll move out in the morning," Jim said.

That night, Jim, Abraham, and Tatame sat around a small radio in the bush and listened to a transmission.

"The armed group of insurgents known as Angels is nothing more than bandit Mai-Mai," a strong voice said. "Bandits fighting other bandits to prey upon the good people of the Democratic Republic of the Congo. For years the government has taken steps to control these types of groups. Yet these 'Angels' are responsible for the murders—yes, murders—of hundreds of peaceful villagers."

"Deputy Minister, surely you are mistaken," came the reply. "The reports are that they are led by a priest, a man of God—"

"A charlatan and disgraced priest. Even the very church he claims and has sworn to support and obey knows his true and violent nature," the deputy minister continued.

"But the reports tell of them freeing people, people kidnapped for unknown purposes by a private militia group."

A heavy sigh from the deputy minister. "False. They are the ones who have assaulted the villagers and taken them. Where is their spokesperson? I ask you that. If they are for the people, they should contact the government to help with the rebuilding of our country. Our president is poised to bring plans to fruition which will help keep our beloved country safe."

"Well, that is all the time we have tonight on this broadcast. Thanks to Deputy Minister of the Interior Jamiz Kueshu. I am Godfried Hinsusu with your Congo News Tonight Radio Hour."

Abraham turned off the radio. The men around him looked to each other after listening to the broadcast, then lay back down to rest.

"Well, it seems we know on which side the government has landed," Jim said.

"It would seem so," Tatame said.

The force had traveled by trucks to the outskirts of the village, Hinta, in the northern highlands. In addition to their vantage point above the town, they had scouts on different peaks watching approaches to the cluster of huts below.

Having arrived before the government forces, Abraham had gone down to the village and warned them of the danger. The brother's renown had grown to the point where even the inhabitants of this small hamlet had heard of and trusted his word. They quickly gathered what they could carry and were moved with assistance to a safe place miles away.

And now the force waited.

"Mr. Jim," Tatame said, having stepped away for a moment.

"Yes?" Jim answered.

"It's Henda and Jambi. They have returned."

"Send them up. We have food," Jim said.

Directly, Henda and Jambi appeared. Both looked dirty and tired but were smiling.

"The government troops are staging about six kilometers from here. It appears they need a meal and some alcohol before they attack," Jambi said.

"So tonight?" Jim asked.

"Yes, most likely, but there is more. We found signs of other men, armed men. Henda says men carrying rifles and equipment are making different tracks."

"More soldiers?" Tatame asked.

"Yes, but not government troops," Jambi replied.

"How do you know?" Abraham asked.

Jambi spoke with Henda.

"No boots. The tracks are regular shoes and bare feet," Jambi translated.

"Who are they?"

"I believe it may be the people's militia we have heard of, the one that has been fighting the ANC troops."

Jim considered the implications. How would a new group of fighters affect the plan?

"Do you think they will attack the troops or us?" he asked.

"Most likely the troops," Jambi replied. "The

militia has been fighting in this area for months in retaliation for some villages being attacked."

"Where are they now?" Jim asked.

"They are about two kilometers away, setting up an ambush on the road. They will let the troops come in and will trap them, and then they will attack. Maybe kill a few, but they usually hit and fade away. They have about thirty fighters," Jambi said.

"We'll wait here until something happens. So check your men and be ready to go if we need to," Jim said to Henda and Tatame.

The force of Angels waited in place as night began to fall. They didn't have to wait long. As the sun touched the horizon, the sounds of automatic weapons and small concussive explosions could be heard.

Jim watched as tracer rounds randomly flickered in the sky. In moments a dull sound prickled his ears, and he turned to scan the sky.

"What is it, Jim?" Abraham asked, noticing his search.

"A jet," Jim said. "It sounds like a jet."

Scanning the skies north of their location, Jim spotted the small dark shape of the MiG in the last rays of the sun. It lined up where the firefight was going on and unleashed its own string of fire toward the ground.

"My," Abraham said. "That's the beast you fought?"

"Maybe. One like it, anyway," Jim said, losing track of the jet as it left the area. "Everyone, get ready. We may need to move out soon."

The presence of the jet was worrisome. They had enough small arms and explosives to attack a ground threat, but an experienced force with air support would quickly annihilate the Angels.

"Stay put," Jim said to the group. "We will go down to investigate after dark."

"What are your thoughts?" Abraham asked.

"We're no match for air-supported troops. If they have laser marking or any other ways of marking a target from the ground, we will be overmatched."

"So we don't engage tonight?" Abraham asked.

"I have a suspicion that the jet will not operate at night. I don't think we're near a base, and that thing can't linger too long. So we wait and see what the outcome is."

"Then what?"

"We wait some more," Jim said. "Abraham, do you think you could find the place where you found me hanging in a tree? It's near here, isn't it?"

Abraham considered the question.

"Yes, I believe so. Why?"

"There were MANPADS in the pallet I was attached to. We may need that edge." Seeing the confused looks, Jim explained, "Shoulder-fired rockets, good enough to snatch that jet from the sky."

"We will send someone immediately," Abraham said as he looked at the ground fires where the jet had attacked. "Beautiful has said that the government forces know that we have formed a base on Kavala. We need to move all our people, including the refugees, from there so that they will be safe. The villages we have helped can now defend themselves, help one another."

Jim watched Henda move through the grass with binoculars. Sending the old hunter down first to scout the area had proved its worth in the past.

Henda reported back that the trucks and lightly armored vehicles had moved out. Jim surveyed the devastation from where the attack had taken place. Tree stumps and denuded bushes were spread over a wide swath of ground. The group that had attacked the convoy of government trucks wasn't hard to track. Blood and equipment littered the trail of their flight.

Jim wanted to see who they were and if they would be possible allies. Henda and Jambi were slipping along as scouts, with the rest of the Angels following behind.

They tracked miles through the jungle until they waited in a small clearing for the two scouts to return.

"They are close," Henda said, startling Jim from his hidden place behind a tree.

"I wish you would stop doing that," Jim said. "How many?"

"About twenty. Ten wounded. In the rocks, about a kilometer," Jambi said, pointing. "The entrance is hidden in the cliffs, but they did not hide their trail very well. So it could be an ambush."

"They could just be hurt," Abraham said.

"Or waiting to hurt who is following," Jim replied.

"If armed men approach, it could be enough to make them fight," Tatame said.

"Suggestions?" Jim asked.

"I will go alone to talk to them. Then maybe they will allow us to help," Abraham said.

"It's dangerous," Jim said.

"If we can ally ourselves, we will be that much stronger. And my faith has protected me thus far," Abraham said, fingering one of the bullet holes in his robe.

"When are you going to replace that?" Jim asked.

Abraham did not reply. He stood up and made his way forward, motioning for the others to stay in place. As Jim watched him disappear into the trees alone, he was again struck by the man's courage and willingness to put himself in danger for his fellow man.

They waited in the heat and bugs for a long time. Jim began to get restless and was just about to order everyone forward when Abraham emerged, with a slightly built man, from the trees ahead. Jim couldn't believe his eyes. It was Erevu, the man whose village he had helped bury a lifetime ago.

"Jim!" Erevu said, spying him in the trees.

"Erevu, it's good to see you," Jim said, standing up and walking toward the man.

"I heard you were dead, Jim," Erevu said.

"Who told you that?"

"Jacques. We bought more ammunition and weapons from him. He has no more pilots. When your plane was shot down, he was nearly ruined. He is smuggling by boat and truck now."

"Your English has improved, Erevu," Jim noted.

"A teacher is in our group," Erevu explained. "A woman. She became my wife. She has taught me much."

"Are those your fighters we saw attack the convoy?"

"My brothers. They escaped the village. They came back, and then we went together to fight," Erevu replied.

"How long have you been fighting?" Jim asked.

"Since I saw you last. This is the first time we have faced a jet. It did not go well."

"How many are you?"

"Thirty men and twenty women, people whose villages have been destroyed in the fighting."

"Are any hurt?" Tatame asked.

"We may be able to help them, Erevu," Jim explained.

"Come then, come, come," Erevu said.

Jim motioned for the squads to move out and followed Erevu to his camp.

The fighters in the camp were surprised when Jim and the others walked in with Erevu. Over half had injuries of some kind, and a few of those injuries were dire. But, with Abraham's help, most of the fighters were stabilized enough to be moved.

"Now what, Erevu?" Jim asked.

"We go back to our camp. On the fire mountain in the north."

"Near Goma?" Abraham asked.

Erevu nodded.

"Is it safe?" Jim asked.

"Enough for our purposes. We are close enough to Uganda to meet with representatives of that country. They have been supplying us with weapons, training, supplies. They are very interested in the election. And they asked about you," Erevu said, addressing Abraham.

"Me?" Abraham asked. "Why me?"

"Because people are speaking of you. They know what you have done. From the radio."

"Why would they care about us?" Jim asked.

"You should ask them yourselves. Would you care to come with us? We could use the help getting back," Erevu said.

Jim looked to Abraham, who nodded his assent.
"Where to, Erevu?"

The journey took the better part of two days, moving
cautiously along little-used trails, avoiding settlements.
They had sent Jambi and Henda with men to find the
rockets and other supplies. Tatame had gone to guide
their remaining people to the camp described by Erevu.
Abraham and Jim found time to discuss the future while
winding through the jungle and scrub.

"Where does it go from here, Abraham?"

"Where it takes us, where the Lord wills it."

"We keep fighting forever?"

"No, I don't think that it would be ideal to keep
fighting forever. A new day for the people of Congo, for
Africa. A new way."

"A lot of people have tried for a very long time."

"I dreamed of a mountain of fire. Back before the
lions came. I do not know why we need to go, only that
we must," Abraham said. "I never realized that it could
be a simple as a volcano."

Erevu had told them of his group's base of
operations. The mountainous terrain in the north of the
country had helped them evade the government forces.
Teeming fields of lava and steep cliffs were difficult to
navigate by heavy equipment. The band stayed in the
mountains, striking far away to keep their position secret.

Jim walked in silence after that. Following a dream
was all he had left. Too many things had happened for
him to discount one out of hand.

They arrived on the outskirts of Goma, a city near
the mountain, tucked into a pocket between Burundi and

Uganda. Abraham and Erevu accompanied the wounded into the city in separate buses they had found. Jim lay down in the back of a truck and went to sleep. He awoke to a foggy scene in the morning and waited until Abraham returned.

"Good news and bad news, Jim," Abraham said.

"I'm listening."

"I met with a representative of Uganda. He is connected with both the government and the church. He says we are welcome to come to Uganda to spread the Word of God. The people have heard of me and want us to come."

"Us or you?"

"There is no me without us, Jim. All of us. We can all go and recuperate. You, me, everyone."

"They want to use you?" Jim asked, suspicious.

"They said that they want the people who have stood up for people in the Congo. So yes, they might have plans that involve us. But it feels as if there is a plan from the Lord as well."

"And the bad news?"

"Beautiful," Abraham said. "She is in danger, I'm afraid."

"For spying?"

"Yes. She is in Kinshasa. We need to get her out. To take her with us."

"Can we fly her out? Have someone help her?"

"She has risked everything for information that is critical to us. She is one of ours. I will go and collect her."

"No way," Jim said. "I don't see that as being very smart. I can go."

"How?"

"Barter a plane ride from Goma, then scoop her up and come back. Jambi and Henda will have gathered everyone else who wants to come and meet you at the mountain. They can collect anything they need. Who did you send to try to locate the crash site where you found me?"

"Louis and his brother Étienne. I sent them by boat, because they know the lake and can move quickly that way. I expect them in a few hours."

"Good, then you'll be ready too, assuming they find the equipment," Jim said. "It seems likely. That's an exceptionally isolated spot. You finding me there like you did was—" He paused.

Abraham grinned. "A miracle?"

The two men laughed together.

"I think this plan can work," Abraham said. "When do you leave?"

"I'll start today," Jim said.

Jack Lyons

Chapter 26

J im was tightly manacled, the handcuffs biting into his wrists.

The trip from the dirty cell in the city had been tortuous and hot. In that cell, he had endured an extensive beating. Unable to defend himself from the kicks and blows, he could only survive. His small cell had been windowless, stained drywall, speckled with dirt and grime and illuminated by a bare bulb, the concrete floor slick and grimy. How long he had lain there, he wasn't sure. Then they had moved him from the cell to an interrogation room. The soldiers had deposited him there roughly, given him a few goodbye kicks, and closed the solid metal door. A mirror that he assumed was for one-way viewing was in the wall opposite him.

The plan and the people had been in motion. Jim had found a small plane willing to fly into Kinshasa. No bartering had been necessary. The pilot had heard of Abraham and his miracles and was glad to help Father Lion. Jim had boarded the plane and watched his friend wave as he departed. Arriving in Kinshasa, Jim had taken a taxi to the address written down by Abraham. Knocking on the apartment door, he had felt it open. Men had surrounded him from all sides. They had been waiting for him; he'd never had a chance.

That had been two weeks ago.

After what seemed like endless hours, his hands

numb and his tongue swollen in his mouth from lack of water, Jim saw the door open. A thin African man dressed in a police uniform entered. He rolled Jim onto his stomach and undid the handcuffs.

Jim flexed his hands, which immediately began to lose their numbness as blood began to scream back into the swollen digits. Other men entered the room, bringing two chairs and a table with a steel ring set in the middle. He was roughly lifted up by two men, set in a chair, and handcuffed to the ring. Two bottles of water were left on the table, and the men exited.

Jim did his best to grab one of the bottles and managed to open the top but could not bring the bottle to his swollen and split lips. The best he could do was to suck on the bottle while squeezing it in his hand.

After he had drained the bottle, he looked up into the mirror for the first time and was shocked by how much he had changed. Both of his eyes were blackened, and his face was swollen. He stared at the stranger in the mirror, with his torn, dirty clothing. He knew he smelled, and his mouth tasted fuzzy.

"You look like shit. What's the other guy look like?" he said to his reflection. For some reason, this made him chuckle.

The door opened again, and Jim was surprised to see a white man in work clothing enter. Older but strong-looking, the man ambled in his square-toed boots to sit in the chair opposite Jim. He sat there staring at Jim, taking in his appearance and something more. Whatever conclusion the man came to must have satisfied him.

"Rough night?" the man asked.

Jim blinked at him, surprised by his deep Texas accent.

"Let me help you with that," the man said as he grabbed the other bottle, opened it, and offered it to Jim.

Jim leaned forward, wincing in pain, and drank the whole bottle from the man's hand.

"Thank you, sir," Jim said.

"My name is Delroy. You can call me Delroy. I don't answer to 'sir.'"

"My name is Dav—"

"I know who you are, son, so let's not pretend."

Jim looked at the mirror.

"Ain't nobody in there. Can't guarantee this place isn't bugged, but from the looks of it, they got bugs enough."

Jim regarded the man.

"Are you CI—"

"Who I work for isn't really important at this time."

"So . . ."

"So, here we are," Delroy said, leaning back in his chair. "Your name is Jim Stabbert. You're a former decorated pilot for the US Marine Corps, call sign Reverend, who disappeared at sea during a training mission off the coast of San Diego and was presumed dead. Good so far?"

Jim sat silently.

"So you and your plane disappeared without a trace. But on the same night, on an island off the coast of Mexico, intelligence was debriefing a Mexican cartel insider, a man arrested in the US for the drunk driving manslaughter of your wife, unborn child, and family friend, but never charged. In exchange for information about the cartel and its activities, this man would not be prosecuted for those deaths.

"This individual was killed either by an asteroid or by a large weapon while standing on the roof of a particular nondescript house on a nondescript part of said island. Heavy gunfire was reported by Mexican and US agents in the compound. Heavy gunfire . . . and the sound of a jet."

Jim stared at his bloodied wrists, the circulation still returning and causing him pain, though he refused to show it. The scene of Champos standing on the roof flashed before his eyes. A lifetime ago. Delroy shifted his seat in the chair as if his hip pained him.

"There's some fuzziness about how you turned up in Africa smuggling guns. Then you dropped off of the map, or rather, out of the sky. Yet here you are again, looking far healthier than your reported death would allow," Delroy said calmly, looking Jim in the eyes.

"You've done some research," Jim said.

"I've read some research," Delroy corrected. "I have people for that. Got people for a lot of things."

"Nice thing to have, people," Jim said.

"Yep. Apparently you found some yourself. Take the priest, what's his name again? Oh yes, Abraham. Brother Abraham Hunt. You two men found each other in the wilds of the jungles of Congo, got together, and started a war. One you can't possibly win. And I only have one question: why?"

"Why what?" Jim asked.

"Why didn't you just stay dead and lost?"

Jim thought about it and then shook his head.

"I guess there's a plan for all of us, and mine apparently didn't include staying lost."

"A higher power, then?"

"I've started to believe a bit more than I did in the

past," Jim said.

"Happens when you get older," Delroy said, shifting again in his chair.

"You need anything else, sir?" Jim asked.

"Name's Delroy, not 'sir.' You avenged your wife on her killer. I can respect that."

"Wife and daughter," Jim said quietly.

"What's that?" Delroy asked.

"Wife and daughter," Jim repeated, looking across the table at Delroy.

Delroy sat observing Jim.

"The fracas over here, though, that's a different story," Delroy continued.

"People were being stolen and murdered," Jim said.

"This is Africa. There ain't been a day gone by in ten thousand years when someone wasn't getting stolen and murdered."

"Where does that leave us?" Jim asked.

"Depends. You think you gonna attack me or do something stupid?"

"No," Jim said.

Delroy leaned forward and tossed a handcuff key on the table, then leaned back.

"Had to make sure I wasn't dangerous?" Jim asked, picking up the key and opening his shackles.

"Son, I know you're dangerous, but I don't think you'll attack me," Delroy said.

"And now?" Jim asked, rubbing his bruised wrists.

"Your group is still out there causing problems. The armed type of problems. But bigger than that, it's rallying people. Pushing back against a government that, at its best times, has a loose grip on the country. That is making people nervous. When it was just a few villages, no one cared. Now your friend has arrived in Goma, which is a small city. And he is preaching. And the people are listening."

"He does like to go on."

"The problem is that while he is rallying people to God, he is also rallying people to him. So which way he's going to point them is the part making people nervous. Nervous people do bad things."

"How so?"

"The current president is up for reelection. He is going to either have to embrace your man or eliminate him. And he's leaning toward the latter," Delroy said.

"Will he attack, do you think?"

"I get paid a lot for what I think, but here is this for free. The general in charge needs to show he can control this. And he is a hammer looking for a nail. He is there now, or on his way, with six tanks and a whole lot of men and support. I don't know what all. Buncha troops. Interests outside the country with interests inside the country are providing support. Heavy support. The fighting will begin at midnight, three hours from now."

"Will he let them surrender?"

Delroy shook his head. "Can't. He needs them gone. Hanging around makes them a rallying point. Martyrs are easier to deal with, as they are dead."

"The Angels can't stand up against armor."

"Seems like they can. They knocked out a tank with an RPG when they drove the garrisoned military out of Goma. But that ain't gonna last."

"So, how are they going to do it?"

"If I understand right, they are going to line all of their tanks up and drive your friends out of the city, then build up some kind of mountain stronghold until they know your friend and his people are dead. Goma politicians support the opposition candidate anyway. I saw the military briefing."

"They'll be slaughtered."

"Yep, but I notice you haven't asked what will happen to you."

"It doesn't matter. I can't help my friends. They're what's important." Jim replied, hanging his head.

"They're working on your extradition. The US never pursued charging you for your Mexican vacation, but they're reassessing now. Seems they knew where you were for a while. You were useful to the intelligence services' interests when you were smuggling. Your boss, Jacques, sold you out when he got jammed up. Something about a planeload of rockets lost."

Jim looked up. "Where are we?"

"Kinshasa airport, military section."

"Can you help me get to them?" Jim asked.

"My influence only goes so far, son. And why should I?"

That one stumped Jim.

"Can't really give you a reason," he said, "other than that some good people I love are going to die. A man who brought me back from the edge of death needs me."

"*Philia*, then?"

"Who's Philia?"

Delroy laughed. "*Philia* is one of the types of love. It's friendship love. *Storge* is family love, *eros* is romantic love, and *agape* is God love. Unconditional."

Jim thought about it. "Yes," he said. "I guess so, but probably closer to *agape*. I'd follow Abraham anywhere."

"You ready to die for him? It seems he has that quality to inspire."

"Yes, if it comes to that."

Delroy sat silently regarding the man before him.

"Someone wants to talk to you," he said finally.

With that, Delroy got up and walked out of the room. Jim watched as the door closed, then a moment later opened. A young woman walked in. He recognized her.

"Hey, Rev," she said, standing by the door holding a backpack and dressed in a flight suit.

"Hey, IRIS," Jim said, smiling through his shock.

"It's Lisa now, just regular Lisa Little," she said, crossing to the table and sitting down across from him.

Jim saw that her hair was longer. The flight suit was not a fighter pilot's pressure suit but a close match to a pilot's coverall. No US flag, just a name tag "Little" and a corporate logo: "Seraph Systems."

"You get out?" he said.

"Honorable discharge, barely. Let me see your wrists," Lisa said, taking medical supplies from her backpack.

"Discharged or drummed out?"

"It was made clear my time was done. I wasn't officially supposed to be on that flight that day. But you disappearing after disabling the jet was too suspicious for some—well, enough people. So I wrapped up my time in a supply office and got out when my time was up."

"I'm sorry about that."

She shrugged and began to clean his cuts with disinfectant.

"How did you trick the location beacon?" she

asked.

"You sure you got out?" Jim asked, watching her face.

"Out of the Marines? Yeah."

"Who is that?" he asked, indicating the corporate logo.

"Defense contractor. I fly for them now."

"What are you flying?"

"A C-5," she said, finishing with his first wrist. "That looks pretty bad. Move your fingers for me."

Jim was still looking closely at his former pilot comrade; she stopped dressing his wrists and met his eyes.

"I'm sorry, Lisa," he said. "I didn't mean for you to lose your career."

Lisa held his gaze and then nodded.

"We had a funeral with an empty casket," she said. "Your parents were torn up but stoic. Didn't even flinch for the rifles. Your mom cried, though, when she got the flag."

Jim heard the emotion in Lisa's voice and decided to change the subject.

"How are you here?" he asked.

"Told you, I'm flying a C-5 for Seraph. It's transporting two Abrams tanks at sixty-seven tons apiece. Fully armed and even fueled. Tank crews provided."

"You gotta be kidding me," Jim said at the ridiculous sum of weight. "That's the C-5 Galaxy? Who the hell owns one of those privately?"

"Lend-lease from the US government, contracted through Seraph," Lisa said, taping a bandage onto his wrist. "I've heard about what you've done over here, Jim. Avenging Angels, freeing the people, arming them.

Teaching people how to defend themselves."

"That wasn't me," Jim said, wincing at the antiseptic applied to his wrists.

"Whoever it is, they have you. And you're gonna get the credit or the blame. The US government doesn't know what to do with you right now, so they're keeping quiet."

"They going to try and take me back?"

"Seraph has some intel contacts. Even they don't know what to think about you. Your little scrap has settled down a country at war and made trade open up again in some parts. Arming the villagers and driving out the bandits made a huge difference. The biggest part is the election. The government needs you and your group to go away."

"What stake do you have in this, Lisa?"

"I saw a fellow Marine being dragged into a building in the last place I would ever have suspected. I happened to talk to Delroy in a bar. He has some major pull in the country. I think he's involved with the oil business. He took a chance to let me see you. You'd have done the same for me."

"I appreciate it, Lisa. I know you didn't have to do that."

Lisa looked away at the mirrored glass.

"I don't much care for what I do now," she said. "The pay is amazing, but flying weapons and mercenaries isn't sitting right with me. Started to see some of the after-action reports of the conflict areas. All the photos were missing was the smell."

"I saw some of it up close. Before I met Abraham, I helped bury a man's village. His whole village. The things . . . well, the things they did to those people were horrific."

"As I said, I . . . well. I'm looking for a new line of work."

Jim regarded the woman whose career—and life—his decisions had ruined. He owed her something more, but it was she who broke the silence.

"I think they will probably kill you, Jim," Lisa said, looking into his eyes. "Never name you, but just put you in a hole somewhere. Your people too. They're already trading shots. A force is surrounding Goma, herding them in and cutting off their escape. I heard it on the radio. The tanks are going to an airstrip where they will then be sent against your friends. We are fueled, pointed, and ready. The mercs are in the barracks. We're just waiting for the sun to come up."

"I—" Jim began.

"Delroy is a shot caller somewhere. The locals defer to him in a big way, but I don't think he likes what he's seeing any more than I do," Lisa said. "You were always a hero, Rev. What you've done over here is just incredible. Noble, even. You changed a country, Rev. It's just stunning."

"How far is Goma from here?" Jim asked. "About a couple of hours east, right?"

"By jet, maybe."

The door opened and Delroy stepped in.

"Time's up, young lady," he said. "The alphabet soup name guy's plane just landed."

"Semper fi, Rev," Lisa said, standing up.

"Semper fi."

Jim looked up at Delroy. "You have a plane?"

"Yep, sitting ready on the tarmac. But I don't think I can get you on it."

"Nope, not me. The Marine needs a ride."

Chapter 27

After Delroy and Lisa departed, Jim got down on his knees and did something he hadn't done since he was a boy. He began to pray. Clasping his hands and bowing his head, he searched for the words until he spoke them aloud.

"Hear me, God, I am Yours. I am Yours to command. Help me to save my friend. He is Your servant, and he's a much better man than I will ever be. And he needs me. I don't know how I will help him, but I will do whatever it takes."

Jim felt the wanting, the emotion in his chest.

Footsteps sounded outside the door. As Jim looked up, three men entered the room. Seeing him on his knees made them startle in surprise. Jim didn't waste a moment. He launched himself from the floor, and his fist crashed into the first guard with a thunderous impact, dropping the man senseless to the ground.

One of the other men, who was unarmed, started to back away as the other guard fumbled with the pistol at his belt. Jim grabbed the unarmed man by his throat and arm, lifting and pivoting his body as if he weighed no more than a feather. He crashed him into the guard who was raising his pistol. A dull thud of impact, and the two dropped to the floor.

Jim felt an energy in him. His body was thrumming with it. All of his fatigue and pain had dropped away. The skin around his eyes felt tighter, his vision sharper. He moved with an economy of purpose.

Jim stepped over the prone men, grabbing the pistol from the still hand of the third guard and collecting the spare magazines on his belt. Opening the door, he saw a guard at the end of the hall walking toward him, head down, with an AK-47 slung over his shoulder. Jim sprinted at the man, who looked up only in time for Jim to slam the heavy pistol into the side of his head. Jim grabbed the rifle from the ground, slipping the pistol into his waistband.

Trotting along the hallway, Jim neared a corner, then slipped around to find two men facing away from him, sitting at a security desk. Jim raised the rifle and crashed its metal butt into the head of one man and then the chin of the other. Jim kept moving past the desk, spying a metal door.

Pushing the door open, he found himself outside in the humid darkness. A sparsely illuminated airfield was before him. He could see two MiGs in a hangar about three hundred yards from him. There were at least five men working on or around the planes.

Farther to his left, about a quarter mile away, was the C-5 Lisa had spoken about. A truly incredible cargo aircraft, it was massive even at this distance.

Jim resumed his trot, scanning around for threats, but no one seemed to have spotted him yet. Then, behind him, headlights swung in his direction. He felt the light hit his face and heard the truck accelerate in his direction. He began to run.

"Halt!" a voice over a speaker shouted at him. "Halt or I'll shoot!"

Jim had no intention of halting, and the sudden

gunfire only made him run faster and start to zigzag like a broken-field runner. On the open airfield, there was no cover. Bullets whined around him, the sharp crack of the supersonic rifle bullets buzzing by, lending him more speed.

His lungs bursting, Jim spun and raised his rifle. He fired off a burst toward the truck, followed by two more. The vehicle swerved and came to a stop. Approaching the door, Jim saw that the driver and passenger were both gone, having run into the night. Jim opened the door and got in.

Just then, an alarm began to sound on the airfield. Jim looked and saw the men in the hangar begin to run around. He needed a distraction.

Gunning the engine, he saw the white, round shapes of a fuel farm to his left. Flooring the truck, he jostled with the wheel and his rifle as he sped toward the aviation gasoline storage tanks. Jamming his rifle into the accelerator, he made sure the truck was aimed at the fuel tanks and rolled out onto the tarmac.

Struggling to his feet, Jim began to run toward the C-5 near the hangar. Looping away from the shouting, he heard a loud crash behind him as he dove down into a ditch. Moments went by as Jim heard the sound of men and vehicles off to his right. The explosion was deafening, a concussive wave of primal force. The heat was intense as flames bloomed a hundred feet in the air. Jim was up on his feet running, careful not to look at the fierce light, though he could see himself outlined from behind, a moving shadow on the ground.

As he came to the edge of the hangar, Jim looked back. All of the attention seemed to be focused on the out-of-control flames. He slipped around the wheel of the immense aircraft and looked for the door.

"And who might you be, mate?" Jim tensed at the voice behind him. "Nothing stupid, boyo. Hands up, there's a good lad. Now turn to me."

Jim put his hands in the air and moved to face the voice. A muscular, compact white man in dark fatigues held a submachine gun steady in his direction.

"What's going on, Brennan?" Lisa's voice came from behind Jim, in the door of the plane.

"Don't know, Miss Lisa. Seems we have an uninvited guest."

Jim stayed still as he heard footsteps behind him and saw Lisa walk behind the commando.

"You're due an extra beer tonight, Brennan," Lisa said. "I'll get help."

"You do that, my new mate, and I will wait for—"

Jim watched Lisa swing a wrench into the man's ear, and he folded up.

"Hope I didn't kill him," Lisa said as she pulled the gun from the man's lifeless fingers. She checked his pulse. "Still breathing. Got a head like a brick, this one. Bit of an asshole."

Jim relaxed his arms. "Thanks, Lisa."

"Let's go," Lisa said as she moved to the door. Jim followed her into the aircraft. Lisa shut the access door behind them.

"I thought you would be—" he began.

"Gone? Well, I didn't think you would be able to get here without some help. I was right."

He followed Lisa through the cargo hold, marveling at the size of the space.

"Up here," Lisa said, climbing the stairs at the front of the plane to the cockpit.

Jim sat down in the copilot's seat. The glow from the fuel fire illuminated a vast array of controls and gauges. Lisa turned on some switches and started the engines, and the gauges lit up. She then gave Jim a quick rundown on how to fly the aircraft.

"I'll drop out of the door when you go," she said. "Press this switch to close it. Here's the radio. I tuned it to ground control in Goma. Take it out past the G-5."

Lisa pointed through the windshield to the white private jet.

"And Delroy said he would give me a lift out," she continued. "Seems he could use a pilot."

Jim looked at the face of the woman who'd had no reason to help him.

"Thank you again, Lisa," he said, returning her smile.

"Semper fi, Marine," Lisa said. "Head east by northeast for a couple of hours at top speed. Don't know what you're going to do there, but you'll be in the vicinity. Maybe you can touch down or something."

With that, Lisa was gone down the stairs.

Jim turned his attention to the controls. Moving the throttle up, he felt the aircraft begin to move. Steering the massive plane across the tarmac at a creeping pace, he saw the figure of Lisa running away toward the G-5 private aircraft, which was about fifty yards away with its lights on.

Once she was clear, Jim pushed the throttles more, the plane's engines rumbling up to speed. A few moments later he was making a turn to the end of the runway. Lining up on the strip of concrete, he could see figures and vehicles moving toward him in the flames from the destroyed fuel farm.

Jim pushed the throttles to their fully engaged position, the plane surging as the four TF39 turbofan engines roared, moving the 247-foot plane forward down the runway. Jim held his hands on the throttles and the yoke as the pursuing vehicles suddenly swerved out of the plane's way. The power of the aircraft was unreal as it quickly picked up speed.

Jim looked out of the cockpit to see the G-5 taking off on a parallel runway. Three fighter jets were starting to move after it on the ground, either to chase him or the G-5. Jim pulled hard on the yoke, and the plane defied gravity and climbed free of the earth.

Leaving the throttles in position, Jim activated the controls to retract the wheels and close the doors. Once the control lights signaled all was secure, he throttled back, placed both hands on the yoke, and banked hard to port.

He felt the massive weight of the aircraft move at his command, still climbing but now turning to face the airport from which it had just taken off. He felt the plane's wings and body flex, taking the structure to its limits as he lined up on the two runways.

Weightless momentarily at the turn and already a mile away, Jim saw the fighters beginning to line up for takeoff. He knew that once the more nimble and, more importantly, armed fighters were in the air, he would be defenseless. Pushing the throttles again, Jim aimed at the glow of the afterburners of the MiGs moving on the ground. The shallow dive made the ground rush under him until he was barely fifteen feet above it. Alarms screamed at him about a collision, but he ignored them.

Just as he passed near the first fighter, he pulled sharply back, tipping the nose up and the tail down toward the three fighters. The planes were blown off the runway like insects by the massive air pressure of the C-5's engines.

Jim struggled with the controls as the plane climbed back into the sky. Banking again, he saw the wreckage of the three fighters like squashed bugs around the runway. Finally, satisfied that the immediate pursuers were down, he leveled off and turned southeast, a man alone in the vast sky over a dark, sleeping landscape as he hurtled toward his friends. The big plane was surprisingly smooth in the air. Some turbulence that would have bucked a regular jet only slightly bumped the giant aircraft.

Jim fiddled with the radio dial. He found the station of the radios Abraham and the others had captured from the government troops. He knew the Angels were using the radios; Abraham had said they would speak the Word to as many people as possible, whether they were from the Congo or Rwanda, Uganda or Burundi, and the call had gone out on the radio stations that were the primary communication and dissemination outlets in the country. Jim began transmitting.

"Angels, this is Angel-1. Do you copy?" Jim spoke into the microphone, then listened into the static. He tried a few more times and received no reply. He was still too far away.

Looking out over the rolling green hills, Jim felt his body coming down from the physical toll of the escape. Lisa and Delroy seemed to have gotten away, and for their help he would be forever grateful. They'd had no reason to help him, but they had.

He consulted the map on the kneeboard Lisa had left him. After consulting the GPS, he decided the lights he saw in front of him were the city of Tsikapa. Looking at the compass, he made the turn to take him to the mountains and specifically Mount Nyiragongo, the fiery heart of the northern mountain range.

Another twenty minutes of flying and he would be there. What he would do when he got there was another story. The darkness was holding and giving him cover. Jim pulled back the yoke to gain altitude, then transmitted again.

"Angels, this is Angel-1. Do you copy?"

"Angel-1, this is Angel-3. I read you. How me? Over." Tatame's voice made him jump in his seat.

"I read you, Angel-3. What is the situation?" Jim replied, relieved.

"About three hundred people are retreating up the volcano. We can see tanks and armored vehicles coming out of Goma, but the single roads hinder them. They have thousands of troops with them," Tatame said.

"Can you make it to the Goma airport?"

"Negative, Jim. The tanks and troops are in our way. We are on the east side, but we are getting pushed back up the mountain. The retreat is cut off."

Jim could see the glow of the volcano in the distance. The sky was beginning to grow brighter, but the deep red of the lava lake inside still stood out. He banked the plane toward the east. Sporadic flashes on the lower slopes winked below. Red tracers from the base to the upper slopes showed him where the attackers were. In his unarmed plane, he was useless.

"Jim, Jim, can you hear me?" Abraham's voice in his headset.

"Yes, Abe, I'm here."

"Praise God, Jim. My prayers are answered."

Jim banked the plane to get a better view. The dark slopes of the volcanic mountain stretched up to the lava lake at the top. A small, pale line snaked its way jaggedly, switchbacking up the face.

"Where are you, Abe?"

"Not far from the summit, north of the cleft in the rim," Abe replied. "The Angels are fighting, but I fear we are outclassed this time."

Jim couldn't disagree with him.

"Can you help us, Jim?"

"The plane I'm in is huge but unarmed. There's not much I can do. Let me think."

Jim put the plane into a sharp bank. Once around, he could see the origin of the tracers. He could fly low over the enemy troops, but that would only give them a startle and a target.

The troops on the ground were milling like ants, judging from the headlights. There seemed to be roadblocks holding up the vehicles. Being shot at by the Angels was not helping them clear the road. Jim straightened the plane and flew away from the mountain, trying to think.

Suddenly a roar came across his windshield. Jim jumped at the controls, desperately craning his neck. Looking at the radar screen, he saw a dot moving away from him. The RWR, or radar warning receiver, suddenly emitted a tone. Jim knew that was a missile lock warning. Something had lined up its sights on him. He dipped to port and then slammed the yoke hard to starboard to put the big jet in a barrel roll. The weightless feeling at the top of the roll made him tighten his leg muscles instinctively, trying not to pass out as the blood rushed away from his head. He was successful in not passing out, and the missile lock warning signal went away.

Now pointed back toward the mountain, Jim pushed the throttles forward to gain more speed.

"Mr. Jim, how have you been?" an accented voice crackled in his headset. "You are an ace now: three jets in one blow. Much like the tailor and his jam. Though you are the giant in this tale."

Damn, Jim thought. *This guy again.*

He saw the jet on the radar moving closer to him.

"Your friends: alas, they are cornered. The general will finish them off. You, on the other hand, could be different."

Jim keyed the mic. "What are you rambling about?"

"He speaks. I am granted an audience."

"Fuck off."

"I am the one positioned to do the fucking here. However, your friend Beautiful was more than willing to make that bargain. Are you?"

Jim was silent. The pilot had gotten to Beautiful.

"Do I have your attention?"

"Listening," Jim said. Not much choice at this point.

As Jim watched, the MiG pulled up on his port side. He could see the pilot in helmet and gear through the window.

"You are carrying some very, very expensive hardware," the pilot said, "not to mention a valuable aircraft. The tanks alone are worth millions."

"To your employer?"

"To us, and, of course, to your former employer, Jacques."

"I'm not really in that line of work anymore."

"No, I suppose not. You're a zealot, a freedom fighter now. A man of God. L'Ange de la Mort. Though an angel without a sword, it seems. You could be rich, millions. I have the coordinates. We fly there, get paid. You leave. Simple."

"My friends deserve more."

"Your friends are dead. They just haven't paid their toll yet. The ferryman is waiting."

Jim suddenly jammed the yoke and accelerated, heaving the massive plane toward the MiG, attempting to swat it out of the air. But instead, the MiG moved more quickly and slipped under and away from the C-5.

Jim had been tempted for a moment. The thoughts of a child: *Let this be over. I wanna go home. Everything will be all right if I just do as I'm told.* But he owed Abraham his life. A man pays what he owes.

Flying closer to the volcano, Jim saw the elite military forces attacking and the Angels firing back, machine guns and rockets. The army moving up the mountain stretched for miles: at least three thousand troops to crush a few hundred. The tanks and troops were halfway up now. Abraham and the rest were effectively cut off. Taking his eyes up, Jim saw the enormous lake of molten magma, held as if in a bowl. It was filled to the brim above the tanks and troops. A desperate plan formed in his head. He scanned the control console, looking at the button labels.

The RWR screamed the sound of a missile launch. Jim glanced at the radar, then searched the console. Finding the button, Jim activated the flare countermeasures. The sky lit up around him as the flares ejected, providing protection, luring the missile away from the cargo plane. Jim felt the explosion of first one missile, then another right after.

"And lo, I did see an angel in the heavens, and it brought me salvation," said Abraham's voice on the radio.

Jim desperately angled the aircraft on a turn. He imagined that Abraham was referring to the pattern the antimissile flares made as they launched from the plane, resembling an angel. Finally the plane leveled out, with Jim guiding it away from the mountain back over the freshwater lake. He was out of options and ideas.

"Well, Mr. Jim, a stunning display. The antimissile flares do look like an angel in the sky. Regrettably, those were my only missiles. I shall have to finish you off with guns. As our forefather pilots did. Knights in the sky."

God, this guy blabbers, Jim thought. *If I was in a jet, you wouldn't be so chatty.*

"Jim," Abraham said in his headset. "Come closer to us, Jim. We began this journey together. I would rather end it with you near. It would give me comfort, my friend. Our entire force has pulled back. The troops are stopped for a moment at the last roadblock. We have chosen to be together here at the end."

Tears came to Jim's eyes as he turned the plane to point once more at the battle. Letting off on the throttle, he settled to cruising speed. The mountain loomed closer. He was resigned to his fate, with no way to outrun the MiG and no weapons to fight it.

"Thank you, Abe. You don't know how much you've meant to me. You found me when I was lost."

"I was ordained a shepherd for years, but you were the first of my flock," Abraham said. "You gave me more than I ever gave you."

Jim looked out at the African landscape, green and

lush. The lake he hadn't noticed passed below him. Everything in these moments, the last moments, was so beautiful. The lake, the sky, the rolling green.

"I've done evil things, Abe. Pride, sloth, lust, rage, greed. Don't know which sin I missed."

"Gluttony and envy," the MiG pilot said over the radio.

"I'm sure I did those as well," Jim said. At this moment, he didn't even hate the other pilot. It seemed the time for such feelings had passed.

"Would you like forgiveness, Jim? Would you like to confess and accept the Lord into your life?"

"Your forgiveness would be enough, Abe."

"I am just the conduit of His love for you. A servant and vessel. Do you accept Him?"

"Yes," Jim said. He felt his being lighten. The full rays of the sun were warm on his face. Tears streamed down his cheeks.

"Do you reject Satan and all his works?"

"I'm not familiar with Satan, Abe. It's a stretch for me."

"Do you deny the miracles you have witnessed? The unexplained coincidences? The dead rising? The faithful walking through a storm of bullets? You are part of these, Jim, and they are a part of you. They happened."

"I believe in you, Abraham, in *philia*, in *agape*. I regret my sins, yes, Abe."

"Someone's been reading," the pilot said.

Jim looked but could not see the jet on the radar or through the windshield. He was approaching the mountain; he could see the glow of the fiery heart of molten rock. It was immense.

"I'll take that as a yes, Jim," Abraham said. "In

---

your repentance, I give you absolution. You are taken in. Marked as one of His. I bless you and forgive you in the name of Almighty God. Go in peace."

Jim bowed his head for a moment, then looked up, smiling.

"And myself, Father? Do you forgive me?" the pilot asked.

Jim could see the shape of the MiG on the radar now, closing in behind him in the perfect firing position. He waited for the end.

"*No, I do not!*" Abraham shouted. "Bank away, Jim!"

The RWR registered a lock with its screeching tone. Jim saw the glow of three missiles rising from near the rim of the volcano. He jerked the yoke to port, and the C-5 moved gracefully as the shoulder-fired rockets raced from the ground to the MiG behind him.

"Merde," the pilot said.

The MiG, crippled by the rockets, fell from the sky at an incredible speed, heading straight for the lip of the volcanic lake, breaking into two pieces. It slammed into the mountain face. An explosion threw dirt high into the air. Jim saw where the jet had impacted and broken the rock; streams of lava now shone through multiple cracks.

"Thank you, Abe," Jim said. "I guess you found the Iglas."

"Yes, we brought them here in case we needed them. Now, Jim, it is over for us. You have done everything that could be expected and more. You need to go."

"I can't leave you to die, Abe."

"What else can you do? The troops are gathering for the final push. We are backed against the mountain with a volcano at our back. The mountain is boiling, Jim, and the jet crash felt like an earthquake. I have given you your absolution and your life for all that you have done for me. There is nothing else you can do."

Jim looked again at the crash site and the troops in the landscape, at the burning jet fuel mixed with what appeared to be fissures in the rock, glowing red.

"Are you behind the promontory point of rock about a quarter mile from the crash site, Abe?"

The radio was silent for a moment. Then Abraham said, "Yes, I guess we are. Why?"

"Get behind it, Abe, all of you, quickly," Jim said, turning the jet away from the mountain. "It's your only chance."

Jim pulled up on the yoke and moved the throttle to the full position, gaining altitude into the sky. Breaking through the puffy clouds of a glorious morning, he reached into the inner pocket of his shirt and retrieved an item carefully hidden and wrapped.

Slipping it out of its plastic, he looked at the picture of Maggie, in her bikini, contemplating her swelling belly with her crooked half smile. The picture was tattered and worn. He smiled back at her and tucked the picture into his pocket again. Jim then took careful note of his heading and turned the yoke while depressing his right foot control.

The plane did an aerobatic pirouette, gracefully turning in the clouds with a smooth rotation of the wings that brought the plane back to the line it had just flown up. The powerful engines roared with the application of the throttles. Aligning to a spot on the ground in the distance, it reached its top speed within seconds, hurtling out of the sky, picking up momentum from gravity as it went.

Abraham looked to the sky. A noise was becoming louder. On the ground, the general stopped talking on the radio in time to see the plane roar over his head and impact the mountain above him. The sound was so loud that it left the soldiers stunned.

Dirt and rock exploded from the impact. A long, eerie silence followed. Then an ominous rumble escaped from deep in the volcano. Time stood still.

The speed and mass of the jet impacting the mountain had shattered rock that had transformed into liquid eons earlier. The fissure from deep in the heart of the earth absorbed the immense force of the crash, and the subsequent explosion of the fuel and tank armaments on board was a shock wave. The shock wave flowed through the lava, a mile deep, until it met the deep sea of molten subterranean rock beneath and started back, gathering speed.

The general turned his attention back to the men staring confused around him.

"Get ready to mo—" he began, then looked up as a new sound was heard.

The entire cauldron of hundreds of millions of gallons of magma roiled and surged, bursting the side of the mountain. The heat was so intense it melted everything in its path, so bright it blinded the eye.

A crashing, roaring tsunami of hot lava, a half mile across, thundered down the mountainside, completely engulfing the troops and vehicles. The lava flowed as it had never flowed since the dawn of time, an unstoppable force, destroying everything and everyone in its path, following the channels of the earth to the lake below, total and complete destruction in moments.

Jim gained consciousness in the air. The parachute harness pulled on his back and neck, which ached from being compressed. Below him he could see the destruction, feel the heat. Magma was flowing over the forces that had been trying to kill his friends, his people. This was a sight that no one had ever seen or would ever see again.

A firm breeze pushed him farther across the landscape, away from the destruction. Impacting the brushy land at speed, Jim bounced across the ground. Extracting himself from his harness, he waited, cradling his ribs.

Abraham and the others walked to where he sat, surrounding him. Abraham sat beside him without a word. The two men watched the sunrise over the steaming lake.

The End

Author Note

Thank you so much for reading this book. I sincerely hoped that you enjoyed the story. If you could take a moment and write a review it would mean a lot and guide my future writing.

Thank you,
Jack Lyons

ABOUT THE AUTHOR

Growing up, Jack Lyons always yearned to see the world. After six years in the US Navy then twenty more as a US Merchant Marine. Jack worked in many different sectors of the seagoing industry. Jack now pursues writing and exploring different genres and story ideas.

Made in the USA
Las Vegas, NV
22 June 2022